Radical

With billions of lives at stake, what would you do?

Paul Scott

Los Angeles, California

This is a work of fiction. It's not intended as a how-to book. Neither the author, nor the publisher, endorse, encourage, or condone violent acts no matter their motivation.

Some of the characters are fictional and some are based on real people. In my book I hope to educate the public as to the harm they're causing in using dirty energy and to encourage them to switch to cleaner alternatives. I also hope this book will compel Congress to put a price on carbon and to overturn *Citizens United v. Federal Election Commission*, 558 U.S. 310 (2010) and *McCutcheon v. Federal Election Commission*, 572 U.S. ___ (2014).

Published in the United States of America
ISBN – 13: 978-1545493496
ISBN – 10: 1545493499
Editing: Rebecca's Author Services
Interior Design: Intention Media
Cover Design: Kim Smith, Designs
Interior Art: Karen Ayers Design
Cover and author photos: Charles-Ryan Barber

Acknowledgements

The idea for this book, my first, was born in a hospital bed. As my body had begun to prematurely break down, I endured several years of health challenges and felt I may not have much time left. That, combined with the devolving world situation destroying much of the environment, compelled me to quit my day job and step up my fight to mitigate the problems.

The following three books crystalized my thinking and were catalysts for the idea for this book: *The Sixth Extinction*, by Elizabeth Kolbert; *This Changes Everything*, by Naomi Klein; and *Merchants of Doubt*, by Naomi Oreskes and Erik M. Conway. Many thanks to these esteemed authors and the hours of research they poured into their projects.

Early on, I sought beginner's guidance at Santa Monica College, a wonderful local community resource, where I took a writing class that gave me the encouragement and confidence I needed to continue—even though I had no clue about the monumental task I was undertaking.

After making some progress, I came down with a bad case of writer's block. Fortunately, writing coach Gemini Adams gave me the tools to complete a first draft, a 131,000 word tome that contained everything I needed in the book—and then some.

To trim the fat and help me structure the book to tell the most compelling, powerful story possible, I relied upon a handful of talented editors. Rebecca Camarena of Rebecca's Author Services provided adroit editing assistance and guided me through the Amazon printing and sales process.

I hope to see Mark Hampton at the movies—he has written a terrific screen play based on the book and had the enormous good sense to convince me to change the book's original title to *Radical.*

Charles-Ryan Barber, one of my chess buddies, shot the book's cover photograph, perfectly capturing the look I was after (if not my knight).

This manuscript would not have been possible without the competent counsel of my First Amendment attorney, Jeffrey Douglas. His understanding of free speech law convinced me I was on solid legal footing.

EV enthusiast Brian Kent, of Negative Carbon Road Trip fame, offered encouragement at a crucial time in my writing process. I entrusted several other friends with early drafts of the manuscript, receiving invaluable feedback—as well as moral support—in return. Most of these friends prefer to remain anonymous.

Of course there wouldn't have been a book to write without all the activists and advocates working ceaselessly toward the goals we all share: electrifying everything and cleaning the grid.

And finally, there is my friend, Barbara. Thank you for being my sounding board at the end of this process.

Dedicated to:

My chess teacher, Mel, who went by the real last name of Bloch, taught me much more than strategy on the board. He broadened my horizons in innumerable ways with the encyclopedic knowledge he picked up from worldwide travels and an insatiable curiosity seasoned with more than a touch of healthy skepticism.

When I first moved to Eugene Oregon as an idealistic young man, Alice Soderwall, the elderly manager of B.R.I.N.G. Recycling, took me under her wing and taught me the importance of efficiency. Alice wasted nothing. As I washed bottles and jars at her kitchen sink for a nickel apiece, she regaled me with stories of her hard life as a child growing up during the Great Depression. I have tried to live my life teaching this ethic to anyone willing to listen, spreading the gospel of Alice, a true radical in her own right.

Table of Contents

PART ONE

LOSS OF INNOCENCE

Chapter 1

Cody studied the map closely. The event was being held at Quartz Mountain State Park on the shore of Lake Altus in the southwest corner of Oklahoma. He'd need to keep the van hidden for a few days while he scouted his route and planned the senator's assassination. It needed to be within a reasonable bike ride so he could quickly get back after the shooting and make his escape.

The surrounding area had several small towns, but one quickly stood out: Granite, OK. With a population of 2,000, it was nestled in the foothills of the Wichita Mountains, about 10 miles from the lake. The road to the lake was an easy ride, with arrow-straight farm roads intersecting it every mile or two. The nearest city, Lawton, was almost 80 miles away, so the emergency response would take well over an hour—long enough for Cody to get back to his van, stash the bike and gun, and quietly drive away, taking farm roads to Hobart and then down Highway 183 to San Antonio.

Cody pulled into Granite after dark and went to the first gas station he could find, Domino's Food & Fuel on 1st St. Before going in, he put on his heaviest coat and a hat that would cover his eyes and face. It seemed every store in the country had surveillance cameras these days, and Cody knew the FBI would check everything in every gas station and store in the entire state looking for any suspicious characters. He looked for, but didn't notice, any cameras by the pumps, so at least his van would not be recorded. That was his biggest worry, since the van could be easily traced.

He got some extra food and a full tank, and then drove north of town a mile or so to a granite quarry. His Google search showed many secluded locations on the quarry property where he could hide the van. He didn't know if the place had security, so he drove past the quarry first, scanning for any signs of a guard. Nothing, not a soul. There was no gate, nothing. He thought how small-town America is still safe from most crime, which worked to his advantage.

He drove back to the quarry, turning into the main entrance. From the Google map, Cody remembered a dirt road off to the left that led up to what appeared to be a good hiding place.

"Holy shit!" he yelled. The road ascended a steep incline, with huge rocks interspersing it. Luckily, the road made a sharp right turn and leveled off, so Cody drove on. He was now in a thick grove of scrub mesquite. The van's lights shone on some very big granite rocks and a few scrub trees. It was actually a beautiful spot. He cut the engine. It was a cloudy and cold Spring evening, but not freezing.

Cody got out to stretch his legs and relieve himself. A light breeze did make it chilly, so he took care of business quickly and got back in the van. He needed to call his parents and Victoria to pretend he was in LA and working on the film.

Lying to people he loved was hard, but Cody's mind was set. Victoria's addition to the short list was problematic, but if he could lie to his parents, he could lie to anyone, even if it felt dirty.

It certainly wasn't harder than murdering someone.

After his calls, he brought up the maps again to study his morning route.

The day broke with clouds still obscuring the sky, but the temperature had begun to rise, so Cody dressed in layers he could remove. Now that it was light, he got a good look at his surroundings. Before leaving, he needed to check if he could leave the quarry without being seen by employees. He walked down the road to where he could see past the trees. He had a good view with the higher elevation. It was Friday and people were arriving for work, maybe a dozen, so there wouldn't be too many eyes to avoid. The main operation was about 300 meters past the gate. As the pick-up trucks drove in, they followed the road to some ramshackle buildings that didn't have a good view of Cody's location. Still, riding a bike down that road to the gate, he'd certainly be visible to anyone entering or exiting. He needed another way out.

Back at the van, he scouted for a direct route north through the scrub and down a steep embankment. He found a point where he could see down to the road. There wasn't even a fence blocking access, just a stretch of barren rock his mountain bike would have no trouble negotiating. Even if someone saw him there, they'd assume he was a bike rider trying out the rocky hills.

His plan was to time his ride to the location and scout the hill from which he'd be shooting. The fundraiser was the next day at 10 am. Cody would need to be in place very early to avoid being seen by anyone who might put two and two together after the fact. His goal was to make the hit, then leave as fast as possible, without leaving a sign that he had been there.

His clothing was not bright and highly visible, as road bikers tended to wear. Cody wanted to blend in to this conservative area and not stand out. Just being on a bicycle was already a huge red flag, since there didn't seem to be many adults riding bikes in this town. If there were any at all, Cody would be surprised.

He stuffed a sandwich, banana, water, and an energy drink in his daypack, pulled the bike out and locked the van. He walked the bike through the scrub mesquite, breathing in the pleasant fragrance of the trees. At the clearing, he mounted the bike and rode across the smooth stone until it petered out just shy of the road. There wasn't a vehicle in sight. The road itself was hard-packed dirt, easy riding. He set off for Highway 6, about a mile east, which wasn't anything more than a single lane in both directions. Traffic was light and nobody paid him any mind. After a couple of miles, he rode into Granite, where he'd bought gas the night before. On the bike, it only took a few minutes to pass through town, and then he was back on Highway 6. Next, he headed west on Farm Road 1465. He rode steadily for two more miles into the hills surrounding Lake Altus.

He admired the beauty of the rocky hills. The road meandered up and through a massive rock formation and became 1470 just before intersection 44A, which went south over a bridge spanning the north fork of the Red river. There was a sad little fun park south of the river that the local kids undoubtedly enjoyed. At least there was something to take their minds off the brutal boredom of living in a conservative rural community.

Cody stopped for a quick drink of water, then continued on 1470 east. The road was now going downhill toward the misnamed lake. The dam on the Red River meant it was artificial and thus a reservoir. Of course, the distinction was lost on most people, so Lake Altus it was.

The downhill was steep in places, so Cody was flying. He zoomed down the southwest side of the lake, winding along the contours of the shoreline until he entered the Quartz Mountain Resort. The parking lot semi-surrounded the main building where Cody assumed the public events were held and, as he rode past, he came upon several residential buildings where overnighters would be staying. The lot had few cars. It appeared most people were not there yet.

At the far end of the property, a trail led down to the lake, which, due to a long-term drought, made this cove dry all the way across to a barely-used dirt trail that hugged the shoreline going north. Cody thought that might be a good route out after the shooting, as most people would assume he'd be using the roads to escape. He'd check it out after scouting the hill above the resort for his duck blind.

Circling back, he noticed a trail going up into the rocks. It was moderately steep, but easy enough to negotiate on the bike. The trail brought him up to the ridge line, which was too far away to make a good shot, so he reversed direction and looked for a way down to a spot that would give him a clear vantage of the parking lot, but also afford good cover.

Cody pretty quickly had to leave the bike behind some large rocks and continue on foot. He soon found the perfect spot. Large granite boulders created a perfect blind with cover in all directions, and there was even a slot between two boulders that let him clearly see the main building and its parking lot. Cody figured that was where the senator would be let out of his vehicle.

He studied people coming and going as he ate. The fundraiser announcement indicated they were expecting a couple of hundred. The event featured a pigeon shoot, with Senator Inhofe as the main draw. How could so many people enjoy killing defenseless birds?

It was almost noon. The clouds were breaking up and the sun made Cody warm. He peeled off a layer before returning to his bike. He rode back down the trail to the residential cabins behind the resort, where the trail led down to the dry cove. No one was outside of the cabins, but that didn't mean that someone couldn't see him from inside. He figured anyone watching would assume he was merely getting some exercise.

Riding down the trail to what would've been the water's edge, he continued across the soft dry dirt to the cove's other side. A different trail then took him to an old dirt road that, sure enough, hugged the shore going north. He was glad to find no sign of life on this road.

Cody rode for a couple of miles before taking a farm road heading west. He remembered several such roads all eventually intersecting Highway 6 where he would turn north. He didn't stop in Granite, the less that saw him the better.

The sun was low in the partly cloudy sky, and the wind continued to blow steadily. He approached his hide out quietly in case anyone happened to be at the van, but found no sign anyone had been there. He grabbed a sandwich and walked through the trees to where he could see workers trying to muscle a large slab of granite onto a small truck. The truck sagged as the massive rock landed on the flatbed. After securing it with tie-downs, the driver headed for the gate.

All the workers were walking back to what looked like the main building. From the pats on the back and handshaking, it was clear everyone was getting ready to leave. He watched as they drove out of the gate, but got nervous when the last one stopped and dragged a heavy chain across the entrance and padlocked it. Cody was locked in.

"Oh fuck!" Cody whispered. He waited a few minutes to make sure no one was coming back and then walked down there. The padlock was big, and the chain was too heavy for the van to break without sustaining serious damage. He needed to deal with this tonight.

He studied the chain, the lock, and the posts it was attached to. He assumed there had to be a weak link. It looked like some vehicle had once hit one of the posts but instead of replacing it, the company bent it back to position. The concrete footing holding the post didn't look substantial. He could rock it back and forth; that might be his salvation.

He jogged over to a shack by the office building and rummaged around until he found a steel cable with a loop on one end and a hook on the other. Perfect. He dragged it up to the van and found the loop fit nicely on the van's trailer hitch. No need to do this while there was still light in the sky, so he climbed in the driver's seat, cranked over the engine, and turned on the heater.

Cody spent the next few hours double-checking everything for tomorrow. He retrieved the hunting rifle from under his mattress and spare clothing. Holding this instrument of death, he thought again, how much his life had changed. He longed for the simpler days of his youth, before the bullying started and before 9/11 put him on a very different trajectory in life. But this was the curse of memory, of knowledge, of purpose.

Cody carefully wrapped the rifle in a towel. He then grabbed several velcro straps from his backpack and secured the rifle to the bike frame. The rifle couldn't interfere with his cycling and it also had to stay hidden. While the whole rifle fit reasonably well, the barrel stuck out pretty far in front of the handlebars. He made sure the towel covered it, but it still looked strange.

Around 10 pm, he figured no one would be traveling the dirt road, so he walked down to the gate. The clouds had moved back in and the wind had picked up. A single light bulb cast light in all directions. From a distance, it looked pretty lonely. He didn't need to see the gate up close, so he jogged back up to the van.

"This fucking road sucks!" he said under his breath. It was rutted and dotted with large rocks, any one of which could render his van inoperable. That'd be the end of his whole plan right there. Cody's heart rate rose as his van descended, very carefully.

Once he negotiated the rocks and got to level ground, he was back in the open. Anyone driving by could see him. He couldn't turn off the lights since he needed to see where he was going. "Just keep going. Get the job done," he thought.

Cody's military training dovetailed well with his track training. The military was all about logistics and strategy, and track prepared him physically to push through to the end. Never give up, and develop the means to last a long time at great effort.

Then there was chess. Cody remembered playing with his father when he was a kid; he had learned long ago to look at the whole board. When something is of consequence, you had damn well better look at all the pieces and their various moves, while also looking forward as many moves as possible. Cody was constantly thinking ahead and envisioning contingencies.

He wrapped the cable's hook around the top of the weakest two poles. Holding the chain, Cody set the hook back on the cable and cinched it as tight as he could, which wasn't much, given the cable's heavy gauge. He then dropped the cable's hoop on the van's trailer hitch. It was loose, but he figured if he pulled slowly, it wouldn't slip off.

Cody jumped into the van and shut the door. He slipped the transmission into drive and inched forward until he felt the cable begin to tighten.

"C'mon, baby, stay on there!"

The van was straining. Cody was freaking. This had to work!

One of the wheels began to spin just slightly.

"No! No spin." Cody pleaded.

There wasn't a sudden give as he'd expected. More of a gradual release of tension. Cody felt a euphoric tingle from his own release of tension. The gate was down. Not all the way, but enough that he could drive over it. He could escape tomorrow.

Cody didn't want to leave the chain down in case someone came tonight or tomorrow morning while he was gone. They might inspect the whole property and find his van.

He pulled the downed pole back up and muscled it close enough to its original position that no one driving by would notice. It was a long shot that anyone would come way out here, anyway. Kind of a spooky place at night.

His sudden elation was quickly tempered by the thought that someone could drive by. It wasn't all that late, and high school kids sometimes drove down desolate lanes to be alone with their dates.

The thought of high school dating sent a pang of grief through him. As Cody stared at the lane, his mind went back over a decade as he thought about Jazzie and the secluded spot where they stood and kissed, both sensing that would be the day they gave up their mutual virginities. He'd hinted the week before about "going all the way," and she'd hinted back that she wanted to as well. Without explicitly asking for sex, they slowly undressed each other, touching, exploring, and kissing.

They arranged their shorts and singlets on the soft dry grass and lay down together, groping and kissing and fumbling, neither exactly sure how to consummate the act, but he managed, with a little help from Jazzie. It was beautiful and brief. But even though he'd come, his desire didn't go away. He was so excited to actually be "doing it," that he kept on going, reading Jazzie's moans and reacting to her non-verbalized desires such that she, too, came beautifully.

They lay together for several minutes staring into each other's wide eyes. Cody slowly caressed her, paying attention to those parts normally kept undercover. The female body fascinated him, and now he not only got to see it, but touch it as well. It was even better than he'd imagined.

Cody stared at the cold dark lane for a long time, remembering. He fought, but failed, to keep out memories of subsequent events. Jazzie's death, 9/11, his military experience, the global confluence of politics and money and short-sighted thinking. He grew angry that these awful, preventable events had polluted his memory. Hell, not just his memory, but his life, and the lives of so many on this planet. He wanted to go back in time to that lovely afternoon when they knew for sure they'd spend their lives together. As they got dressed, Cody paid close attention to how Jazzie covered up her beautiful, sexy body. He wanted to remember every detail so he could replay it all in his head whenever he felt the desire, which proved to be often.

But that was the past.

Cody had to drive back up the steep, rocky hill—in the dark. Even with his headlights on, the steepness of the terrain, combined with the stark, high contrast lighting, and the huge fucking rocks, gave Cody all he could handle. The van bounced and the tires slipped, but eventually he made it up to the level road and into his hideout.

Cody turned the engine off and stared into the darkness. His heart rate subsided, but his anxiety didn't. He envisioned Mel's face; his grey ponytail, the thin beard, the aviator glasses. And that stare. When Mel taught chess, he gave you everything you needed to know, but you had to apply it. When there was an obvious move and you didn't see it, you got that stare.

It meant there was an obvious move. He only needed to see it.

Cody sat for over an hour. The only thing he could think was to check the Inhofe website that everything was set for morning. Nothing had changed. Cody checked the local weather for tomorrow. Clear to partly cloudy, temps in the 50s. Not bad. He'd need a few layers, but not too much.

Most importantly, what time was sunrise? He needed to be in place before dawn.

Sunrise, 6:58 a.m. the screen said. It was already after 11 p.m., He'd need to sleep soon.

He wrote a quick email to Victoria.

"Hey, sweetie. Miss you! Had a long day. Tomorrow's more of the same. I'll call tomorrow night. C"

He set the alarm on his iPhone for 5 am and crawled into the sleeping bag. Sleep didn't come quickly. This would be the fourth life he'd taken. All were arguably legitimate. This one more than any other given the damage Inhofe had perpetrated. He didn't need to rethink the decision to kill him, but thinking about the reasons made him more comfortable, sort of.

The iPhone xylophone startled Cody out of a pleasant dream. It'd been about a nonspecific woman/girl whom he loved. She seemed to be a mix of Jazzie and Victoria, someone he desired. Had the dream continued, there would have been a nocturnal emission. Coitus interruptus of a kind...

Cody sprang into action, dressing with several layers to guard against the cold.

Jumping out of the van to pee, he was treated to a cascade of bright stars splayed across the cloudless sky. With no air or light pollution to dim the brilliant celestial view, rural dwellers lived with this incredible sight most every night. A beautiful day was in store.

As he stood there, a warm stream of pee steaming in a pool on the ground, he stared up at the sky. This might be the last time he'd be able to take in such majesty.

He would soon change the world and his life was in the balance.

In the moonlight, the giant granite slabs sparkled bright around their edges. As Cody scanned the scabbed, rocky land, he thought of the photons that mere minutes ago had left the sun's fiery interior, shooting toward our blue planet and its moon. After bouncing off the moon, a few trillion photons struck the granite and were reflected into Cody's pupils, where they activated an electric signal that traveled along his optic nerve and into his visual cortex, his brain interpreting the electrons as light.

Cody marveled at this understanding of physics, biology, and neuroscience, something he'd picked up just reading online. Why were people capable of learning all these wonderful things, but couldn't live together. He returned to the van to remove the bike. The rifle was wrapped tightly in the towel and strapped to the frame. He remained bothered by the barrel sticking out a full foot but he'd already exhausted all of the alternatives the night before.

He grabbed three energy drinks from the ice chest, stuffing two in his pack and downing the third. He'd already stashed a sandwich and a couple of energy bars in the pack. Spying the box of ammo, he stuffed that in, thinking that one of the shells would likely end a senator's life.

5:18—time to go.

He clicked on the headlight. The bright LED cast a strong beam, illuminating the scrub mesquite through which he had to bushwhack to get down to the open flat rock. Once through, he saw the road some 200 meters distant. There was nothing else as far as he could see in all directions. At the road, he lifted the bike, heavier with the addition of the rifle, over the fence. He then followed, being careful of the barbed wire.

The light helped him avoid the dirt road's rocks and ruts, but once he got on Highway 6 with its smooth, clean pavement, he turned off the light. He knew from the previous ride that, if he rode conservatively, he had plenty of time. His nervousness, however, compelled him to crank hard, and soon he was averaging a solid 20 miles per hour. He made it through Granite without seeing a single car, but began encountering a few as he rode south. He'd turned on his bike light in Granite just in case, and left it on to make sure any vehicles would see him.

The turn off Highway 6 to the lake went smoothly. The descent down to the lake's edge felt good after pushing so hard. Ahead were the lights of the Quartz Mountain Resort. Cody turned off his headlight.

It was still dark, but dawn was only minutes away. The resort was lit up like a casino. Way too many lights in the parking lot and on every building. Were they so concerned about theft they were willing to pollute the skies with light and waste all that electricity?

"Sheesh, what assholes! Overkill, just like everything else in this country. What they should be watching for are assassins." He smiled as he glided silently through the parking area, past the main building, and around to the residential building to the trailhead.

He pulled to a stop and quietly dismounted to walk the bike up the steepest part of the hill. Dawn was just breaking, but he still needed the light once he got on the trail. He was concerned the rifle's additional weight and the barrel sticking so far out might cause him to fall or hit a tree limb. Once he was on a decent trail, he jumped back on and made his way to the rocks he'd located the day before. By now, the ambient light was almost enough to read by. He turned off the light and leaned the bike against the rocks. This part of the trail wasn't visible from below, but his shooting position was a good twenty exposed meters below the trail.

Cody unfastened the Winchester and unwrapped it. He pulled out the box of Winchester Supreme 140 grain cartridges from his pack and loaded four into the rifle. He then attached the suppressor to the barrel.

No second guessing. That had all been done before he left Seattle.

He scrambled down the open slope to the big rocks that gave him cover and a perfect view of the main building's entrance. He was about 200 meters to the edge of the parking lot where Inhofe would probably be dropped off.

Cody hoped his target would be in the open long enough that he could take the shot. He didn't want collateral injuries, though he assumed anyone surrounding Inhofe was a bird of his feather.

He'd started to sweat while riding, and now that he was stationary, the chill air became uncomfortable. He remembered similar circumstances from Iraq when he and his buddies were either too hot or too cold, but the very real possibility of dying provided ample incentive to bear it. There was little chance of his being killed here, but getting caught was almost as bad. He did some push-ups on the limited level ground next to the rocks. That helped some.

The sun was now peeking over the horizon, and there was activity below. A catering truck was delivering food, and a few people were arriving in cars and SUVs. He had no idea when the senator was scheduled to arrive, so all he could do was wait. He had to pay close attention, because he'd only have one chance to make the shot. An hour went by. The sun was now hitting Cody, its warmth welcoming. Cody allowed no doubts to enter his mind. He kept thinking of contingencies.

What if Inhofe was surrounded by people? Cody would take the shot and risk collateral damage.

What if he took the shot and was seen? Cody would ride as fast as possible down the trail and across the dry cove and hope they couldn't follow.

If people were at the quarry when he returned, what then? He'd have to play that by ear. Maybe he'd drive down and out without anyone seeing him. If people were by the gate, he might wait them out until nighttime.

Cody retrieved a Red Bull from his pack and downed it. He needed to be sharp and have plenty of energy to ride back to the quarry.

By 9 am, a steady line of vehicles was entering the parking lot. Cody examined each one for telltale signs of Oklahoma's senior senator, James Mountain Inhofe. He assumed the vehicle would be substantial—possibly a large SUV limo, or maybe a vehicle with some official emblem signifying the senator's office. Most vehicles were parking in the lot, and their passengers had walked into the building. Some people waited outside and talked in small groups.

About an hour had passed when Cody sensed something was happening. A sheriff's patrol car drove up and parked by the entrance. Two officers got out and began shaking hands with and talking to a group of men who looked like they might be event organizers. Cody's heart rate bumped up a notch. He scanned the parking lot's entrance for an official-looking vehicle.

And then it came. A shiny, clean, black Suburban, the kind favored by those who don't give a rat's ass about the environment, drove into the parking lot. The group that had gathered at the entrance were all watching the approaching SUV. This was it! Cody had studied photos of Inhofe so he'd have no problem picking him out.

Cody clicked the safety off. The Army had trained him to control his breathing if he wanted to make a long shot. Deep breaths calmed his nerves. Looking through the scope, he tried to see inside the windows, but tinting prevented it.

The Suburban drove slowly up to the entrance and stopped. "Shit!" thought Cody. The vehicle parked with its passenger's side toward the entrance, which hid the exiting passenger. He wouldn't be able to take the shot immediately, but would have to wait until the man began walking to the building. His view through the scope held steady on the Suburban. The driver's door opened and a large, well-built man exited the driver's side, walked around to the rear passenger door, and opened it. Senator Inhofe got out.

Cody could see his head, but he was moving too much for Cody to take a shot. Inhofe then walked a few feet away from the Suburban and began shaking hands. Two sheriff's deputies stood off to the side watching. The driver got back in and pulled away to park. Cody sighted in on the now exposed and steady senator's head. He squeezed the trigger.

The silencer kept the sound to a minimum. No one in the vicinity heard the shot. What they did hear was the sickening sound of the senator's head being hit by a copper-coated lead projectile traveling at 3,000 feet per second

Cody quickly glanced through the scope, trying to see if anyone was looking his way. Some people were running, others stood around looking confused, as if they didn't quite grasp what they had seen. More cars were coming into the parking lot, unaware of what had happened.

The sheriff's deputies had drawn their service weapons and were scouring the crowd. Cody could see no one looking his way.

Cody put the spent shell in his pocket. He scrambled up the twenty exposed meters to the trail where he was out of sight. He wrapped the rifle with the towel and strapped it to the bike. He then jumped on the bike, jammed his Nikes into the toe clips, and started cranking down the trail. By the time he reached the trail's exposed section, he was out of sight of the building. Going down the steep section, his adrenaline provided superb control over his physical actions.

Cody heard shouting but never looked back. He didn't even slow down when he got to the dry cove, just blasting across the 50 meters of soft dirt to the trail on the other side.

Once he was on the dirt trail, and could pick up speed on the packed surface, he glanced over his shoulder. Nobody there. A good thing since he was still about 12 miles from the van.

He was still in military mode. This felt different than murdering the dog-fighter scum. He felt strange murdering that guy, but he wasn't too worried about getting caught. But this! He'd assassinated a sitting senator. Time was on his side, but not by a lot.

By now, he guessed the state police were on their way, but given that Lawton was 80 miles away, he had time to get back to the van. The only thing he needed to worry about was standing out too much. He was on a bike, the only one on these farm roads, and his bike had this thing strapped to it that definitely looked out of place. But so far, not a single vehicle had passed him, and he was almost to Highway 6.

The only Granite police officer on duty had already left town, heading south on Highway 6, and had passed Farm Road E1440 before Cody got close to the two-lane Highway. But now a Highway patrol officer, who had been eating lunch at the Domino Food & Fuel, was speeding south on the same road, his siren wailing. Cody heard the siren and spotted the flashing lights as he was getting close to the intersection, so he stopped and waited for the officer to go by, hoping that was the only one coming. He remounted the bike and rode to the corner of Highway 6. Turning right, he put his head down and rode hard. There were some cars and trucks by now. It was late morning, the sky was clear and temperatures were chilly, but warming. The locals were headed to the lake for fishing and these folks didn't pay much mind to this guy on a bicycle with a backpack, and what might have been a fishing pole strapped to his bike. Cody didn't raise any concern, or even much interest.

It was only a quick flat mile to the Domino Food & Fuel. Now he was in Granite and there was no way he'd get through without being seen. Luckily, it was less than half a mile before he was on the other side of town, where Highway 6 curved right before turning left again and skirting the granite hill that was the town's namesake. He was getting winded. His escape had been at race pace the whole way. He backed off a bit now that he was on the quarry road.

He rode past the broken gate, wanting to see if it had been discovered. He scanned the area. Nobody inside the gate, the chain and pole were still propped up as he'd left it earlier. He dismounted, threw his bike over the chain and rode like crazy up to the van. He quickly placed the bike, rifle and all, in the back, threw his pack in the passenger seat, and started the van.

He had to pee real bad, but getting out took precedence over everything.

He carefully maneuvered down the steep dirt road, bouncing over the bigger rocks and trying hard not to get stuck. "Careful. Don't fuck up now. C'mon..."

Pulling up to the gate, he threw the transmission into park and ran over to the pole he'd propped up the night before, wrenching it hard and throwing it down as flat as it would go. The chain was still almost a foot off the ground, but if he came at the chain from an angle, the first tire would pull it completely down. Pulling up slowly, he leaned out the window, straining to see the tire against the chain. Sure enough, as soon as the tire got a little traction, the pole dropped, and the van rolled over it.

Once he'd gone a few miles and began to calm down, he turned on his iPhone's radio to see if the news had picked up the story. It'd been about 60 minutes since the murder. The story was indeed ripping across the airwaves. He listened to KCRW, his favorite NPR station from Santa Monica. They had news breaks on the hour Saturday mornings, and it was coming up on noon.

"KCRW news at noon. We have a breaking story out of Oklahoma. State police report that Republican Senator James Inhofe has been shot. Preliminary reports say the senator died at the scene. Inhofe, a conservative who chaired the Senate's Energy and Environment Committee, was attending a fundraiser at the Quartz Mountain Resort in southern Oklahoma. The FBI is sending agents to the scene. They're classifying this as an assassination."

Cody turned down the volume, but kept it on so he could listen to updates.

His mind was reeling with the importance of his action. He'd set in motion something that could end his life. But he'd also ended the life of someone responsible, in large measure, for the miserable state of the world. As he stared at the empty road, white lines passing rhythmically by, he began to smile. Maybe his plan would work. Maybe he could kill the bastards after all.

Chapter 2

"Checkmate!" Cody cried.

Mark stared at the chessboard, then looked up to see a grinning and obviously happy little boy. "Set 'em up again!" Mark exclaimed. "The TV distracted me."

Playing chess with his son was a welcome distraction. They were having dinner on January 17th 1991, the day coalition forces launched their aerial bombardment of Iraqi forces in Kuwait as part of the Gulf War. Grandpa Paul, Cody's paternal grandfather, had driven down from Seattle for dinner as the news discussed efforts to drive Saddam Hussein's army out of Kuwait. Mark, a Vietnam vet, and Grandpa Paul, who fought in the Battle of the Bulge in WWII, were watching the war coverage on TV when Cody and their dog Cooper came bounding into the room and sat on the floor in front of them. Paul had never talked about his time in the military. He'd been able to bottle up his emotions after returning from the war in 1945 and never suffered outwardly from PTSD.

Mark, however, had been in a unit that participated in the massacres of small villages in 1968. While he was one of the few who did not shoot the civilians, he'd witnessed wholesale murder of old men, women, and children. He testified against his own command and individual soldiers during the investigation of My Lai, and he was dishonorably discharged based on fabricated charges of insubordination. It took Mark many years of therapy to come to terms with his involvement in that war. He grew to hate the U.S. government and the military establishment in particular. To this day, the sound of a helicopter could trigger his PTSD.

Both Mark and Paul, glued to the TV, were silent at first, but after Cody prodded them, they opened up and began talking about their experiences. Cody's mother Debra glanced nervously at Mark. She didn't wish for Cody to hear about these things, but it was clear Cody wanted to know. At nine years old, he could understand both what he was seeing on TV and the context his father and grandfather provided.

Grandpa Paul broke down in tears. He was telling, for the first time, his story of killing another human being. He was with the American First Army in December and January of 1944–1945. His division was involved in the battle for Ardennes when the German tanks rolled through in an attempt to break the allied forces and drive through to Antwerp. He told of coming face to face with a German soldier in the deep snowy woods and, acting on instinct, he leveled his rifle and fired directly into the man's body, dropping him instantly. The room grew silent as Debra quietly turned off the TV and everyone stared at their patriarch, a stoic man who rarely showed emotion. As he finished, a tear traced a crease down his weathered face.

After a moment, it was Mark's turn. Cody stayed on the floor with Cooper, absentmindedly stroking his dog's head.

Like his father, Mark had never talked about his time in the war. He'd been drafted right out of college. Initially, he intended to avoid the draft by taking the well-worn path to Vancouver, BC, as some of his friends had, but after talking with Paul who was very pro-war at the time, Mark accepted his fate and was inducted into the Army.

After a brief training, he was shipped off to fight. It wasn't long after landing in Saigon that he knew his decision was a mistake. All the GIs he met told him the war was a sham. They hated being there, and, to a man, they wanted to get out—alive if possible—but out any way they could.

He heard stories of GIs "fragging," throwing hand grenades at their superior officers for making bone-headed decisions and sending troops into dangerous battles for no discernible reason.

As a FNG (Fucking New Guy), Mark was derided and made to do the menial, disgusting, and difficult jobs until he proved himself worthy of better treatment. All new recruits were treated this way.

He was among the first soldiers to arrive in My Lai after the massacre and was tasked with burying the bodies of civilians murdered by William Calley's Charlie Company. Telling the story to his family, he couldn't bring himself to describe what he saw and choked up immediately. After fighting back tears, he finally burst into a sad, lonely howl and cried. Debra rose from her chair and stood behind him, her arms enveloping him from behind. "It's OK, honey, you're not in Vietnam anymore, you're here among family." She glanced around the room at her children, her father-in-law, and her husband. All were in tears.

Cody stared open-mouthed at his father and grandfather. He'd never seen this level of emotion from either of them, and it struck him not only as odd but profoundly sad. Cody never cried much except when he was physically hurt. This was hard for him to understand.

Cody asked, "Why do we fight wars if everyone is against them? I mean, you guys and everyone at school says war is wrong, so why do we fight?"

Grandpa Paul said, "Politics is a messy business. People running the military machine make money off of war, and the oil industry wants access to the oil in Iraq."

The matter-of-fact nature of his comment was not lost on anyone. Paul, a veteran of one of the more significant WWII campaigns in Europe, elaborated. "You're old enough to have read about General Eisenhower, who was the supreme commander of the war effort and who became our 34th president. He gave a great farewell speech back in 1960 prior to leaving the presidency in which he famously warned of the military industrial complex: *'In the councils of government, we must guard against the acquisition of unwarranted influence, whether sought or unsought, by the military industrial complex. The potential for the disastrous rise of misplaced power exists and will persist.'*"

"There's another quote in the same speech that hasn't gotten the attention it deserves, Paul continued. *'Another factor in maintaining balance involves the element of time. As we peer into society's future, we—you and I, and our government—must avoid the impulse to live only for today, plundering, for our own ease and convenience, the precious resources of tomorrow. We cannot mortgage the material assets of our grandchildren without risking the loss also of their political and spiritual heritage. We want democracy to survive for all generations to come, not to become the insolvent phantom of tomorrow.'*"

Everyone was stunned. They'd never heard Grandpa Paul recite anything from memory. But they also thought the quotes were appropriate to the situation in which the country now found itself. We were fighting a war for material gain not because we were attacked, but because some people stood in the way of our access to their resource—oil.

The three adults agreed this whole mess was the result of the U.S.'s desperate need for Middle East oil. Cody and Jennifer had heard this conversation many times. The world was addicted to oil—especially the U.S. The kids were too young to understand the reasons, but they gleaned enough to know the adults didn't trust the government's or corporations' motives. Mark, Debra, and Paul were not radicals, but they were open minded and paid attention.

"I'm going to take a nap," Grandpa Paul said, breaking the silence. As Debra helped Paul into the guest bedroom, Mark stood up and tried not to pace. He walked over to the cupboard and took out the family's chess set. Mark had never been a good chess player; he picked up the game in the military, but hadn't spent the time or effort to learn strategies. However, after Cody turned nine, Mark had begun to teach him. Cody had grasped the basics quickly, and they had played a few games on weekend afternoons. So far, Mark had won all of them.

The loose pieces rattled in the cardboard box as Mark retrieved the game, making Cody turn away from the bright green missile strikes on TV. Mark smiled as Cody snatched the box out of his hand and began setting up the pieces. With the war on in the background, they sat down to play. Maybe it was the distraction of the TV, or the confessions of his father, but Mark found himself in deep trouble after a few moves and soon was checkmated. It wasn't a fluke. Cody beat him three games straight. Mark, however, was not upset. On the contrary, he loved watching his young son methodically develop his pieces and thwart every move he made to set up an attack. Maybe his son had some talent with this game?

Debra had been half-paying attention to the game while she watched TV. "Hey, Cody, you know there's a chess group at the library?" she offered. "I think they have a coach or teacher or something who could make you better. Want to try it?"

"Yeah! Can we go tomorrow?"

"I've got work tomorrow, but Saturday's good. I'll call to make sure it's a good day for them."

On Saturday, Debra drove Cody to the library. It was warm and sunny, perfect for playing outside, but all Cody wanted to do was play chess.

Debra parked next to an old beat-up white 1972 Datsun 1200. The car didn't look like much, covered in political and environmental bumper stickers, racing decals, and sporting more than a few dents and scratches. It actually looked like crap—but a special kind of crap.

What Cody found interesting were the racing decals and the overly large rear tires. Was this somebody's idea of a joke car? Dressing up a junker to look fast when it clearly couldn't beat the local meter maid in her little golf cart.

They noticed a man behind the wheel sitting motionless as if in a trance. He had long, grey hair in a ponytail and a scraggly beard. His eyes hid behind yellow-tinted aviator sunglasses.

When Cody slammed his door shut, the man, whose driver's window was open, slowly turned to face Cody. He stared briefly before lowering his glasses with his index finger. Speaking slowly, he said, "So much for my meditation time. Guess I have to go to work."

This sounded like a mild rebuke for waking him up, but there was just enough irony in his voice to indicate he meant it in jest.

He opened his door with a loud metallic squeak, stopping just shy of dinging Cody's door. Cody met eyes with the old man, who looked angry but greeted him with a friendly, "Howdy, little partner." This surprised Cody, but he responded, "Howdy to you, too, sir!"

Polite to a fault: that was Cody.

Cody wasn't attuned to social nuance as most kids his age were. Mark and Debra had detected signs of Aspergers over the years, a suspicion this interaction supported. His interest in this strange man overcame his fear and allowed him to stare as the man exited his car.

Debra walked around to join the two. She sized up this somewhat stern but frail-looking man and realized he wasn't dangerous. That said, he definitely wasn't your normal library patron. There was his appearance—an aging hippy look he sported without effort.

And then there was the car.

"I hope my son didn't disturb you," Debra said. "Sometimes he doesn't understand boundaries very well."

Cody didn't react to this. He just continued looking quizzically at the man.

The man turned to Debra and said, "I was meditating before chess class. There are some rowdy kids in there, and I have to wrangle them into conformity without my bullwhip. The library administrator has forbidden me using that after 'the incident.' Meditation helps."

Seeing Debra's eyes widen, he smiled and introduced himself as Mel, the chess instructor. Debra smiled; she remembered hearing stories from friends about this 63-year-old iconoclast with the varied background. He'd been in Army intelligence during the early years of the Vietnam War and then in the late 60s he'd worked as a roadie for some big acts, The 5th Dimension and Frank Sinatra among others. His military and professional life let him travel the world, and his inquisitive mind ensured he was eclectically educated. He spoke four languages and could hold his own on most subjects. He was smart about the money he'd earned, salting it away in a variety of investments including stocks and property in gentrifying neighborhoods. He bought Apple early and often.

Now, Mel was retired and spent his time teaching chess to kids and sometimes traveling to far corners of the world. He was a wonderful chess teacher, especially with kids.

Mel noticed Cody's bag of chess pieces and asked if he was there for the chess club. "Yeah, my mom said she saw people playing here and I've been beating my dad too easily, so I want to play some better players." He looked down in embarrassment, thinking he'd disrespected his father to a total stranger, but the man looked at him with approving eyes. "Well, unless you're a budding Bobby Fischer, there might be a player or two here who can give you a good game. Follow me."

Cody went with Mel into a large community room filled with long tables and chairs. An expanse of windows filled the space with bright daylight. More than a dozen kids and a few adults were setting up games or already playing. Learning the basics of chess was easy, but to be really good, you needed to think spatially and consider every possibility, of which there were many. Mel took Cody over to a smaller boy of about seven and introduced him to Jesse. "Beat 'im up for me," Mel told Jesse. He said this with a smile, and Cody realized he was about to get schooled by a little kid.

Jesse was rather quiet and shy normally, but when it came to chess, he was fearless. He wasn't the best player in the group, but he was up there. After setting up the pieces, Jesse pulled out a clock. Cody asked what it was for, and Jesse explained he would set it for 10 minutes for each side. All Cody had to do was hit the button on his side when he made a move, and the clock would begin counting down the seconds for his opponent.

Right away, Cody got nervous. He'd never played on the clock before. He and his dad just moved when they were ready.

The first game was over quickly. Jesse opened with a standard combination and within just a few moves, he captured one of Cody's rooks. Cody never saw it coming. But this was why he wanted to play better players. How else would he learn?

Mel had been watching them play. He came over as they were setting up for the next game. He chuckled at Cody and said, "There's a lot to this game, and I'll teach you as much as I can over time, but for now, just play Jesse and notice how he moves. See if you can detect any patterns or tactics. We'll get into the instruction next time you come."

Jesse proceeded to destroy Cody five games straight. When Debra came in toward the end of the last game, she stood quietly behind Cody. She knew next to nothing about the game, so she didn't know what had happened when Cody threw up his hands in defeat. But Cody knew. A young kid who was a significantly better player had schooled him.

Mel walked them out. "How did you do today?" he asked Cody, knowing full well he'd lost every game.

"Ha! You saw it. Jesse beat the pants off me. No matter what I did, he beat me. Will I ever get good enough to beat a guy like that?"

"Chess is a great game. You'll grow to love it the better you get. You'll always find people you can't beat. The top players have incredible minds. I'm a decent player myself, but there's one boy in the club, the kid with the bright red hair who was playing the older gentleman by the windows. I've played that boy close to a hundred games, and I've only beaten him twice. His rating is just over 1950. Do you know what that means?"

Cody shook his head. "No."

"Well, the numbers start at about 800 for novices, which is where you are now. Jesse, the kid you played, is about 1600, a decent level for a seven year old. The red-headed kid is bumping up against the masters level at 2000. Really good players, those over 2000, are very strong at the national level, but to compete internationally, you need to be over 2400. You'd never beat anyone at that level, ever!" Realizing he'd just put a limit on someone he barely knew, Mel added, "unless you're reeeeally special! Maybe you'll get there if you apply yourself."

Reaching into a folder, Mel handed Cody a sheet of paper labeled "Chess Goop." He explained that these were quick one-line instructions that would help his game immediately.

Cody looked at the paper, thanked Mel, and as he started to get into the car, he offhandedly asked about the Datsun.

"No offense, Mr. Mel, but that's one funky-looking car you got there. Are the racing stickers keeping it from falling apart?" Debra looked at Cody with surprise and disapproval. It was out of character for Cody to disrespect an elder. Cody didn't mean to disparage the man's car, but he'd detected a sense of humor in Mel that gave him the courage to say such a thing, hoping it would be taken in jest.

Mel glared at Cody in an intimidating manner and stated that his dilapidated Datsun could beat anything in town. "Do you want to know why?" he asked. "You can drop the Mr., by the way. To you, I'm just Mel."

Cody smiled and said, "Yeah, Mel, why?"

"This doesn't burn gas, just tires. And I don't mean it burns tires for fuel. The car is electric, and I burn tires by smoking people off the line. Do you know anything about drag racing?"

"Not much, but my friend's father has a Corvette and that's pretty fast."

"Is it a red Corvette?" Mel asked.

"Yeah, they live over on Cedar Ave. You know them?"

"As a matter of fact, I do. He won't race me anymore. Last time was pretty embarrassing for him. No one in town will race me anymore. I have to go up to Olympia or Seattle to get any action these days. Electric cars are vastly superior to gas burners in many ways, but acceleration is the most obvious. You might want to look in to them some time. Might be a career in there for you at some point."

With this, Mel bid them adieu and returned to his chess charges.

Cody couldn't stop talking as they drove home. Mel enthralled him, both for the chess and for the fast car. He'd never been into cars like some boys, seeing them as tools for getting places, not as status symbols. But this little Datsun that Mel had converted to electric, it was a cool car! And it didn't need a drop of gasoline.

Chapter 3

Principal James Edwards rolled his eyes when Gary Cheney entered his office. He knew there wasn't much he could do. Cheney's father, with his hefty donations, had already made his position clear to the school district. Money and power talk loudly in Congress, but in small town Eatonville, WA, where few of means exist, even a little money gives you power. David Cheney had a lot of money. He built a new football field for the high school with his son's quarterback career in mind. When he insisted, he got his way. It was understood that the money would stop if his kid was disciplined.

Freshman Gary Cheney had made the football team as second-string quarterback. His father's donation of the new football field didn't hurt, but Cheney did have some skills, if muscles and unfocused aggression can be described as skills. Cheney, having been let off with just a slap on the wrist for his bullying in eighth grade, felt emboldened to continue tormenting smaller students in high school. He wasn't big enough to take on the older kids, but Cody and his group of friends were easy fodder.

Early in the fall, only a couple weeks after school had started, freshman Cody was walking with some friends to class when Cheney and three other football players confronted them.

The football players were much larger than Cody and his friends. Cody's friend Jeremy, a wisp of a boy who preferred reading to sports, was pushed to the floor, dropping his books and papers. Cody yelled at Cheney, who instantly popped him in the face, bloodying his nose. The commotion drew teachers to the hall, and they broke up the fight before it could escalate. Jeremy, Cody and the four football players were hustled into the principal's office.

The students were seated on opposite sides of the room, which meant the smaller kids had to face their tormentors while waiting. The bullies glared at Cody and Jeremy, who both were now regretting coming to school that day.

When questioned, the Cheney and his gang said they were just messing around and didn't mean to do any harm. The principal let them off with a warning to play nice, a mere admonishment that told Cody and Jeremy they were on their own with these guys.

****

Now in his junior year, Cody had gotten stronger and faster at running, and his performance at track meets was very good. Not as good as his sister Jennifer, but good. He always scored points for the team, if not with a win with a solid second or third place. He was strong enough to double in the 800m and 1,500m, earning even more points.

Jennifer had graduated the year before, having won the state meet in the 1,500m in both her junior and senior years. She'd won the cross country title all four years and exulted in receiving a full athletic scholarship to the University of Oregon, a track powerhouse.

Cody's grades were fine, and he had lots of friends, but he still struggled with Cheney and his gang of toughs. Cody was haunted by multiple incidents from the years before: while Cheney and his gang had to be circumspect, they still made life difficult for Cody. Words were exchanged, there was constant taunting and the occasional shove in the hallway. When Cody complained to teachers or the principal, he was essentially told to just deal with it.

Cheney and his friends had all grown since freshman year and towered over Cody. Cheney was now the first-string quarterback, which made things worse because the football coach would always take Cheney's side whenever anyone complained about bullying.

One day in the winter of Cody's junior year, after cross-country season was over and before track started in the spring, he was walking with Jazzie to a shared class when Cheney and his toughs appeared before them, blocking their way. This was new. They'd never involved Jazzie before. Cody became alarmed. He didn't want to be humiliated in front of his girlfriend.

The two tried to go around the four boys, but they blocked their path and two of them pushed Cody against the lockers. "Leave me alone!" Cody demanded, but this had no effect. He was about to raise his voice, hoping to draw the attention of a teacher, when Cheney pulled out a plastic bag of fresh dog shit and emptied it on Cody's head. Cody reached up and realizing what this disgusting substance was, went ballistic. He shoved a handful of it into Cheney's face, smearing it into his nose and eyes.

The hallway became a battle zone as the four big boys began pummeling Cody. Hearing the yelling and screaming, teachers rushed into the hall and the principal ran from his office.

Jazzie tried to pull the boys off Cody, but she was powerless against the football players. Quickly, the adults separated the boys while everyone was overwhelmed by the stink of the excrement. All were hauled off to the office, with Cody and Cheney making separate trips to the bathroom to get cleaned up. The principal called parents and told them to come pick up their kids, as all were being suspended for fighting.

It took Cody several hours to calm down. He'd never reacted with such anger and force. It was the first time he had purposely harmed another, and he was still trying to process his feelings when the family sat down for dinner.

Jazzie and some of Cody's friends had come over after school to see how he was doing and congratulate him for taking on four football players. Jazzie was more concerned with how Cody was handling the stress. He could be moody at times, although rarely when he was with her.

During dinner, Mark and Debra wanted to know how the fight started. They were upset Cody had been suspended, since he clearly didn't start the fight. Mark took the incident especially hard. He knew the unfairness of bullying stressed Cody out, and he wanted to protect his son and prepare him for a life that would be filled with bullies, both physical and emotional.

Cody answered their questions matter-of-factly. He was calm, almost emotionless. Even his voice seemed different. He was thinking through his options. He asked Mark what he should do.

Mark tried to keep his rage from showing.

"I'm going to talk to principal Edwards tomorrow," he said. "This suspension's not going to stand. We'll get it taken off your record, too. It's all BS."

"I'm going with you," Cody said in a calm, determined voice.

"I don't think that's a good idea. Better I go alone."

"No, I'm going with you." Cody got up and walked to his room.

Debra and Mark looked at each other. Both felt such sadness. Their youngest child had been brutalized and humiliated. What would the long term consequences be?

The next morning, Mark took a personal day from his teaching job in Olympia. He and Cody drove to school, and Mark parked in the teacher's lot, ignoring the rules against doing so. As they walked down the hall to the office, students stared and made hushed comments. Cody was now sporting a huge black eye and his face was swollen and red from being pummeled.

Mark had not called ahead, so when he asked for Principal Edwards, his office manager said the principal was busy. Mark asked when he could see him, and was told it was normal policy to call ahead for an appointment. Mark said slowly, "Yesterday, my son was attacked and beaten in this school when Principal Edwards should've protected him. Go in there and tell him I'm coming in—now!"

The woman was stunned at the intensity of this command, then looked at Cody's face. She went into Edward's office, and moments later, returned saying they could go in.

James Edwards had been the school principal for ten years. He started his career as an inner city teacher in Los Angeles, but eventually burned out and moved to small-town Washington where he figured the kids wouldn't be so difficult. He was thrilled when they accepted him as an administrator and hired him as principal at Eatonville High. No more gang bangers to worry about. But, as he would find out, bullies with powerful fathers could be just as bad.

Edwards was almost old enough to be Mark's father, but when he was sitting across the desk from this agitated man, he felt like the child who had gotten all Fs on his report card standing before his own father.

"Why did you suspend my son for fighting? He only defended himself." Mark let the question lie there.

"I'm very sorry for what happened to Cody," Edwards replied. "Those boys will be dealt with, but we have zero tolerance for fighting, so school rules dictate that all parties in a fight are suspended. I'm very sorry," he repeated.

"That's not fair!" Cody said.

Mark could barely contain himself. "I understand there's zero tolerance for bullying, too, but those boys have been getting away with it for at least three years."

Edwards was sweating profusely. Mark was right, but Edwards would be unable to make anything stick against the Cheney boy. He was starting to hate his job again.

"Look, I agree this policy isn't being enforced fairly. But I have problems with Cheney. His father has power over the school board. There's nothing I can do about it."

"It's illegal to assault another person," Mark said. "We're going to see if Mr. Cheney's influence extends to the police as well." And with that, he got up, motioned for Cody to follow, and left.

They drove to the police station. As Cody and Mark walked in, a jovial officer at the front desk asked with a big smile, "What're you guys in for?" Laughing, he lamely explained that was their standard inside joke.

"We're here to file assault charges against a boy named Gary Cheney. He's a student at Eatonville High. You can see what he did to my son." Mark indicated the black eye and swollen face.

The desk sergeant, Officer Cleek, looked at Cody and whistled. "Wow, that's quite the shiner you got there, boy. I hope you put some ice on it to keep the swelling down."

Cody was surprised at the policeman's joviality. "Yes, sir, I did, but it still hurts."

"What is the procedure to file charges, officer, uh, Cleek?" Mark said, looking at the man's name badge.

Officer Cleek, reading their moods, assumed a more professional demeanor and said he'd assign someone to take their statement and, after that, the department would determine if there was a reason to investigate. He then buzzed the adjoining room, asking for Robin to come in.

Robin Cheshire was 55, a divorced woman not quite grandmotherly in appearance, but edging that way. She'd been with the department for 25 years and was the first woman ever hired by the Eatonville police department. She had endured many insults along the way, as any woman attempting to break through the myriad glass ceilings had, but her endurance and pleasant, albeit no-nonsense demeanor, eventually earned her the department's admiration. She was also a mother and would treat young Cody with age-appropriate respect.

Robin greeted Mark warmly and seeing Cody's face, asked how he was doing."I got beat up yesterday at school. I want Gary Cheney to get punished for doing this to me."

Robin was surprised he didn't defer to his parent, as most boys his age in a police station did. Officer Cleek explained there'd been an altercation at the high school, and they wished to press charges. He asked Robin to take Cody's statement and determine if there were grounds for such an action.

Robin invited Mark and Cody into her office and motioned for them to sit. After offering them drinks, which they declined, she opened a notebook and began asking Cody questions.

"When did this incident happen?"

"Yesterday, between second and third period. I was walking to class with my girlfriend when Cheney and three of his football friends started pushing me and calling me names."

Robin asked for Cheney's full name. "Please continue. What happened next? How did you react?"

"I was embarrassed they were doing this in front of my girlfriend. They're bullies and the teachers and coaches let them get away with it. It's not fair. Someone should make them stop."

Mark said, "That's why we're here. Principal Edwards says Cheney's father has influence with the school board. Plus he's the quarterback on the football team. Edwards refused to punish the boy beyond suspension. Assault is a serious crime. I want to know if that holds true for kids, as well."

Robin kept writing without looking up. When she finished, she looked at Cody. "How did you get the black eye?"

Cody looked down. The dog shit on his head had been humiliating in the extreme. Even worse was the look on Jazzie's face when Cody made eye contact with her.

"After Cheney pushed me against the lockers..." Cody looked up at Robin, "...he dumped a bag of dog shit on my head. Fresh dog shit. It got in my hair and everything."

Robin's eyes widened. "What did you do then?"

"I kinda went crazy, I guess. I reached up to feel what it was, and then grabbed it off my head to look at it. The guys were all laughing at me, and all I could think about was that

Jazzie had seen them do this to me." He was almost in tears as he said this.

"I smashed the shit right in Cheney's face!" He said this with a smidgen of pride. "That's when they all started beating me. Cheney hit me in the eye, but the other guys punched me, too. All of them were beating on me and kicking me until the teachers came out and made them stop."

Mark looked at his son and then at Robin. Barely holding his outrage in check, he said, "That's clearly assault, right? You'll arrest them? I will not allow these boys to go unpunished!"

Robin drew a deep breath. Her notes complete, she said with sincerity, "I'm so sorry you had to experience that. I can only imagine how it must have felt. I'm going to request we bring in the other boys for questioning, and after we've gotten both sides of the story, I'll take it to our DA."

"Thanks for listening to Cody's side of things," Mark said. "I'm disgusted with how the school is treating this incident. Hopefully, we'll get justice from the police. Please call me when you have some news." He motioned for Cody to get up and leave.

In the car, Cody was moody. Mark didn't know what to say, so he let him be, but after a few minutes of silence, he said, "Cody, the world can be pretty nasty sometimes. Remember when Grandpa Paul and I told you about our experiences in the war? What you experienced yesterday and today is sort of like the root cause of wars. Bad people taking advantage of others and no good authority to stop them. In going to the police, we've taken it up with the United Nations. Now we find out if they'll send in the troops to deal with the bad guys. Hopefully, they will."

"But what if they don't?" Cody asked. "What if Cheney's father intimidates the police, too?"

Mark tried to come up with a good answer but could find none. He said, "We'll cross that bridge when we come to it." Cody didn't like that answer and settled back into his bad mood. He did not want to go to school with those boys.

The next morning, Cody's eye looked even worse. He was suspended for two more days, so Debra took it upon herself to contact his teachers for homework assignments. With Jennifer off to college, she was happy to have her boy home for a few days to keep her company. She tried to make the best of the situation by fixing him a good lunch and talking to him about his schoolwork. This helped a little, but there was no denying Cody's mood. He'd been shaken by the humiliation and needed justice—or revenge.

Cody had been developing a need for justice in everything in his life. Having endured low-level bullying for years and feeling the injustice of it, he was careful never to be mean to anyone, not to hurt any animal. He'd grown to really hate people who purposely caused harm to others, or the flora and fauna of the earth. This shift in his personality was not evident to his family or friends, but subtle hints were seeping through. After his first lunch with Jazzie, he'd become a vegetarian. When asked, he said he could not stand to see how the animals were treated before being slaughtered. He didn't want to be a part of that.

He was never the type to belittle someone, but like any kid, he'd occasionally tease people. As he got older, however, he realized that some teasing can be a form of bullying, so he tried to be aware of personalities and gauge when someone would take his actions or words as an attempt at humor—or if they might bother them. His awareness of right and wrong, good and bad, became highly attuned. This is why this latest and most egregious episode hurt him. He'd done nothing to bring this on himself, and those who perpetrated the bullying were, so far, getting away with it. For him to recover, he needed justice.

Officer Cheshire requested that Gary Cheney and the other three boys be brought in. When Cheney's father arrived with Gary in tow, he was not happy. His wife insisted he take care of this. They had a difficult marriage, and their tyrant of a son was a big contributing factor.

David Cheney was a mid-management executive with Weyerhaueser and an acolyte of Albert Wilcox. Albert had become the head of a division of Weyerhaueser shortly after his daughter, Jazzie, was born. Years ago, during protests against clearcutting old growth forests, Albert used Cheney to organize wood workers as an intimidation force against the environmentalists.

Like father, like son.

David entered Robin's office. "What's this about?" he said. "Why'd you bring me and my boy here? I don't have time to deal with bullshit!" Robin took notice of his temper and calmly replied, "Your son has been accused of assault, which is a very serious crime. You've been brought here so I can ask some questions."

"What? Are you serious?" he bellowed. "This is nothing more than a schoolyard fight. There's no reason to bring in the police!"

"Our laws governing assault do not have an age limit, Mr. Cheney. Now, if you'll allow me, I need to ask Gary some questions."

David immediately pulled out his phone, flipped it open, and pressed speed dial for his attorney. While doing so, he stuck his palm out to Robin and said, "My boy is not going to answer any questions without my lawyer present!"

"Your son is not under arrest. We merely want to get his side of the story to determine whether the police need to be involved."

"He's not talking without my attorney! Gary, don't say a word." David began barking into his phone while Gary sat back and smiled.

Once the attorney arrived, there were heated discussions, with the lawyer threatening lawsuits against the police department. Robin knew her job well, but given the circumstances, she decided to call the chief of police.

When Chief Walters arrived, she explained the reason they'd requested Gary come in, but the attorney immediately cut her off, saying that unless Gary was being arrested, there'd be no further discussion. Chief Walters was in no mood to get into a fight with Cheney. He'd run into him back during the protest days and found him not only distasteful, but ready to bring all his extensive resources to whatever fight he took on. He motioned for Robin to join him in the hall.

When they closed the door, Walters explained that under no circumstances would they bring charges against this boy for a schoolyard fight. Cheney would make their lives miserable, he explained, and besides, they didn't have the resources to deal with kids fighting at school. Robin tried to explain how badly Cody had been beaten, but Chief Walters just motioned for her to stop talking.

They returned to Robin's office and the chief informed the attorney and Cheney they were free to go, but to tell the kids to knock off the fighting.

Robin watched with disgust as the three of them filed out. Gary laughed as he walked by, muttering under his breath, "Fuckin' pig! Can't touch me." It was all Robin could do to keep from punching the brat.

After they left, Robin went to Chief Walter's office, closed the door and sat down. She just stared at Walters.

"What?" he said. "You heard my explanation. What more do you want?"

"Did you hear what the little monster said to me as he walked out? I didn't sign up to be humiliated by some fucking punk bully!"

"Whoa, hold on there, Robin, no need to use that kind of language with me! I know you're upset, but you know the reality is we wouldn't get anywhere with that attorney. Our DA won't touch this. That's up to the parents and school to deal with, not the police."

"What's Cody to do?"

"Who's Cody?"

"He's the kid who got the crap beaten out of him by four big football players in front of his girlfriend. They dumped dog shit on his head, and when he retaliated, they beat him. He got suspended, too! How do you think that boy feels?"

Chief Walters looked down and said, "Life can be very unfair sometimes."

"I thought our job was to keep it from being unfair, boss," Robin replied, revulsion in her voice. She walked out feeling disgusted with her job, and especially with the chief. She now had to call Mark Benson and tell him there'd be no help from the police.

Mark answered his cell on the first ring. He'd been anticipating Robin's call since leaving her office. He was ready to go to court to take this bully down.

"Mr. Benson?" she asked.

"Yes, Officer Cheshire, what did you find out from Gary?"

"I don't have good news. Cheney lawyered up and Chief Walters said to let this drop. He said the DA won't prosecute a schoolyard fight. He wouldn't even let me question Gary." After a beat, she added, "I'm very sorry, but there's nothing we'll be doing for you. If it means anything, I think you would've had a good case."

This last comment hurt the most. Knowing they were in the right, yet would have to swallow their pride and deal with it. How would he explain this to Cody?

Mark thanked Robin. He would talk to Debra first to get her take on how to approach Cody. They'd have to come up with a plan to try to make the remainder of his time at school safe. But how?

Debra couldn't believe what Mark was saying. "You mean some punks can beat up our child and neither the school nor the police will do anything about it? That's bullshit! What'll we tell Cody?"

"The truth. Anything less will disappoint him even more. We have to let him know we're there for him." She agreed and they both walked to Cody's room, where he'd been reading his history lesson.

Mark and Debra sat on Cody's bed, and Cody turned his chair around at his desk to face them. He could tell from their expressions they didn't have good news.

"I got a call from Robin at the station." Mark looked down before continuing. "Unfortunately, Robin says the police will not be getting involved. She says the chief of police, some guy named Walters, thinks the DA won't prosecute a schoolyard fight, so they're not going to take up the matter."

"These guys beat me up and put dog shit on my head and both the school and the police won't do anything?" Cody's temper, a rare thing, was exploding to the surface.

Debra tried to calm him down, but all she could offer was a feeble, "It'll be OK. We're going to talk to the principal again and—"

Cody screamed, "Principal Edwards won't do shit!"

He'd never cussed in front of his parents before, he almost never uttered profanity to anyone. But this was the new Cody. A Cody the world was reshaping in spite of Mark and Debra's efforts.

"I'll have to deal with these guys on my own then, and it won't be pretty!"

This statement alarmed Mark and Debra.

"Cody, please! That's not who you are," Debra said.

"Violence is never the answer," Mark told Cody. We'll be there for you. Just call us when something happens again."

All they got in return was a cold, intense thousand-yard stare. Cody sunk into a silent funk and remained mute until they left his room.

Chapter 4

The next morning, Jazzie dropped by on her way to school to see how Cody was doing. Debra met her at the door and let her in. She told Jazzie about the day before and that Cody's mood hadn't improved.

Jazzie and Cody had become a well-known couple at Eatonville High. Intelligent and athletic, they ran with a fun crowd of similar bent. Cody had liked her instantly when they met at a track meet. There was something irresistible about a girl who could not only keep up with him on the field, but in conversation, too. They had become close and reveled in the ever-present sexual tension which they occasionally indulged, safely of course. While on an easy run exploring new deer trails, they had discovered a nice secluded spot near the river. It was a small grassy clearing surrounded by trees and far enough from the main trail that no one would hear them. On warm dry days, that became their go-to place for exploring each other. They taught each other what felt good, and Cody made sure that Jazzie always had at least one orgasm. He told her it was only fair since his was never in doubt. They were in love, still too young to fully understand it, but they often talked about their feelings. They were exceptionally happy.

Jazzie opened his bedroom door and walked in. Cody was seated at his desk in his comfy chair. Hearing Jazzie walk in, and feeling her warm gaze like a sunbeam cutting through a cool forest canopy in spring, he slowly spun around. Nothing in the world could right how wronged he felt, except the feeling he got when he looked at her face. It was almost like their minds melded. All at once, he broke into sobs.

Jazzie turned around and gently closed the door. She walked over and leaned into him, pressing her right breast into his cheek. She knew how much Cody loved her breasts. He'd get excited just seeing any hint of her nipple. It seemed to help as he pulled her tight.

Cody broke the embrace. "Remember when you were a kid? Little kid? You knew right from wrong, right?"

Jazzie's response was barely audible, "Sure." She kept her gaze on him and tried to maintain a calm exterior. Her dealings with her father, Albert, gave her insight on how not to make a bad situation worse.

Cody said, "I thought my school...or at least the police, would do something. Nothing! Cheney's father can do that!" His voice dripped with incredulity.

"Debra told me. I can't believe it either." Jazzie paused. "She said you were justifiably upset." This elicited a slight, but perceptible chuckle from Cody.

"What should I do?" he asked.

"I think we should organize."

"Organize?"

"Yeah. Get our friends and the track team and their friends, and go to the principal. This isn't how our school should be run!" Now Jazzie was getting heated.

"I don't know. You didn't see Edwards' face when he told us there was nothing he could do. It's like Cheney's father has something on everyone in town."

"Probably true, but my dad used to complain like hell about the 'fucking protesters!' as he loved to call them. It pissed him off when people organized. He was afraid of them."

She watched his expression for signs he was mellowing. Maybe a hint. Cody could lose himself in thought. This was one of those times.

Outside the door, Debra waited patiently, wondering if Jazzie could boost Cody's mood.A good thirty minutes later, Cody and Jazzie emerged quietly. Debra exchanged glances with the girl. Jazzie slightly raised her eyebrow, but Debra wasn't sure what this meant. It seemed more a positive sign than not, so maybe things had improved.

"Jazzie, are you running in the meet this weekend?" Debra asked.

"Yep, running the 1,500 again," said Jazzie, relieved at the upbeat change of subject. "Coach says I should get a PR since that Wilkerson girl from Seattle will be down. I'm gonna hang on her shoulder as long as possible. She just ran 4:23 two weeks ago. That'd be a 12-second PR for me. You and Mark coming?" She glanced at Cody, hoping this wasn't pushing any buttons. No indication. He seemed a tad more resigned, but still very moody.

"Yeah, we'll be there for sure. Cody's shooting for a personal record, too. He's got a lot of PRs in his future. We want to see them all."

They both looked at Cody for a response. He glanced up when he felt the silence that followed. "What?"

"Nothing. We were just talking about seeing you get another PR this weekend. Feel like you can do it?"

Cody had to think. He'd backed off his training a little since getting suspended, but felt good—nice and rested actually.

"It could happen," he said. Another sign he was improving.

****

Friday morning, Cody's first day back at school, Debra made Cody his favorite oatmeal with brown sugar, raisins, and blueberries picked last summer from their bushes, then frozen.

Mark looked up from his paper. "How you feeling, boy?" Like his son, he was beginning to think of the world in not-so-gentle terms.

"I'm going to do the best I can given the bizarreness of this whole thing." Cody ate a spoonful of oatmeal. "It's good to know you guys are behind me. The world's a little crazier than I'd hoped."

Hearing this from his young son, Mark felt a heavy pain. Watching his changed high schooler walk out the door, he felt a deep sadness.

Cody rode up on his bike as Jazzie was locking hers to the rack. She smiled at him, and it was the best he'd felt since the incident.

"Your eye looks killer!" she said. "I want to get a picture before it starts going away. This is your badge of honor, pretty boy!"

Cody almost didn't know whether to laugh or be offended, so the rational side of his personality kicked in and he cracked a small smile. He hadn't given any thought to preserving this massive bruise for posterity, but then, he had been humiliated in front of his girlfriend while getting the damn thing.

Jazzie and her friends saw it differently. After seeing Cody on Thursday, she'd invited some friends over for a talk. She needed a reality check. The black eye was pretty nasty, but his attitude toward life had changed. She needed to vent and plan how to get him back to normal.

Five of her friends were there and all agreed that none of this was Cody's fault, and he had no reason to feel bad that Jazzie had witnessed the assault. But that was the girls talking. Cody's perspective was completely different.

Knowing this, the girls concocted an idea to make Cody feel good about the black eye. That's why she'd asked to take his picture.

Cody locked his bike next to hers and then embraced her, giving her a long, tight hug. "Do you really want to take a picture of this thing? I don't feel like it's a badge of honor. Pretty embarrassed about it, actually."

"No need to be embarrassed. You took on four football players, two of them linemen! From what I heard, Cheney's got a black eye, too, heh heh. I'll load up some Kodachrome in my Nikon in photo class and get some shots before we go for our run this afternoon."

With that, they parted to go to their respective classes.

Fortunately, Cody didn't have any classes with his assailants. But the hallways were another matter. He wasn't scared of them so much as just wanting to avoid them—for the rest of his life. He managed to get through his morning classes with no problem, but then lunch time came, and it was unlikely he'd be able to avoid them there.

Sure enough, the same four guys were holding court at the football table with other members of the team. Cody saw them before they saw him and abruptly turned to go to another part of the caféteria. He was just settling in to eat with some friends when he heard from behind, "Shiner man is back! Let's see that thing." It was one of the idiots who had assaulted him. His friends at the table groaned in unison. A couple of them left the table, not wanting to get involved in a scuffle.

Cody didn't respond, didn't even turn around to see who it was. He was resigned to his fate. Whatever happened, happened. But he would not take physical abuse. That's where he'd draw the line.

Cody looked for a teacher or someone of authority, but the two boys who'd left the table walked straight to principal Edwards' office and told him what was going on. Edwards walked briskly toward the caféteria. He arrived to see the four football players surrounding Cody, who was still sitting, calmly eating his lunch. The remaining friends looked nervous.

Cheney didn't notice Edwards' arrival as he taunted Cody. "You think the police can help protect you? Fucking perv, I'm going to make your life miserable. No one can protect you from me!" Edwards heard all this as he walked up. Cheney abruptly turned and walked away, as did his friends.

The caféteria had been abuzz with normal high school noise, but as Cheney raised his voice, everyone grew silent. Then the whole room turned to watch the principal. As the bullies walked away, Edwards sat next to Cody and told him not to worry, he'd do what he could to protect him.

"Thanks, but it doesn't really matter," Cody said. "I can take care of myself. Just tell coach Rove that if he wants his quarterback to be able to use both legs in future games that Gary better not touch me again." He turned back to his lunch. One of the boys at the table blew a low whistle. The others were similarly impressed by Cody's nerve. Cody had never spoken to teachers or administrators like this. But this was the new Cody. The new Cody had to deal with these guys himself.

Edwards walked back to his office and summoned the football coach, Rove, and the track coach, KC Bosworth.

Richard Rove had been a quarterback himself when he played for Pershing High School in St. Louis back in the late '60s. He'd also been involved in a little bullying. He wasn't a big guy, but he'd been raised in a tough neighborhood and had learned to fight. When he found out he could easily intimidate others by threatening them, he felt a sense of power lacking in his home life. He didn't consider himself a bully then, and still didn't think bullying was anything to get upset about.

Principal Edwards was about to change that.

When both men arrived, Edwards said, "I just witnessed Cheney giving Cody Benson a hard time in the caféteria." Looking at Rove, he continued, "You need to tell that boy and his three henchmen to lay off. Cheney's father may have been able to get him some leniency this time, but I swear to god I'll kick that little bastard out of this school if he touches anyone else! You understand?"

Rove was not used to being upbraided. He'd had a decent relationship with the principal for many years, and the team had performed well in the district. "Look, kids fight. What can I do?"

Ignoring the question, Edwards told coach Bosworth that Cody seemed to be a changed person. He relayed what Cody had just said in the caféteria, and the eerie, calm demeanor he exhibited while saying it. "I remember Cody Benson as a nice, chess-playing kid. Maybe a little shy, but certainly not someone capable of causing harm to anyone. The boy I saw down there scares me."

Then, Edwards turned to Rove. "The way he talked about Cheney—it sounds like he's going to take matters into his own hands. It could get very ugly. I want you to talk to these four boys and tell them they're off the team if they so much as talk to the Benson kid. You understand? I want this shit to stop—today."

Rove started to ask a question but the principal waved him off.

"No more questions, Richard. Talk to them immediately." Both coaches left, but on the way out, Bosworth gave Edwards a nod indicating he understood the seriousness of the situation.

That afternoon, Rove called the boys into his office and closed the door. "You boys want to play football for this school?" he asked, looking them over one by one. The boys looked quizzically at each other, then back to the coach. While they were nodding yes, Cheney said nervously, "Sure, coach, what's up?"

"I just got called on the carpet for the shit you guys did to Cody Benson. He ran to the principal instead of taking care of the matter himself. Goddammit, we got a big game tonight, and they're threatening to kick you guys off the team."

This startled the boys, who had no idea the principal was taking this matter so seriously.

"We didn't do anything to the twerp!" Cheney blurted. "He's just a cry baby."

"I know, those track kids can't take a little ribbing," Rove replied. "But I got my orders to let you know you can be kicked off the team if anything more happens—at least on campus." He winked at Cheney. "Now get out of here and get your heads right for the game!"

Rove had never much liked Cheney. The kid had a snotty attitude, which everyone knew came from his father. But he was a decent quarterback and they didn't have a good back-up. Cheney knew this, which made him even harder to control.

Cheney walked out without saying a word as the others mumbled their assent.

****

Cody jogged up to Jazzie at track practice. She was standing with a few other girls who were stretching and warming up. Seeing Cody, she embraced and kissed him on the mouth. She was displaying genuine affection while letting everyone know she was standing by her man. Then she turned and grabbed her bag, pulling out her Nikon. "OK, stand over here and face the sun. I want good light on this thing."

Zooming in close, Jazzie took tight shots of Cody's face from several angles, trying to get the best look. Then she asked one of her friends to take a picture of the two of them. Jazzie embraced her boyfriend and pulled him tight, nuzzling her face against his. Cody felt good in her arms.

There were only two more football games this season. The team had a chance to beat last year's district champions if they could pull out a win tonight. In fact, the team won, and the whole school, sans certain track-team members, were enthusiastic about the bigger game the following week.

Chapter 5

Cody hoped to put the whole mess of the previous week behind him and concentrate on his school work and running. Cross-country season was over and he'd done very well. Track season was in the spring, so practice through the early winter was not as intense to let the cross-country runners recuperate before increasing their workout intensity for track.

The final game was in a few days and the football players were all wearing their jackets emblazoned with a big "E" for Eatonville. They were called the Cruisers, named for timber cruisers, and the mascot was a prototypical lumberjack holding a double-sided axe. Cheney's team had easily won the previous game, and he was getting praise for leading them to the district championships. This made him feel invincible, which he liked: he could finally look his father in the eye without being afraid of what the old man might say.

But Cheney's father's approval wasn't everything. Monday and Tuesday, Cody ate lunch with his girlfriend and avoided eye contact with Cheney. Cheney was angry that Cody was ignoring him. His attitude made him appear as if he were unafraid. Cody, he decided, needed another lesson. He needed to know who was in control.

After football practice on Wednesday, Cody was in the locker room getting dressed. The football players dominated the showers after their workout, so Cody made a point of getting done with his shower before they arrived. He'd hoped to get out of the building before they came in, but didn't quite make it.

"Well, look who's here!" Cheney announced to everyone, moving next to Cody. "Can't take care of himself, so he runs to the principal for protection."

Cody didn't even look up. He was calm and collected on the outside, but he was roiling on the inside. He didn't want to be there, he didn't like his violent thoughts.

Under his breath, so no one else could hear, Cheney said to Cody, "You and I are far from done."

With that, Cody looked up and stared. He had finished getting dressed, so he stood up, walked over to the rack of baseball bats, and chose one. He took a practice swing, looked at Cheney one more time, then left. He took the bat with him.

Everyone noticed. Cheney laughed nervously. "The punk thinks he can scare me with a fucking bat! Fuck him! I don't scare."

Coach Rove walked in and noticed something was up. "Everything OK?" he asked. Everyone just stared at Cheney who in turn smiled at Rove. "Everything's fine, coach. We're going to win the game Friday and make you happy." His insincerity was obvious. But Cheney grinned widely at the room of attentive players before getting dressed.

After coach left, Cheney gathered his henchmen to tell them he planned to catch up with Cody after school and teach him a lesson. They jumped into his black BMW M3, a gift from Cheney's daddy for his 16th birthday. Cheney raced out of the student parking lot, almost hitting several people in the process.

They sped along the route they figured Cody would take home and very quickly spotted Cody and Jazzie riding their bikes. The neighborhood had little traffic and no one in sight.

Cheney drove very close to Cody, who was riding to Jazzie's left. He then pulled in front of them, hitting his brakes hard and almost causing both to crash into him.

"You fucking asshole!" Jazzie screamed. "You almost killed us!"

"You OK?" Cody jumped off his bike to help her.

The boys piled out of the car and surrounded the couple. "Leave us the fuck alone!" Jazzie said. "We didn't do anything to you."

"Pussy whipped!" Cheney shouted. "You can't stand up for yourself, so your girlfriend has to do it for you! What a punk!" The other boys laughed and closed in tighter.

As Cody glared at them, his right hand unfastened the velcro straps holding the baseball bat to his bike frame. He dropped the bike and stood with the bat. He was scared as hell, but he remained outwardly calm, staring at Cheney and mentally considering his options, should he be attacked.

"Ooohh, look at the runner with a bat! Are you going out for the baseball team now?" Cheney sneered while stepping back just a bit. All four boys had moved back, seeing Cody's aggressive stance. He'd played enough little league in his younger years to know how to swing a bat, and everyone there knew the damage a hard-swung Louisville Slugger could do to a human. The question was, would he use it?

While Cody sized up his opponents, Jazzie pulled out her phone and dialed 911. She knew he would use the bat if they advanced on him. When the operator answered, Jazzie said they were being attacked by four boys and gave the location. She implored they send police immediately. She then relayed the bullies' names and described them.

The football players had heard all of this. They were looking to Cheney to make the first move, but they were getting nervous. A police report linking them to an action against Cody would likely result in a suspension and getting kicked off the team. One of them said that maybe they should leave the baby alone. This only further angered Cheney, who'd never learned the better part of valor.

Ducking low, Cheney went in for a tackle. Cody's reflexes were equal to his, and he dodged the move. As he did so, he swung the bat low and hard against the side of Cheney's right knee, hitting a home run. The crack of the bat echoed the crack of the bone as it shattered, and Cheney crumpled to the ground.

Jazzie screamed as the big football player went after her boyfriend, and the other football players groaned seeing their quarterback writhing in pain. Now, Cheney was screaming bloody murder. He'd never hurt this badly, and as he thought of his football career, he wailed even louder.

Cody remained ready with the bat should the other boys attempt to attack him. None dared. Moments later, a siren in the distance gradually grew louder than Cheney's screams.

****

Cody's parents arrived at the police station just in time to hear David Cheney yelling at the police to throw the book at Cody for assaulting his son. Robin ushered the couple into a separate room and told them to wait for Chief Walters. They could hear the elder Cheney continuing his rant, even as Walters did his best to calm him down. "His football career is finished!" they heard Cheney yell. "He could've gotten a scholarship. I'm going to sue the shit out of his fucking parents!"

After a few more obscenities, Walters calmed him and put him in his own room, then talked to the Bensons.

"Well, I guess we can't be too surprised this happened." he said. "Cody is being held for assault with a deadly weapon." His parents gasped. "You need to get yourself a good lawyer. Cheney is going to go after you big time."

"So Cheney can assault my kid, but when my son defends himself, he gets in trouble? That's insane!" Mark yelled.

Debra jumped in. "Bullshit! This is nothing but bullshit!"

"I know it doesn't look good—" Walters began.

"You're goddamned right it doesn't look good!" Mark spat back at him.

"It's because of the bat. It's considered a deadly weapon, and the law is very clear on the use of such a weapon in a fight like this."

"There were four big football players against one small boy. What the hell was he supposed to do, just let them beat him up again? You didn't do shit to protect him last time," Mark said.

"Understood," Walters said. "But he used a deadly weapon and caused serious injury. There will be repercussions."

"We want to see Cody now!" Debra demanded.

"OK, I'll have Robin bring him in." Walters left them alone.

Debra began to cry, sobbing softly on Mark's shoulder. "Poor Cody. How could we have let this happen to him?"

Mark held her tight. "We did all we could. This is that shit of a boy's fault, and the school and police department. Society failed to protect him. We'll fix this somehow."

A light knock on the door and then Robin lead Cody into the room. "I'll leave you alone for a few minutes," she said.

Debra embraced Cody like never before, her tears flowing freely. "We're so sorry this happened to you! We're going to get you out of this mess, whatever it takes."

Mark noticed Cody's calm demeanor. "It's OK, mom. I'm just glad it's over. Whatever happens, I won't get bullied again."

Mark was concerned that Cody had no idea of the potential consequences of his actions. The correctional institutions to which "dangerous" juveniles could be sent were filled with bullies who were much worse than Cheney.

Mark asked him to describe what happened in as much detail as he could remember. He needed to relay this information to the attorney he'd have to hire. He'd brought a notebook and took down the pertinent points as Cody described them. They were almost finished when Robin knocked and entered the room.

"Please give us another moment, Officer Cheshire," Mark said. Robin nodded, but remained in the room.

Cody continued. "So when Gary charged at me, I knew I had to hit him as hard as a I could or I'd be beaten by all four again. I also thought they might hurt Jazzie. I dodged him and swung the bat at his legs, figuring that would stop him. I didn't swing at his head for a reason. I wasn't trying to kill him. I just wanted him to stop."

Mark and Debra looked at Robin, who was slowly shaking her head in sadness. She was hating her job even more now. She was 100 percent on this family's side. She even thought the boy was right in using a bat to protect himself. It was the school and the police who should be on trial for not doing their job. She took Cody to a holding cell after final hugs and tears from his parents. He would have to remain in custody until a judge could set bail.

Chapter 6

When Mel Beckman, Cody's chess teacher, heard of the incident, he called Debra and asked if they could meet. Mark and Debra arrived at the Cottage Bakery & Café ahead of Mel and grabbed a table by the window. They watched as Mel's old white Datsun glided into a parking space at the far end of the building. He got out and removed a long cord from his trunk, which he plugged into an outlet on the building. The other end went into a hidden receptacle in the front of his beat-up old car.

Maria greeted him as he came in. Mel was a regular and had arranged to use their plug to charge his car's batteries whenever he ate at the restaurant. He always tipped big. Partly for the electricity, and partly because he had a crush on the much younger Maria. She liked him back, but more as a father figure, much to Mel's dismay.

Mark motioned for Mel to join them. Debra had met Mel several times, but this was Mark's first time meeting the strange man that Cody and Debra had described as a brilliant hippy environmentalist polymath.

With his long grey hair tied in a ponytail and his John Lennon-style granny glasses, Mel did look the part. Reaching out to shake Mark's hand, he peered over his glasses and said, "I'm profoundly sorry for what happened to Cody. No one should experience the treatment those boys inflicted on him. It saddens me no end." He bowed to Debra and sat down.

Mark thanked Mel for wanting to help. "Cody is an exceptional kid," Mel said, "but you no doubt know that. How is he handling being locked up?"

"He's OK, given the circumstances," Mark replied. "We're looking for an attorney. Cody's got to go back and finish school and get into a good college, but if they convict him of assault, his chances will be limited."

"That's what I wanted to talk to you about. I know a guy," Mel said cryptically. "He's a criminal defense attorney who helped me out of a jam a long time ago. I keep in touch with him."

Mark looked at Debra, his eyes slightly widened, wondering if Mel was legit. Noticing this, Mel said, "I take this matter very seriously, and I wouldn't offer any help I didn't think was useful. Consider talking to this man. His name is Zak." Mel slid a note across the table to Mark. "Here's his contact info."

"I didn't mean to ..." Mark stammered.

"Not a problem, Mr. Benson. We all want the best for Cody. I do think Zak can help. Now, can we get some food? I'm starving." Mel signaled for Maria to come take their order, and they spent the rest of the hour getting to know one another. By the end of the lunch, both Mark and Debra were comfortable with Mel. His breadth of knowledge was remarkable.

As soon as they got home, Mark called Zak. The phone rang, and rang, and rang. No machine picked up and no one answered. Mark was thinking "Who doesn't have voicema ..." .

"Zak here!" His voice was deep, resonant. He was clearly breathing hard, probably from running to get the phone.

"My name is Mark Benson. Mel Beckman said I should call."

"Good ole Uncle Mel!" He chuckled. "He told me you might be calling."

"Uncle? Are you two related? He didn't mention that."

"No, sorry, it's just something I've called him since our time working together years ago. Mel's a special guy, but since you've met him, you know that. What can I do for you? You the one with the boy and the bat?"

Mark was unsettled by his flip tone but decided to forge ahead. "Um, yeah. My son, he..."

"It's OK Just tell me what happened. I got some of this from Mel, but I want to hear it from you."

Mark appreciated Zak trying to reassure him. He seemed to read people's needs quickly and respond appropriately.

Mark started at the beginning, going into more detail when Zak asked about what got the youths to the point of violence. He was particularly interested in the years-long campaign of bullying that the school had made only minimal efforts to stop.

Mark and Zak talked for over half an hour. Zak eventually said he had enough for now, but he would drive down from Seattle to meet with them in two days. He wanted to do some research first.

It was raining hard the next morning as Debra and Mark drove to the police station with some food and reading material for Cody. Eatonville didn't have a juvenile facility, so kids in trouble were kept in the adult jail until their parents got them out, or until they were remanded to a juvenile jail in Olympia or

Seattle. Robin greeted them and walked them back to Cody's cell. It was a small, dank room with a toilet and bed, and not much else. Debra broke down when she saw him behind actual bars like some criminal.

"Mom! Dad! I hate it here! Can I go home now?" He'd been up since dawn, his body's rhythms used to rising early and a morning run, or a bike ride to school.

Hearing his plea only made Debra cry harder. Robin realized she should've brought them to the waiting room where they'd been the day before. "I'm so sorry," Robin said. "Let's go to the conference room where it's more comfortable."

There, Debra managed to compose herself enough to bring out the food she'd carefully prepared and wrapped. "I hope you're hungry. I brought you some soup, a sandwich, and juice."

"I'm starving," Cody said as he dug in to the food. His athletic body required lots of calories, so he was always hungry. "You should see what they offered me for breakfast a while ago," he said with his mouth full. Decorum took a backseat to hunger.

Robin almost told them that prisoners were not allowed outside food, but remained mum. If anyone caught her in this breach of the rules, she'd just deal with the consequences.

Mark spoke calmly to Cody. "We talked to Mel yesterday, and he gave us the name of an attorney in Seattle."

"Can I go home today?" Cody asked. Seeing Mark lower his eyes told him all he needed to know, but Mark continued. "Not today, buddy, but the attorney, Zak, will be here tomorrow, and we think you can go home then." Mark looked at Robin to see if this was accurate. Robin shrugged ever so slightly.

Cody grew silent again, but kept eating.

"We know this is hard, and it's incredibly unfair," Debra said, "but you will get out and this matter will get settled and your life will get back on track." She hoped her son understood they were doing everything they could.

They spent the rest of the time with Cody eating and everyone making small talk. Mark and Debra left even more depressed than before.

Meanwhile, the school was abuzz over the fight. Jazzie held court as the only reliable eyewitness, telling anyone who would listen what happened in great detail. She did this in part to counter any lies the three football players might tell and also to help rally people to Cody's defense. She was particularly incensed by the talk she'd had with her father Albert the night before.

Albert had received a call from David Cheney telling him about the incident and suggesting he assist in hurting the Benson family. Wasn't his daughter the boy's girlfriend? Maybe he could convince her to stop seeing him?

When Albert brought up the topic at dinner, Jazzie explained what had happened. She was extremely agitated and in no mood to take any crap from her father. When he tried to bring up the subject of her relationship with Cody and how maybe he wasn't emotionally stable, she just stared at him.

"Are you suggesting this was his fault?" she demanded incredulously.

"Well, look, the boy used a bat!"

He wasn't used to being on the defensive with anyone, especially his daughters.

"OK, dad, tell us what you would've done if you were in Cody's shoes." Jazzie said this with a smart-ass tone she'd never used with her father before.

"Don't you ever talk to me with that tone young lady!"

Marlene and Jazzie sat there dumbfounded at their father's vitriol. Glancing at their mother, they saw she was equally shocked.

Jazzie went for broke. In a calm, but steady voice that rose in volume as she spoke, she said, "Sorry if I used an improper tone, dad, but my boyfriend was jumped by four big football players who could've turned on me as well. So I ask again, in all seriousness: what would you have done?"

Albert considered his children subject to his commands in the same way his employees were. He even considered his wife less than his equal. He blew up.

"I forbid you to see that Benson boy ever again!" Albert screamed at Jazzie, stabbing at the air with his fork.

Jazzie didn't know whether to run from the table or scream back at him. Alexandra and Marlene were just as shocked. Albert had never before been violent. His flushed face and belligerent tone gave the impression he might hit Jazzie.

"You can't stop me!" she said. Her lower lip quivered, partly from fear, and partly from sadness. Her father was a real asshole. And with that, Jazzie pushed away from the table, no hurry evident. She got up, took her plate of food, and walked up to her room.

This was new territory for Albert. He didn't take that sort of response from anyone, let alone his own daughter. He just sat there and stared.

Marlene was waiting for her mother to stand up for Jazzie, but Alexandra also sat stone faced, afraid of her husband's wrath. Marlene was afraid of her dad, but not to the point of acquiescence. She thought her mother's silence condoned her father's behavior.

"Dad, Jazzie loves Cody. He's her first boyfriend. You—"

Albert stood and pointed his finger at Marlene. "You shut the fuck up! You aren't in charge of this family. I am!" He stormed out of the room.

Marlene was stunned. She'd never heard her father cuss, and to have him direct such language at her, at the family dinner table, was more than she could take. She broke into tears and buried her face in her hands. Alexandra got up to wrap her arms around Marlene. "My god, I am so sorry, Marlene. I had no idea he could...that he was capable of … ." She started to sob.

"Mom, what happened?" Marlene cried. "Why'd he say that to me?"

"I don't know what the hell's wrong with him." She glanced in the direction of Albert's exit, afraid he'd returned and had overheard. This was the first time she really feared Albert.

Marlene went to Jazzie's room, calling for her mom to follow. They found Jazzie sitting at her desk, typing on the emerald green iMac she'd gotten for her birthday. "Honey, I'm so sorry!" Alexandra said, her tearful voice quavering. "Daddy didn't mean what he said."

Jazzie stopped typing and turned to face the two members of her family she still loved. Her eyes were red and watery, but her demeanor was that of a warrior. As far as she was concerned, her father had burned a bridge, and she wanted nothing more to do with him. She'd never felt love and warmth from him like she got from her mom. She'd accepted this—that the nice house and things his income afforded the family were compensation for his lack of love.

But trying to keep her from her boyfriend was too much.

"What did he say?" Jazzie wanted to know what transpired after she left. "What was the yelling? It sounded bad." She looked at Marlene. "Did he go after you, too?"

"He told me to 'shut the fuck up!' What the hell? I couldn't believe it!" Marlene said.

"I've never seen him so mad," Alexandra added. "So, what are you going to do about Cody?"

"I'm going to the police station to bring him some homework. I'm sure as hell not going to stop seeing him because of some 'order' from that asshole!" Alexandra recoiled at the venom. "I've got to live under his roof for another year, then I'm outta here! Screw him!"

Alexandra started to weep. Within ten minutes, she had seen her family disintegrating before her eyes.

****

Jazzie remained in warrior mode the next day at school. When some football players teased her about Cody's violence, she pointedly reminded them of their quarterback's current inability to walk and hinted the same could happen to them.

The track team, which contained a few football players among its ranks, were solidly behind Cody and Jazzie. Track and field rarely generated bullies as football did.

KC, the track coach, was very popular. He loved coaching track and field and had seen a few of his student athletes get scholarships to run for PAC10 schools.

When news of the incident with Cody and Cheney reached him, he was intensely disappointed his school had failed Cody. He also felt guilty. He'd been aware of the bullying, but didn't realize how bad it had become. Had Cody reached out to him, KC would've tried to help Cody and probably would have prevented him from taking a bat to Cheney. Now, one of his top middle distance runners was gone from the team, and probably gone from school.

Everyone was curious about what would happen to Cody in the legal system, especially with a bulldog like David Cheney going after him.

Principal Edwards called KC and Rove into his office. They arrived together, their tension evident. Both coaches had lost valuable players, although the loss to the football team was arguably greater since the season's final big game was on Friday, and their back-up quarterback was mediocre, at best. Cross-country season was over, and it would be a couple of months before track season started.

Edwards closed the door before walking back to his desk where he remained standing. "Guys, we all fucked up."

Bosworth stepped back when he heard his principal say "fuck." Rove stood stoically, but his blood pressure crept up, and he used his sleeve to wipe sweat from his face.

"I'm going to take the blame because I let Cheney off when I should've kicked his ass out. All three of us knew that prick was bullying kids. His old man intimidated me." He looked down as he said this. "God damn that boy!" He plopped down in chair, his shoulders slumped.

Looking up at the two coaches, he started to say something, but couldn't get it out, so Bosworth stepped in. "Look, I hate to point fingers since I should've spoken up, but Cheney and his pig of a father are at fault. I want to know why Cody is still in custody."

"I hear his attorney will be here tomorrow to get him out," Edwards said. "The police say it was the bat that made the difference. I guess fists, superior strength, and numbers are OK." Both looked at Rove, who looked down and shuffled his feet, his blood pressure still rising.

"I don't know what will happen to us," Edwards continued, "but we should assume there will be repercussions. I've spoken to the district's legal office, and they're sending someone out tomorrow to talk to everyone, so expect to be called in."

Rove's silence pissed off Edwards. "Do you have anything to say, Richard?"

"Nothing I say will help at this point. I won't take all the blame, but, yeah, I wish I'd done more. I guess I'm sorry."

"You 'guess' you're sorry?" Edwards spat. "You guess? Get the f…, please leave. I'll talk to you tomorrow."

****

The next day, Zak Stolar arrived to Eatonville midmorning. He went directly to the police station where he'd agreed to meet Mark and Debra.

Robin took one look at Zak and thought "trouble." He was a large man, but it was his countenance that had the most effect. Like Mel, he sported long hair, greying a little on the sides and tied in a ponytail. His full beard had been trimmed ever so slightly, maybe in deference to meeting the police, maybe not. His eyes, however, cut right through any bullshit in the room.

His voice, on the other hand, had a calming effect. Asking to meet with Debra and Mark, Robin could hear the rough, gravelly delivery of someone who could, and probably did, scream bloody murder when such a response was called for. Yet, Zak also somehow sounded mellow. In spite of herself, Robin liked him.

Although Zak was only 47, he looked like a man in his late 50s. His daily relationship with alcohol and pot had not been good to his body, but it was how he coped with living in a world he was hell-bent on changing.

He'd chosen to follow his father into law after learning how he had taken on the McCarthy gang during the '50s blacklisting era. He'd grown up in a Jewish neighborhood in Brooklyn where his father was a minor celebrity for hammering the right-wing on behalf of writers and actors who'd been caught up in the red-baiting witch hunts after WWII. Being Jewish in the late '50s- and early '60s-New York, Zak had experienced his share of bullying and earned a reputation as one who would fight back ferociously, at first with his fists, but eventually with his words. At Columbia Law, he excelled at debate and dispatched opponents with glee.

Robin opened the door to the conference room where Mark and Debra were waiting. When Zak followed, both looked up, surprised. They'd never seen an attorney who looked the way Zak did—although after thinking about Mel for a moment, it made sense.

"Howdy, I'm Zak." He first greeted Debra, then Mark, with a friendly smile and a firm handshake. Then he addressed Robin. "Officer Cheshire, would you please bring me the file on Cody? And if you have good coffee, I could sure use a cup." Robin, feeling charmed a bit, exited the room.

"Mr. and Ms. Benson, may I call you Mark and Debra?"

"Sure, we don't mind. We just want Cody to come home with us today."

"I should be able to arrange that. Has bail been set?"

"We were confused about that," Mark said. "Robin said they had to wait for his representation before he could leave."

"These little towns sometimes operate differently than the big city. Had it been Seattle, Cody would have gone home the day of the fight. When Officer Cheshire brings me the file..." And right on cue, Robin walked in with a large cup of coffee and a thin file.

"Here you go." Robin laid the file in front of Zak.

"Thanks. What's the bail status for Cody?"

"The judge just got back to us this morning. Bail is set at $5,000. We thought that seemed high, but this particular judge is hard on assault cases. Plus, Mr. Cheney helped get him elected," Robin added sotto voce.

"I guess that explains why he wasn't released on his own recognizance," Zak said. He explained to Cody's parents, "You can get a bail bondsman for 10%. Or the better option is to write the check for the full amount, then get most all of it refunded when you show up for trial."

Mark looked at Debra, who nodded. She took out her checkbook and asked Robin who to make the check out to.

After dealing with the paperwork, Zak requested that Cody be brought to the room. Robin, smiling, said, "Absolutely! Be right back."

Cody rushed into the room and hugged his mom and dad. "You're going home with us, baby," Debra said.

Zak stood quietly next to Robin.

After a semi-private moment with his parents, Cody asked Zak, "You my attorney?" To which Zak replied with a smile. "Yeah, I'm that guy!"

"How much do you know about what happened?" Cody asked.

"Well, not all the details, but from what I do know, you have a good case. But let's go where we can talk freely." He turned to Robin. "No disrespect."

"None taken, Mr. Stolar. Let me know if there's anything I can do for you." She watched Zak with an intensity Mark and

Debra picked up on. Realizing her indiscretion, she lowered her eyes and turned to open the door for them.

Zak followed the Bensons to their house. Debra brewed a fresh pot of coffee and Zak got down to work with Cody at the kitchen table.

"We can sue the school for failure to protect Cody from assault and for failing to punish the boy who assaulted him," Zak said. "We can win that suit easy. Going after the police is another thing."

Mark looked at Debra, and when she nodded, he turned to Zak. "Let's do it. We like his school for the most part, but the administration failed us."

"What about defending Cody from Cheney?" Debra asked. "Isn't that more important than playing offense against the school and police?"

"You know the old saying, sometimes the best defense is a good offense?" Zak replied. "I've heard the elder Cheney is a real piece of work. If we can win against the school, that'll help us in our case against him, since we'll have established the years of abuse, including several assaults."

****

In the months that followed, Cody's life returned to normal, but he was no longer an innocent kid. He was still very nice, and he loved Jazzie even more after her full tilt effort to stop bullying at their school. But there was a new edge to his personality.

Jazzie used the pictures she'd taken of Cody's black eye to make graphic posters highlighting the damage bullies were capable of. Everyone knew the damage Cody had done to Cheney, and other than a few of the nastier football players, they were pleased.

Zak took on the school district's attorneys in court and destroyed them with his withering attack, detailing every instance of bullying Cody had related to him, and the school's indifference. The judge ruled in Cody's favor, awarding a $500,000 judgment against the district. Mark and Debra put the balance, after Zak's fee, into a college fund for Cody.

On April 20th, 1999, shortly after Cody's acquittal, the news erupted with the mass shooting of students at Columbine High School in Colorado. In the aftermath, when it became evident that bullying might have played a role in the shootings, schools across the country adopted strict zero-tolerance policies.

Back at Eatonville High, principal Edwards was forced into retirement. Coach Rove was fired after it came to light that he'd encouraged Cheney and his toughs to go after Cody off campus.

The legal team David Cheney had put together followed the school district case and, after watching Zak in action, told the elder Cheney to drop his case against Cody. His boy was guilty of years of abuse, and they knew Zak would demand a jury trial. It was very likely the twelve jurors would have sympathy for Cody.

But Gary Cheney wanted revenge.

Chapter 7

Even on a tiny TV, Gary Cheney found the black-and-white security footage of the Columbine shooting compelling. Sitting just outside the high school's new principal's office, he released his balled fists as the footage got to the good part. Boom! He chuckled. Another whiny loser down.

The principal's door swung open, and Cheney's hands tightened right back into fists. Principal Geraldine Rosen frowned at him.

"I've called the police," she said finally.

"What?!" Cheney shouted. "I wasn't even--what the hell!"

"Language," Principal Rosen said dryly. "Not that's it really going to help you at this point. The cops have the incident on record, Mr. Cheney. At 7:35 this morning, you recklessly endangered Cody and Jazzie by almost hitting them on the road with your car while they were walking to school."

"That's bullshit!" Cheney yelled, remembering the crunch of leaves under his tires as he had veered off the road and snuck up behind the pair that morning, the way the bitch's head had turned suddenly, how her eyes had widened. He'd never seen terror like that before. "Cody is such a whiny punk-ass. I didn't even see them."

"Given your past history with Mr. Benson, consider this to be your lucky break, Mr. Cheney. The police are sending an officer out to perform a breathalyzer test on you. I hope, for your sake, you haven't been drinking."

"Football players don't drink!" Cheney rocketed up from his chair and immediately winced; his knee still ached, especially when it rained. He bent over and kneaded his flesh.

"I don't see how that's relevant, considering you are no longer a football player," Principal Rosen said. She walked across the office and snapped off the TV. "The officer will be here within the hour. You can wait in the nurse's office."

Cheney picked up his backpack and slowly limped along the frosted-glass corridor. Three grass-stained boys sat in the office, happily nursing cuts and abrasions. They still hadn't changed out of their football uniforms. Cheney heard their laughter stop as soon as he came into sight.

"Rodriguez. Hansen. Smith," Cheney called out, as if he were back on the field, barking out strategy before a pass. But the boys only glared at him. Rodriguez folded his arms across his chest.

"What did you do now, Cheney?" Smith said finally. "Rape a cow?"

"Shut up," Cheney said.

"Cheney's got a chode for cattle," Hansen said. "Classic."

"Cattle chode!" Rodriguez laughed.

A silhouette loomed up on the frosted glass, and the door opened. Cody stepped inside.

"Hey! Cody, my man," Hansen said. Smith and Rodriguez smiled at him.

"Hey guys," Cody said, then went quiet as he saw Cheney.

"Oh, don't mind cattle chode here," Rodriguez said. "He's just getting some medicine for his chafed dick. Moooooo!"

Cheney swung out and punched the wall. Bits of plaster covered his bleeding knuckles. All of the boys laughed.

Cody walked down the corridor toward the principal's office. Cheney watched Cody go, cradling his fist as the blood ran over his knuckles and splattered onto the floor.

****

As traumatic as the previous school year had been for Cody and his family, it had ended well. He and Jazzie trained hard, partly because they enjoyed it, but also to cleanse their heads of the craziness they'd experienced. Both performed well at local high school meets, although not quite good enough to make it to the state meet.

They spent the summer before their senior year running, biking, going to movies, and hanging out with their friends. Cody's dog Cooper was showing his age a bit, but he could still run shorter distances on the trails in the woods. His companionship was second only to Jazzie in making Cody happy.

Sadly, Grandpa Paul was diagnosed with stage four bladder cancer and opted out of treatment after learning it would involve several surgeries plus heavy chemo. His decision depressed the family, but he was resigned to it. Tobacco had killed his beloved wife Millie years earlier, and he still missed her. Toward the end, as the pain became harder to control, he arranged to stay with a friend in Portland where assisted suicide was legal.

On the day he chose, the family drove down to be with him one more time. Debra and Mark talked about the days back when the kids were small and Grandma Millie had supplied them with baked goods and fresh-squeezed lemonade.

But as Cody sat by his Granpda's bedside, he was remembering something else: the hunting trip they had taken six years previous. It was one of those male-bonding things. Cody didn't want to disappoint his Grandpa and his Dad by not going, so one bright, clear Saturday morning, the three of them, all dressed in camo gear, drove the Subaru deep into the woods to a trail head, then walked for miles past the hiking trails, bushwhacking much of the way.

Mark had sensed Cody was afraid, so he paid close attention to him during the hunt. Mark wasn't much of a hunter himself, having last hunted over a decade earlier, back when Debra was carrying Cody.

Cody proved to be adept at walking quietly in the woods so as not to scare off the prey. It didn't take long before they spotted a six-point buck with two doe. Grandpa Paul used hand signals he'd taught Cody on the drive out, instructing him to take the shot. Cody leaned against a tree for stability and carefully took aim through the scope, zeroing in on the buck's head. The deer was standing, watching out as the two doe fed on grass in the small clearing.

Cody steadied his breathing as his finger wrapped around the trigger. He tried to block the fact that he was about to shoot a beautiful and graceful animal. He'd often seen deer while running or riding his bike in the woods, and now he was going to kill one.

The shell's explosion startled him out of his deep concentration, and he saw the buck collapse to the ground. His bullet to the animal's head killed it instantly.

The two doe leapt out of the clearing and were gone, their mate dead.

"Great shot, Cody!" Grandpa Paul congratulated him.

Cody burst into tears and buried his head against his father's chest. Mark hugged him tightly. "It's OK, Cody, this is what hunting is all about. You didn't do anything wrong."

Cody was inconsolable. He had hurt—no, killed!—another being. Mark and Paul looked at each other with a sadness that surprised them both.

Cody never hunted with them again. He locked the rifle away in Mark's gun cabinet and forgot about it. Grandpa Paul regretted giving the gun to Cody as a gift, but Cody never spoke of the incident again.

But was now the time to bring it back up? What purpose would it serve, exactly? Cody watched his Grandpa Paul's papery hands as he gave the signal for the meds. Cody clasped his Grandpa's hand.

"I know you're going to a better place," Cody said. Grandpa Paul weakly squeezed his grandson's hand, but he didn't speak. His eyelids were already beginning to flutter.

The drive back to Eatonville was miserable. Mark had to stop and let Debra drive at one point because he was having a hard time seeing the road through his tears.

****

Cody and Jazzie ran together when they could, but some days, their schedules didn't allow it, so they'd run on their own. They were both busy. Jazzie's efforts to rid the school of bullying gave her confidence that other students saw as leadership and they overwhelmingly elected her class president. She saw many things that could be improved and set about organizing committees to accomplish them. Even as early as fall, most of the seniors were talking about electing Cody and Jazzie prom king and queen the following spring.

Today, Jazzie would be running solo. She bundled up against the cold and headed out from home for an easy late-afternoon four-mile run. Since she wouldn't have Cody to talk to, she grabbed her discman and cranked the music. The sun was close to setting, but there was plenty of light for the next 30 minutes, more than enough for her to get the run done before dark.

The clouds moved east, leaving clear blue skies and cold temps. Track season was still a couple months away, but the serious runners trained year round. Still, there was hardly anyone out this afternoon. The freshly repainted blacktop of the road sprawled out like a track lane. Jazzie hugged the shoulder as she ran and lost herself in the rhythm of her breathing; it was meditative to be inhaling this air, to be so focused as to somehow be outside of her own body. Her muscles worked; her mind soared.

After a bend in the road, Jazzie saw the giant oak up ahead that marked the halfway point of her run. The sinking sun flashed in her eyes; the music in her ears reached a noisy chorus.

There was no way to hear Gary Cheney's black BMW coming up fast behind her...

****

Cody was eating dinner with his parents when the phone rang. Debra excused herself and went to the kitchen to answer. Cody and Mark heard an audible gasp followed by "Oh no!" Mark and Cody scrambled from the table and into the kitchen.

"What happened?" Mark asked.

Debra hung up the phone and walked to Cody embrace him, tears flowing from her eyes.

"What's the matter, mom?" Cody was upset seeing his mother in such a state.

Debra pushed Cody to arm's length, holding his arms tightly and said, "Jazzie was hit by a car." She could barely get the next part out. "She was killed. She's gone..."

It took a moment for Cody to process this information. Mark also gasped, and then Cody collapsed to his knees and let out a mournful wail unlike anything they'd ever heard from him.

After Mark and Debra made some calls to get more information, they all drove to Jazzie's house. Several cars were already parked out front, a police cruiser among them.

Marlene, eyes red from crying, answered the door and ushered them in from the bitter cold. Several people were standing in small groups talking in hushed tones, but when they saw Cody, everyone grew silent. All eyes were on him as he walked over to Alexandra, who was sitting on a large plush chair surrounded by close friends. She stood and embraced him, saying, "Oh, Cody, our poor Jazzie...Oh god...I can't..."

Albert wasn't home. He had been gone for two days in Seattle for meetings at Weyerhaeuser. Alexandra had called him as soon as she heard from the police, but it'd be a couple more hours before he could drive down.

Cody had been mute except to ask his mother in the car ride over how Jazzie had been killed. Everyone could see something in the way he carried himself wasn't right. It was as if he were trying to channel Jazzie in the afterlife. He didn't acknowledge anyone who tried to console him. He was in his own thoughts, not wanting to live.

PART TWO:

DESCENT INTO RADICALIZATION

Chapter 8

Cody had been home from Iraq for two weeks when he got an email from Mel asking to meet. He suggested the Cottage Café late on a Tuesday afternoon after the lunch crowd was gone and before the dinner crowd came. It was the same day and time of their previous chess games.

When he arrived, the White Zombie was plugged in on the side of the building, and Mel was sitting at his regular table, a coffee already in front of him. Maria saw Cody coming in and brought him his favorite, a latte with honey on the side.

"Thanks, Maria, it's so good to see you again." Cody gave her a friendly hug. Maria had been so saddened by Jazzie's death.

"Mel, it's been too long, man."

"Yes, it has. Please sit down, take a load off."

"Before we get started, I need to say you were right about everything. Joining up was the biggest mistake of my life. I thought I was doing the right thing, but..."

Mel looked down. He wasn't the type to rub it in. He gave good advice, whether about chess, about love, or about fighting wars for your country. He'd served in Army intelligence back during the early days of the Vietnam war, several years before Cody's father had been drafted. What he learned there had colored everything he knew about the military and the federal government.

"We all do what we think is right at the time, Cody. Your decision was understandable given what you'd been through. I'm sorry it turned out the way it did. How're you holding up?"

"Not too great." Cody studied the foam on his latte. "I didn't want to go to Iraq, but I didn't have a choice. I was out for revenge against Bin Laden, and maybe Cheney. They sent me to a country that hadn't attacked us to kill..." he stopped and began to choke up some.

He thought about that day when the twin towers came down and the constant drumbeat for war to avenge the 3,000 lives lost. The anger he felt toward Gary Cheney was morphing into anger toward the perpetrators of 9/11. His anti-war stance began to evolve.

Cody had enlisted in the Army in the winter of 2002, just before the Bush administration launched their campaign against the Taliban in Afghanistan. He didn't tell his parents or Mel. He just drove to Seattle and did it. He was going to get his revenge one way or the other. Mark and Debra were devastated. Mel was greatly disappointed. But the Army didn't have a grace period during which you could change your mind. Besides, Cody wanted to go deal with his anger toward Cheney and the Taliban, and in his convoluted thinking, this would solve the problem. But my god. As if anything could be solved that way.

Cody steadied himself and looked at Mel. "I killed two men. They were only defending their country against a fucking invading force. They hadn't done anything to me, although if given the chance, they sure would have. It happened quick... over in seconds. The guys...the guys back at base cheered for me. Can you fucking believe it? Some of them were bloodthirsty motherfuckers! It was like all they wanted to do was kill people. They didn't even care why we were there. Shit, I wish I could go back in time and follow your advice. Dad and Grandpa said the same as you, but I ignored you all, and now I gotta live with that goddamn memory. Every time I try to go to sleep, it comes flooding into my head. I see them raise their weapons and I just open up on 'em. What I did to human bodies... fuck!"

Mel let Cody get as much out as possible. He took a sip of his coffee, then asked, "You seeing anybody about this yet?"

"No. Dad suggested the VA, or maybe some private therapist. Mom wanted me to talk to you first. I liked that idea. When you emailed me, I figured we could talk, and maybe you could point me in the right direction."

"I'm not a therapist, but if it helps, I know what you're going through. For what it's worth, it'll get better—and it won't get better. You should see somebody, absolutely. I think the VA has some good people, but they're overwhelmed. Seeing somebody outside the VA is also a good idea. You got insurance?"

"No. I need to get a job. Life is hard out of the service. Back there, you knew what was expected every day, but now, I'm just floating. Gives me too much time to think about shit I don't want to think about."

"Right."

"Anyway, I'm thinking of getting into visual effects. My friend in LA was doing it when I visited before the Army. He says there's lots of contract work I could get. Pays well at least."

"Sounds like a decent plan. Would you have to move?"

"Maybe to Seattle. There's a good school there. I could still see the folks, and I wouldn't have to live in LA."

"Zak is up there. You been in touch with him since returning?"

"No, I haven't seen or talked to Zak since the trial. It'd be good to see that crazy guy."

Mel detected a note of optimism in Cody's response.

"Let me know when you go up and maybe the three of us can get together. I haven't seen him for a few months myself."

That night, Cody talked this plan over with his parents. They, too, detected a slight brightening in Cody's demeanor when he talked about moving to Seattle, going to school, and seeing Zak. Both were happy he had a plan, and that he'd come up with it while talking to Mel gave it even more credibility. Zak, too, had made a great impression on them, so they encouraged Cody to go for it.

"Do you want the Prius? We can do without it. I know you've got the bike, but with the rain and all," Mark offered.

"I really don't want a car, but you're right about the rain. Let me see what kind of living arrangements I can get. If I'm close to school, or there's a bus I can use, that might work OK."

Four days later, on a Saturday morning, Cooper didn't wake up. He'd died peacefully in his sleep at the foot of Cody's bed. The family mourned together all day. They called Jennifer in Eugene and had a family conference where they all cried together, reminiscing about the good times they'd had with that wonderful dog. The Man Eater was no more.

Cooper's passing cut the final cord holding Cody to Eatonville. He moved to Seattle a couple weeks later, renting a small apartment not far from the trade school he attended for visual effects. It was early October, and the weather was cooling, the days getting shorter, but still very dry.

The settlement money, plus the GI bill, meant he was not hurting for funds. His parents had invested his money in the stock market, buying a lot of Apple and some other tech stocks that had done well in spite of the Y2K scare. He'd had access to the money since turning 18, but he barely used any of it, instead letting it ride in the market.

Cody enjoyed the school work. Visual effects, VFX as it was known in the film industry, was booming. It took a couple of years to get through the program, but he was a good student and plowed through the work. Not having a girlfriend helped, of course, and he didn't have many vices beyond occasionally enjoying pot, a habit he'd picked up in the Army.

He and Zak would sometimes meet in a bar for drinks, and Zak always invited him out to his car for a little smoke first. They got along really well. Maybe it was the alcohol and pot, but Zak was also a hell of a fun guy to be around. He knew almost as much as Mel about the world. This, combined with his gregarious nature, made for some outrageous conversations. On the occasions Mel drove up in the White Zombie, the name he'd given his electrified dilapidated Datsun, the two would hold court in the bar with two dozen patrons listening closely. Cody would sit and watch, mesmerized.

Zak invited Cody to move into his house after school was over. He owned a large Victorian on Queen Anne Hill, a tony older neighborhood just north of downtown Seattle with a terrific view of the Space Needle. There was a large bedroom on the third floor that Zak had rented out to friends in the past, and since it was empty, he offered it to Cody for a decent price. Cody jumped at the chance to share such a nice space with Zak.

Now that he was out of school, Cody contacted his friend, Ian, in LA, who by now had risen through the VFX ranks and was a producer who hired contract workers when his staff couldn't finish a job in the allotted time. The schedules could be brutal, but the pay was good, and there was almost always a break between jobs. This was perfect for Cody, since he lived frugally and had that sizable stock portfolio.

As good as things were, they weren't perfect. The ghosts haunting Cody visited often, and they sometimes brought him to the edge of an abyss. He'd been visiting a VA therapist who diagnosed PTSD on Cody's first visit. The therapist was not "one of the good ones" Mel had talked about. Nevertheless Cody stuck to his schedule and visited the doc when he was supposed to.

Part of the problem was the news. Cody had been a news junkie since childhood. His parents subscribed to the Seattle Times, and the whole family devoured it every day. On Sundays, they got the New York Times, a paper Cody grew to love for its great writing and a decent grasp of reality. As news moved online, Cody followed and became addicted to various progressive blogs and news sources to which he contributed his highly-opinionated comments.

What he was learning was infuriating. Iraq and Afghanistan were still seething with brutality from all sides. Iraq, particularly, was metastasizing into a fractious war with new groups of combatants being radicalized by all manner of atrocities. Soldiers and civilians were still dying in large numbers, and there seemed to be no end in sight.

The Bush administration had started two huge wars on credit, with money mostly borrowed from the Chinese, and was in the process of tanking the economy. Republicans were supposed to be the party of business, but they had taken Bill Clinton's budget surplus and squandered it on wars and huge tax breaks for the wealthiest one percent. Gas prices were rising fast, adding what amounted to a huge tax on everyone, but hitting the poor especially hard.

And soldiers were still dying. Civilians were still dying. Cody had seen this up close, and it drove him crazy knowing the war mongers continued to put young men and women in harm's way for illegitimate reasons.

Unbeknownst to him, his therapist at the VA had been noting his anger and was creating a red-flag file for those who could present a danger to themselves or to others. Cody's discussions with this man warranted inclusion on the list of potentially dangerous vets.

The following years proved problematic for Cody. He had a decent career working for Ian at the powerhouse, Digital Domain, in Venice. He'd make periodic trips there to work on projects, always staying at his friend's condo near the beach in Santa Monica. He tried dating, both in LA and Seattle. There was no shortage of attractive women everywhere he looked and having a good job and being attractive helped, but he never progressed past two or three consecutive dates—never got close to a sexual encounter. He kept comparing women to Jazzie and, of course, they never measured up.

His PTSD was gradually getting worse. He'd have bursts of anger, always in private, so no one knew, but he was beginning to hold grudges against those who he thought were responsible for the shit going down in the world.

He was also mad at the general public for not taking a stronger stance against the war. Sure, a small percentage of people were active in the anti-war movement. But, in spite of their actions, the same asshole politicians were being reelected, and they continued to vote unlimited budgets for the military while simultaneously cutting funds for education, healthcare, the environment, and just about anything else Cody believed was needed to start turning things around.

Despite his anger, Cody maintained a very close relationship with his family, driving down from Seattle every month for dinner. Jennifer was living in Eugene, where she'd landed a job as an assistant women's track coach at the University of Oregon. Her running career with the Ducks had been stellar, and it turned out she had a knack for coaching. She continued to run post-collegiately, earning an occasional payday in a road race. Cody was quite proud of his sister's accomplishments. His family was his anchor.

In the spring of 2008, on his birthday, Cody drove down to Eatonville. Jennifer, having a rare weekend off, drove up from Eugene. Spring was track season and the Ducks always had a heavy schedule, but Jennifer hadn't seen her brother for over a year, so she pleaded for the weekend off.

Cody walked up to his parent's house lost in his thoughts. Instead of walking in like normal, he knocked on the front door. Gone was the carefree little boy who played with Cooper. Gone was the young man deeply in love with his high school sweetheart. Gone was the young patriot off to war to avenge his country. He'd devolved into a depressed, angry young man.

Cody almost didn't register that his mom was standing before him waiting for his hug.

"Oh, hi mom," he said, leaning in to embrace her. Debra didn't ask why he'd knocked. She and Mark had seen their boy sink into this PTSD cloud over the years since returning from Iraq. It saddened them, and it was starting to scare them.

"Hi, sweetheart. Jenn is here, and dinner's almost ready. You want something to drink?"

"Sure, got any fresh orange juice?" Cody had recently stopped drinking alcohol. His VA therapist had convinced him that down that path lay misery, and potentially worse. Four of his fellow troopers had survived the war only to come home and kill themselves in drunken rages. One of them had taken out three others in a bar fight before shooting himself.

Mark walked in from the back yard, where he'd been planting the last of the hothouse tomatoes into the ground. Embracing his son, he said, "Hey, buddy! How was the drive down? Traffic in the big city still bad as ever?"

"Hey, dad. Yeah, it's way worse. Some pretty stupid drivers out there." He stopped before mentioning how they could kill someone. The thought of Jazzie's broken body on the side of the road was one he'd never be rid of. Any talk of traffic conjured this for him. Between the war and Jazzie, Cody had more than his share of bad memories.

"Come check out the garden. We expanded it a lot. Mom and I are taking canning classes at the co-op so we can manage the waste better. We hate seeing so much food go bad, especially after all the work growing the stuff."

Mark led Cody out back in the fading evening light. Mud was everywhere, the norm for a garden in the Pacific Northwest in springtime. Regular rains kept everything moist and muddy until at least July when the dry season necessitated watering.

"Oh, man, I want some of those raspberries!" Cody exclaimed as he greedily began picking and scarfing them down.

"Hey, leave those alone, you'll ruin dinner," Debra scolded as she brought out his orange juice.

"They're so damn good, though, mom. I haven't had fresh berries since last year. What else you planting?" His mood brightening, Cody marveled at the scope of the garden, almost double in size from when, as a teenager, he'd helped turn the soil every spring and get the planting done. The whole family spent Saturdays and Sundays prepping the garden back then, and all of them had great memories of those days.

Sitting at the dinner table, Jennifer excitedly shared some good news. "Mom, you know that boy I told you about last month, the one who asked me out to the Pre meet?"

"What was his name—Bill?"

"William,"she corrected. "It's William Seibert. He's from LA, or Orange County, actually. They say there's a difference, but it's all LA to me. Anyway, he bought tickets near the finish line. He must've gotten them early. They're very hard to get, you know. This is him..." She whipped out her new iPhone and began swiping across the screen until William's picture appeared.

"I still can't believe how those phones work!" Debra said. "How do they do that?"

"It's magic, mom," Jenn teased. "Look at him. Cute, huh?"

The boy was tall and lean and had his right arm around her shoulder. She was leaning into him. They made a nice looking couple.

"Lemme see." Cody leaned in from the other side. "Looks nice. What's he do?"

"He's poly-sci. Probably the most political person I've ever known. His family is in the solar business and all he talks about is pollution this, climate-change that. I hope you get to meet him some day. You two'd get along really well. Oh, and he drives an electric car!" She said this enthusiastically, given that Cody had recently converted his Prius to a plug-in.

"What'd he convert?"

"It's not a conversion. He got one of those RAV4 EVs that were in the movie."

"No shit! Color me impressed. Those are hard to come by. Most of 'em were crushed, you know."

"I know all about it. He even knows the director of that movie about killing electric cars. Wait'll you drive this thing. It's amazing!"

"I might be going down to Portland soon on a job at Will Vinton. I'll pop down if I do and meet this guy. I like him already. Does he know about Mel?"

"He says everyone in the EV world knows about Mel. The White Zombie's famous!" Jenn mentioned the name of Mel's now very famous electric hot rod. "You've heard about the Tesla, right?"

"Yeah, a friend of mine was in LA last month and got to drive one. He couldn't believe how fast the damn car was. He says it hits 60 in less than four seconds! Holy shit!"

Mark and Debra loved seeing their kids bonding over boyfriends and electric cars. This was the happiest they'd seen Cody in months.

Maybe Cody could get back to normal, or close to it. Debra desperately wanted to ask Cody about his love life, but since Jazzie's tragic and violent death, Cody was unable to talk about girls, sex, his love life, or anything related to it at all. He also put up a stone wall around his war experiences— being forced by circumstances to brutalize other human beings is not something you want to talk about.—which were arguably worse than losing his love.

"How's Zak these days?" Mark asked. Still suing the bad guys?"

"Zak is fine, amazingly so. And yeah, he's busy as hell suing everyone in sight. He wins most of the time, too. You should see the room I have. The house is a three story in Queen Anne and my room is on the top floor overlooking downtown and the Space Needle. He's giving it to me for a song. I owe him big time for being so generous."

"Tell him we say hi. He's still the most interesting person I've ever met—him and Mel both. What a pair!"

"Mel drives the White Zombie up once a month or so for races, so I see him a lot," Cody said. "I'm back playing chess because of him. Zak and I play a lot. We're about even, so it's fun."

Cody sipped his orange juice. "What do you guys think of this Obama guy? Think he has a chance?"

Jennifer piped up immediately. "Oh man, he's going to obliterate McCain! Have you seen how stupid that Palin woman is? Can't wait for the debates. And Jon Stewart'll have the best time ever!"

"I started watching The Daily Show when I got back stateside," Cody said. "He's incredible! Why doesn't 'real' media cover things like he does? It's crazy we get our news from a comedian, but he's better than anyone else at explaining reality."

"We watch him and Colbert every night," Debra offered. "Election season is going to be a hoot!"

****

What Cody hadn't shared with his family were the late night conversations he'd been having with Zak. They began the first night he stayed in Zak's magnificent home.

"Cody, you see "An Inconvenient Truth" yet?"

"I saw it in LA. Pretty scary stuff. Mel says it's accurate. What's your take?"

"If anything it's worse. Shit's getting bad fast. People are dying now. Species are going extinct now by the thousands, every year. Yeah, it's bad. I've got some books you need to read."

Despite Zak's sense of humor, he grew serious when he talked about the state of the world. Climate change had started to dominate his thoughts. He was reading books, going to lectures, and researching online. He was gradually coming to the same conclusion to which most of the world's climate scientists had already arrived. This motivated a lot of his work. He actively sought cases that involved pollution, but if a case had to do with pollution contributing to climate change, he went after the perpetrators with a vengeance.

Zak began to share his reading lists with Cody, and they talked regularly about the growing environmental problems facing humanity. Cody began to realize there were people who didn't care how their action affected others. Some were negligent; others seemed to be actively trying to hurt people. The military was rife with the latter, and some corporations were led by people driven to make money above all else. They had no regard for those they hurt in the process.

As he learned more about climate change, he could see that humanity itself was at stake.

Chapter 9

Having a lot of downtime between VFX jobs, Cody began to volunteer at a local animal shelter. Zak loved animals, but his family never had dogs or cats, and he wasn't home enough to care for a dog. So to get his animal fix, Cody found a great shelter that rescued abandoned and abused animals. Helping homeless animals gave him something to hold on to and helped him cope with his PTSD and his growing hatred of the world's horrible people.

Heather Reinkoff, a 46-year-old heavyset woman, had worked at the shelter for 25 years. She ran the place like a military operation, scrutinizing every potential adoptee, making sure they were worthy of the animal she'd place in their care. Most rescue operations began working this way after they learned that assholes were "adopting" pets and then selling the animals to medical researchers or worse.

She knew every animal in the facility and their chances of being adopted. A long time PETA member, she took shit from no one when it came to abusing animals. She and her girlfriend had both been arrested several times for protesting against stores selling furs, and through years of persistent activism she had helped rid Seattle of the trade.

Heather and Cody bonded over their mutual hatred of animal abuse. But more than that, they both believed in punishing abusers severely. Other employees and volunteers didn't share this view, so they learned to keep these conversations to themselves.

Animal-abuse had made headlines the year before when Michael Vick was accused of running a dog-fighting ring. Stories of his torturing and killing dogs were all over the media. Within weeks the once-popular NFL quarterback became the most hated man in America.

The story led to other dog-fighting groups being investigated. One particularly noxious group on the Big Island of Hawaii "adopted" bait dogs from the local Humane Society. They used the dogs to train their fighting dogs. Severely injured by the fighting dogs, most bait dogs died from their wounds. A local rescue group tried to have this ring shut down, but the police were mostly native Hawaiians who were friendly with the locals in the dog-fighting gang. It drove Cody and Heather spitting mad.

Cody set up a Google Alert for stories of this type.

"Oh god, not another one," Cody exclaimed one day in the break room. The Los Angeles Times ran a story about a high-desert resident in a Southern California town near LA who'd recently been released from jail after being convicted a second time for running a dog-fighting ring. The story went into great detail about the horrific abuse his ring had inflicted on dogs.

"What's it this time, Cody?" asked Heather. She walked behind him and read over his shoulder.

"This fucker was convicted twice for running a dog-fighting ring, and he's just been released from jail. He's going to do it again, I just know it. Those assholes don't learn."

He looked up at Heather and their eyes met. Cody whispered, "Fucker needs to die." Her slight nod of assent indicated where she stood on the question.

"I've got to go to work." Cody abruptly stood and walked out of the room. He was thinking about how he could find this guy and kill him without getting caught. The government had trained him to kill, and he'd already ended two men's lives for what he now considered illegitimate reasons. If someone deserved to die, it was this guy.

He began to wonder if he could actually go through with murder. He obsessed over the question all day. He thought through the logistics: getting the gun, which had sat unused at his parent's house for over a decade; driving down to LA; locating the guy; and, finally, pulling the trigger.

He decided to try.

Getting the rifle proved easy. He knew when his folks were at work, so he just drove down to Eatonville, used his key to let himself in, and walked out with the rifle. Since it'd been stashed away in a little-used storage closet, there was faint chance anyone would notice, possibly for years.

Next step? Getting himself to his target's territory.

Cody didn't want to take the Prius. No need to involve a car that could be traced. Plus he wanted to bring his bike so he could scout the target's house without raising suspicion. He decided to get a U-Haul van since those were nondescript, and it wasn't that unusual for one to show up in any given neighborhood.

He informed Zak he was going to LA for a short VFX job. He told Heather the same story—although she raised an eyebrow when he did.

The drive from Tacoma to Southern California took two days. Cody spent his time obsessing over the article he'd read, generating sufficient anger to kill.

The Army taught Cody that it was OK to kill if the reason was just. This reasoning kept his foot on the accelerator and his van pointed south. He felt justified in his mission to end the pain of innocent animals. Anyone willing to torture animals for sport needed to be put down.

The article said the dog fighting ring was located in Littlerock, a small town north of LA. Cody's iPhone told him to turn off the freeway at Highway 138 and drive over to Lancaster, a small, bustling high-desert town. He was tired, stinky, and needed a room as a base to organize his search.

He pulled into the first clean-looking motel he found and paid cash for a room. He told the proprietor he was in town looking for work and might be there for a few days. Cody asked if anyone was hiring, and the proprietor said the Chinese company BYD was advertising for people in their electric bus assembly plant. And with that, Cody felt he had his cover handled.

He drove around back to his room and parked the van. He would leave most of his stuff in the vehicle until after dark, when he'd bring in the bike and rifle. No need to arouse suspicion or lure thieves.

Cody needed food, so after a quick shower, he set off to eat. The desert community was very different from the Pacific Northwest. Few trees offered shade from the blazing sun and a chilly wind blew the heat away at night. He found a small family café and ordered his usual veggie burger.

When Cody's food arrived, a couple with a Lab mix sat next to him on the patio and asked if he was OK with dogs. Cody looked at the medium-sized pooch sitting perfectly, staring hard at its owners. "Of course, I love doggies," he said as he reached over to let the dog sniff his hand.

As they spoke, Cody asked if there was an animal shelter where he might see some rescues. They were happy to offer what they knew about the local city shelter but also mentioned a rescue group that usually had lots of dogs from all over the high desert. They seemed sad as they talked of this, and Cody asked if the dogs there were OK. They told him a dog-fighting ring had been broken up in a neighboring town and rescue groups had taken in most of the canines. The man telling him this could barely hold back his anger when describing the bait dogs' conditions.

Stolen from homes or adopted from shelters, bait dogs are sold to evil, pathological humans and used to train the fighting dogs. They are usually torn to shreds after several bouts with big pit bulls. If they survive, they're allowed to recover enough until they're again thrust into the ring until the opposing dog finally kills them.

Based on the ramshackle housing Cody saw as he drove, Littlerock, CA was clearly lower income. The newspaper article about the dog fighting king pin described the community as just down the road from Palmdale, a sparsely populated town where retired folks lived next to some of the desert's poorest inhabitants.

Cody pulled into a gas station to fill up and ask questions. The attendant was a scruffy young man, maybe 25 or so.

"Marines and Mexicans is all you got here," he said with a combination of pride and prejudice. Cody shivered at the attendant's bigotry, but allowed the comment to pass.

The attendant took his silence in stride and completed the transaction, giving Cody his change. Before he left, Cody asked if the man knew where he could find a guy buying dogs. He explained he'd heard of someone looking to buy some pits.

The attendant sized up Cody, who was unshaven and in old clothes. "Nobody's looking for prize winners out here, just some good watchdogs is all. What you got?"

Bingo! The location was just a few blocks away off 34th street, a dusty, dreary lane with junk cars and drooping fences unlikely to keep anyone out, but lots of barking dogs that would.

Cody drove further, looking for the home the attendant had described. Sure enough, at the end of a cul-de-sac was a brown house with white gutters and a particularly mean looking pit bull chained up outside. Cody circled the cul-de-sac and left. He now knew where to find his mark.

Back at his motel, he studied Google Earth to discover that there was a view of the back of the house from one treeless street over. Maybe he could get a clean shot from there if his target came to a window.

Early the next day, before temperatures rose into the 90s, Cody drove back to Littlerock and parked a few blocks away from his destination. He pulled his bike from the van and rode up and down all the adjoining streets, trying to look like a lost cyclist finding his way. When he arrived at the spot where he could see through to the house, he stopped and got his water out for a long drink. He took a few pictures with his phone, as well. The back of the house was clearly visible, with nothing blocking his view. The trick would be to avoid drawing any attention to himself while parked in the van. He might need to wait for a long time, which meant the neighbors could notice him. With all the druggies in the area, they might suspect he was a cop or a criminal.

Cody noticed that the car parked at the house was an old GM SUV. He hated to think of the poor animals that had been transported in that clunker. Dogs trained to fight other dogs purely for the entertainment of the lowest of lowlifes.

As he watched, he saw movement at the kitchen window. A man fitting the gas-station attendant's description was doing something at the sink. He spent the better part of a minute standing still—a perfect target. Cody wished he had his gun, but he had to wait. Broad daylight was not a good time to commit murder, not if you wanted to get away with it.

The heat was getting to Cody and he had all he needed for now, so he rode back to the van and stashed his bike. He'd return after dark.

After a cool shower and some diner food, he returned to the motel for final preparations. He took out the rifle, remembering how he had killed that deer with his grandfather and father, and how its death nipped his hunting career in the bud. But after killing two men in the war, Cody was now ready, willing, and able to hunt bigger, more lethal game.

When the sun finally dropped below the horizon, the desert twilight reminded Cody of his time in Iraq. There, the beauty of his natural surroundings contrasted starkly with the violence all around him. He might have been a participant in that mayhem, but it wasn't of his making. This time, he'd be the one initiating the violence.

It was after 9 pm when Cody carried the wrapped rifle to his van. The bike and all of his belongings were already packed, and he'd filled the gas tank just in case. If he was successful, he'd leave immediately and make the drive in one long stretch, stopping only to grab a few hours sleep in southern Oregon.

Nighttime in the small desert community was pretty quiet. Certain people, however, crawled out to scout neighborhoods for anything to steal, or possibly find some unsuspecting stranger who could easily be rolled. Unaware of this aspect of the community, Cody drove as normally as possible to his destination.

Coming up the block, he noticed another car driving slowly in the opposite direction. He grew anxious, since he was almost to where he needed to park. If this person lived there, or knew the neighborhood, Cody's van could easily raise suspicion. He still had Washington tags and regretted not changing the plates.

But as the approaching car got closer, it sped off. Its two gang bangers inside were as worried about Cody as Cody was about them. Still, was the noise from their low rider enough to rouse the neighbors' suspicion? A dog barked in the distance, but otherwise, all looked OK.

Cody eased to a stop at the spot with the perfect view of his target's house. He shut off the engine and lights and sat quietly while observing the houses immediately surrounding him. He kept an eye on the kitchen window. There seemed to be no activity anywhere, so he retrieved the rifle, unwrapped it from its blanket, and confirmed a cartridge was in the chamber.

His head suddenly filled with images of war. He hadn't held a weapon since returning, but now the heft and feel of a rifle, even though quite different from the automatic weapons he'd used in Iraq, was enough to bring him back to the conflict he so desperately wanted to forget. But could he go through with cold-blooded murder? Did he want that on his mind, as well?

Suddenly, snarling, barking dogs shook him from his thoughts. The noise was coming from the house he was watching, but not from inside. Two pit bulls were fighting in the back yard. A flood light snapped on, startling Cody and causing him to hunker down, even though he was a good 50 meters away. He recoiled at the sound of dogs in pain, dogs hurting each other. His adrenaline level, already rising, spiked as the back door slammed open, and the man he was hunting started screaming at his dogs. He was speaking a mixture of Spanish and English, but Cody caught enough to understand.

Apparently, this outburst was typical, since Cody heard no rustling, saw no neighbors coming out. It was just him and his target, and the asshole had been nice enough to light up his back yard like a prison during a nighttime escape.

Cody's military training kicked in. He'd been taught to be ready to use his weapon the instant shit went down, which happened a lot in Iraq. He raised the rifle to his cheek and looked through the scope, zeroing in on the man's head. He tracked him as he tried to control his two dogs, and as soon as the man bent down to tie up one of the dogs, Cody squeezed off a shot. The noise was much louder than he remembered as a child. The bullet struck the man's head, and he crumpled to the ground.

Cody set the rifle on the passenger seat and started his van but kept his lights off for the first block. If anyone saw him, they wouldn't be able to read his plates. He drove away at a normal speed without seeing any lights flick on at the neighboring houses. As far as he could tell, no one had seen him.

He made his way back to the highway and headed north.

The drive back was uneventful, but Cody couldn't stop thinking about the two men he'd killed in Iraq. They were clearly enemy combatants, and his kills were considered legitimate by the military, if not by Cody. But taking a human's life is not a thing normal people do. Maybe they were normal before, but they were never normal after. Still, once you'd killed, it became easier the next time. Cody told himself that the asshole would torture no more dogs. And as the miles slid slowly by on I-5, he became comfortable with what he'd done.

Chapter 10

When he arrived home, Cody told Zak about his brief gig at Digital Domain. He was surprised at how easy it was to lie. He felt a little guilty. Probably because the good little boy still lived within him even though he'd been dirtied by life.

The hard part came when he returned to work at the animal shelter. A few of the volunteers welcomed him back and asked about his trip to LA. Everyone loved Cody and admired his skills with dogs, and they were all eager to hear of his film work.

When Heather heard he was back she went looking and found Cody cleaning out cages in the main dog-holding room.

"Hey, welcome back, stranger!" She practically hollered while slapping him on the back. "How was the film job? Are we going to see your work on the big screen?"

"It went fine. It's a new James Cameron flick and I got to work on removing zits from some actor's face. Not even a known actor. At least I'd never heard of him." He laughed. "Not everything in the film world is glamorous."

He couldn't tell if she bought the story. Heather played her cards close.

"Hey, can you come into my office for a second?" she said. "I have something I want to show you."

Cody followed her into the tiny space stacked with paperwork and cases of donated food. Pictures of adopted animals covered the walls. Sitting at her computer, she typed a few characters and up popped a small article from the Antelope Valley Press, the paper of record for the Palmdale area. The article's headline sent a shiver down Cody's spine.

"Convicted Dog-Fighting Kingpin Shot to Death." The article contained little information since there was scant evidence and no witnesses. Reading that, Cody felt relieved.

"Hmmm...that's interesting," he mumbled, trying to act nonchalant. "Can't say I'm sorry it happened. He was clearly a piece of shit, and deserved whatever fate he got."

Heather stared at Cody. She suspected him, but nothing in his demeanor gave her any clues. After an awkward moment, Cody raised his eyebrows. "Yeah, he deserved death all right," Heather said. "One less asshole torturing dogs. I call that a good day! Whoever did it deserves a medal."

On her way out, she slapped him on the back. "Good job helping these doggies. I'm sure dogs everywhere appreciate what you do for them." Cody took this to mean she was glad if he had in fact done it. He'd never admit to murder, however, and she never mentioned the incident again.

The '08 election was heating up, with the whole country going nuts over the idea of a black president. Some loved the idea, others hated it. McCain screwed the pooch by selecting Sarah Palin as his running mate, so those who were paying attention knew the good guys would win.

The right wing, meanwhile, grew ever more vitriolic in their denunciations of Obama. A meme surfaced suggesting he was not born in the US, but in Kenya, his father's birthplace. The conservative media cesspool festered, with more and more pundits calling for investigations into his origins.

After an interminably long election season, the day to cast votes arrived with a steady, cold Seattle rain. Zak and Cody drove the Prius to the elementary school serving as their gateway to democracy and proudly cast their votes for Obama.

Zak had depositions to take, so he was gone all day. Cody spent the rest of his day working at the shelter. He was always happiest among the needy animals.

As the polls closed on the eastern seaboard, followed by central and mountain time zones, both Cody and Zak followed the election results on NPR. It began to look very good for the Dems, which brought smiles to millions hungering to replace the evil George W. Bush with someone who promised them change.

When Zak had moved from Brooklyn to Seattle two decades earlier, he'd searched for a boozy hangout near Pike Place Market, a tourist draw with some old derelict bars on its perimeter imbued with the character Zak preferred in his drinking establishments. Kells Pub, an Irish-themed bar with an excellent selection of whiskeys, it fit the bill and for years had been Zak's favorite. It was as close to his native Brooklyn as he could find in Seattle.

He and Cody drove into Kells' lot and parked in the far corner. Zak produced his pipe and a small stash of pot which they smoked. They were in a celebratory mood.

It was about 7:30 when they burst through the front door, Zak bellowing his customary "howdy" to various regulars, hugging a few as they got up to greet him. The two friends grabbed the last available table. The TVs were all tuned to election returns, which pissed off the patrons who were decidedly apolitical. Tough for them since the owner was a huge Obama supporter, like so many in the liberal bastion of Seattle.

The mood in the room grew increasingly festive as state after state was called for the Democrat. Once it was apparent Obama had it in the bag, the few remaining conservatives left amid the winning side's cheers. By the time the election was confirmed in Obama's favor, everyone was celebrating in earnest.

Kells' owner was making the rounds, high-fiving and hugging his regular patrons. When he came to their table, Zak stood up to his full 6'3" and gave the man a bear hug. They'd known each other for many years and talked politics all the time. They had a strong mutual respect.

Cody also stood and shook the owner's hand. He was happy for the first time in a long time. The murder he'd committed, the two enemy combatants he'd killed, all was stashed away in a corner of his mind he normally had to fight to secure.

Chapter 11

The heady first two years of Obama's administration were tempered after the mid-term election. The House went back to Republican control and the Democrats barely kept hold of the Senate. The celebrations had long since diminished as it became clear to progressives that the Republicans were willing to do whatever it took to limit the president's effectiveness.

Cody's PTSD was mostly under control, but there were times when crowds or certain sounds would snap him back to Iraq, and especially to the day he killed.

When this happened, Zak would come home and find Cody sitting at his desk in his room staring out at the Seattle skyline.

On a rainy day in the winter of 2010 Zak knocked on Cody's door. "C'mon in," Cody murmured. Zak opened the door to see his friend once again sitting at his desk, a joint smoldering in the ashtray.

Zak had just won a case against a local independent gas station that for years had been dumping cleaning solvent into a storm drain. A runner spotted an oil slick in a small stream and followed it up to the drain next to the station. Then he watched aghast as the gas station attendant poured solvent into the drain.

The runner went apoplectic and cussed out the attendant. He then reported it to the local office of the Washington State Department of the Ecology, which initiated an investigation. It took over a year to get to court, but once Zak took the case, it ended quickly. The judge imposed the maximum fine, making Zak ready to celebrate.

"What's up, buddy?" Zak asked.

"Just thinking about stuff," Cody responded dully.

"Want to talk about it?" Zak asked, helping himself to the joint. "Is it Iraq again?"

Cody looked up at him, eyes red from the pot. "I dunno. Maybe."

Zak exhaled. "Get your coat, it's wet out. Let's head down to Fiore for some coffee. The walk will do us both good." Zak was partial to Caffe Fiore, a rustic coffee shop a few blocks down the hill.

A blustery wind knifed into them as soon as they exited the house. "This reminds me of training runs back in high school," Cody said. "I kinda liked it when it was windy like this, but without the rain. Jazzie really liked it when it rained..."

Of all that had happened to him in his short 28-year life, losing Jazzie was hardest to take. His heart still ached for her, and the impossibility of her return was something he could never accept. Often the thought of her brought him to tears.

It being late afternoon, the cafe was only half full, so they grabbed a table by a window and settled in, Zak with his large black coffee and Cody with his medium latte. They always got the same thing, so they switched off buying for each other.

"Man, you should have seen the judge throw that station a huge fine. It was fantastic! We had them by the short hairs, and their attorney knew it. They were hoping for a lenient judge who wouldn't sting them too bad, but they drew Osblom, the poor fuckers. Osblom hates polluters! Fined 'em $600K! Ha! That'll fuckin' teach those bastards."

It wasn't rare that Zak won, but it didn't happen often enough to suit him. Big polluters tended to have deep pockets and hire competent counsel who could bury most prosecutors under mountains of legal bullshit that would take years to work through, depleting the budgets of those trying to win judgments. But since this was an independent station, they went cheap on legal counsel, a move they now regretted.

"So tell me what's up. Open up to me, buddy." The effects of the pot combined with his big legal win and a $120K payday made Zak happy. Maybe some of his joy would rub off on his friend.

"You know those two guys I killed?"

"What about 'em?"

"I keep thinking about who they were and why they were there. Hell, why was I there? It doesn't seem right." Cody stared into the space between them.

Zak looked at his coffee, black with no cream to soften its edge, no sugar to sweeten its bitterness. "Yeah, I wondered when you'd want to talk about that. Kind of a heavy thing to hold inside. Is the guy at the VA any help?" His voice was low and measured.

"Not much. I tried asking for another doc, but they wouldn't switch me. Just pisses me off. I stopped seeing him quite a while ago."

"Yeah, the Republicans won't fund them, so they're always short staffed. Fuckin' assholes. Those guys are quick to spend trillions of fucking dollars to go fight the goddamn wars, but when it comes to taking care of soldiers they send to kill or be killed, they get tight ass. And to top it off, most of 'em never wore a fuckin' uniform themselves."

While true, this didn't make Cody feel any better. It wasn't just the two he shot in Iraq. The dog fighter he'd killed also weighed heavily on him. In his head, it was more justified than his two military kills. But it was cold blooded murder, not sanctioned by any government.

"Those two guys were probably just protecting their country. I have no idea why they were fighting, but the way they just kept coming at us, with no regard for their own safety. I mean, you shoulda seen how they'd fight! We had all kinds of firepower we'd throw at 'em, but nothing scared them. Shit, I sure wasn't into the war like they were. I had no idea why we were there. Me and the guys used to talk about that a lot. No one knew. There were guys who said we had to fight so they wouldn't invade us back home, but—shit—there was no chance any of those people would ever get to us here. That was just some bullshit they got from Fox-fucking News."

"Don't get me started on those assholes," Zak responded. "If I could strangle them, I'd do one a day until they were all gone. It'd feel so good to squeeze the life out of 'em. I mean, they were cheerleading the wars! None of 'em—or their children—joined the fight. They were all like, 'Yeah, let's kill those fuckin' Muslims!' But them fight? Shit no!"

Both men were getting riled up, and as their volume increased, people began to look. Noticing this, Zak hunched over his ceramic cup and lowered his voice. "How's the PTSD these days? Is that what this is?"

"Yeah, I guess. I don't know how anyone could do what I did, or see what I saw, and not come home pretty fucked up." A moment passed, and then Cody asked, "You ever see someone get shot?"

"No, never saw anything get shot, 'cept maybe a tin can or something. Nothing living at least."

"It's not pretty." Cody lifted his bloodshot eyes to stare at Zak. "Their bodies do weird shit. Depending on where they get hit, and with what caliber round, their bodies crumple to the ground like a rag doll, no control, no life. Just blam! And they fall in a second... You ever hear about 'pink mist'?"

"No, what's that?"

"If a guy gets hit with a big round, especially a 50 cal, it destroys a good portion of his body, which poofs into a pink mist. Tiny bits of flesh and blood. They never know what hit 'em."

"Jeez, did you see that a lot?"

"No, not a lot, but a few times. You shoulda heard how some of the guys responded. Man, they were cheering like it was some sort of big fucking game. I got really tired of that. A lot of the guys were really into the killing. I think that's why they were over there. Not to protect the good ole U. S. of fucking A."

"Jeez! Did you use a 50 caliber?"

"No, I never got the opportunity, but guys in my unit did. It's a pretty badass weapon."

"If you're willing to talk about it, what was the circumstance of your kills?"

"It wasn't anything special, just a normal day going out on patrol. Lots of IEDs were being planted along this one road, so we were tasked with keeping an eye on it and asking locals for intel on who was doing it. We approached this one house, and before we could get close, shit got real. The guy next to me, Randy, took a direct hit in the face and dropped. There were shots coming from three windows, so we opened up on them while running for cover. We had two down, both dead, and three wounded who'd gotten under cover. I got behind a low wall with a good view of the front of the house and started laying down suppressive fire. Man, when you're being shot at, adrenaline just courses through you. It's like nothing you've ever experienced. One of the guys upstairs was shooting at my buddies who were exposed, so I opened up on him and hit him directly. He disappeared from the window, and no one shot from there again.

"We were still getting fire from two windows downstairs, and it was hard to make anyone out. There were several people shooting at us, but they were back enough that you couldn't see them. By now, we were laying down a lot of fire, so they were hunkered down for the most part, but then one of them poked his head up to try and get a look, and I happened to be aiming right where he was, so I opened up and he dropped out of sight.

"One of our guys managed to get a grenade in the room right after that and got the rest of them. That's it. It was over. My cherry was popped and everyone congratulated me back at the base."

"Jeezus!" Zak said. "War is fucked up."

"It's way worse than you can imagine. There are things I saw I'll never talk about." Cody looked down and became quiet.

Zak was a smart man, but counseling a soldier suffering from PTSD was not his strong suit. He was no longer in a good mood. It sounded as if Cody hadn't told the story many times, if at all. He presented it as a factual retelling of an enormously important day in his life, one that clearly changed him.

In October of 2011, President Obama declared the combat mission in Iraq over, but that didn't stop the vets coming home from needing help. More and more were becoming aware of the true reason they were over there and this drove many to levels of anger they were ill-equipped to handle.

Cody's mood hadn't improved much, so at Zak's insistence, he called the VA and got in a queue to see a different therapist. The people at the VA were mostly good at their jobs, but some were just government employees doing the bare minimum. Hopefully, Cody would get to speak with one of the former.

The day of his appointment was clear and cold. A high-pressure system had moved in and pushed the rain out of the Pacific NW, leaving the temperature near freezing, but skies sparkling blue. Cody geared up for what would be a frigid six-mile bike ride. After arriving, he checked in and sat in a drab waiting room reading old Car & Driver magazines. Some of the older vets didn't look so good, some were clearly homeless. He imagined their lives were especially miserable in the winter.

"Cody Benson?" the aide called. Cody followed the matronly woman to a tiny office down the hall where she told him to sit and wait for the doctor. She wasn't rude, but neither was she particularly friendly.

He spent another ten minutes waiting in this dreary, bare room. Cody wondered what kind of doctor would work in an office with so little visual stimulation.

With a soft knock at the door, a genial African American man of about 60 entered. "Hello, I'm Dr. William Drexel, but please call me Bill." He reached out to shake Cody's hand.

"Hi Bill, thanks for seeing me. It took a while to get in. You guys are pretty busy, huh?"

"Well, we aren't supposed to discuss politics here, but it's pretty clear our budget could use some help. We need to hire more people so we can give you folks the assistance you deserve. You follow the news?"

"Sure. I've been paying particular attention to the Republicans and their budget cuts for everything except the war machine. It's clear to anyone watching what's going on."

"So tell me, what is going on? I mean, what's going on with you?" The doctor knew a good segue when he heard one.

Cody had been sitting erect, but hearing the question, he sat back and slouched. Had he been able, he would've melted right into the big plush chair. After all this waiting to see the VA doctor, he suddenly didn't want to open up. The talk with Zak a few weeks earlier had been fueled by pot and strong coffee, neither of which were available to him now. Had he known how he'd feel, he would've toked up before entering the building.

"So, how much can I say off the record? Is everything here confidential?"

The doctor looked him over before calmly explaining the doctor-patient contract precluded him from telling anyone about the counseling he provided unless it was to prevent a suicide or aggression toward another person. He didn't tell Cody his file contained a red flag from the previous VA therapist who had detected a potential for aggression or violence.

"I killed a couple of guys in Iraq, all legal. The guys in my unit praised me for it. But that's not the issue."

"Please tell me about the issue, then," Dr. Drexel said.

"I'm pretty sure the war was based on lies. All those people who died...those two guys I killed...they were only fighting an invading force. We attacked them, and they were defending their country against us infidels, who were killing them wholesale. Bush said they were a danger to us, but that was never true. It was so goddamned clear that whole shit storm was about the oil."

It was not the first time Drexel had heard this from a vet who'd served in Iraq. Vets who'd served in Afghanistan and not Iraq had their own issues, but at least they felt they were fighting a just war. More and more of the Iraq vets were talking about how the pretense for the war was a huge lie. The wasted human lives and the massive waste of our country's capital were all so the oil companies could get access to the black liquid under the sand. The anger was too much for many vets and the divorces, fights, and suicides were growing as more of them returned after multiple tours.

Adding to vets' problems was the public's disassociation from the war. Only about one percent of American families had any skin in the game. Without a draft, the country had a 100-percent volunteer military, which was significantly more professional than the military in Vietnam.

However, the military was being used as a cudgel against recalcitrant countries that were led by brutal dictators like Saddam Hussein, but only those countries that had oil. The first Gulf war was over oil. The attacks of 9/11 opened the door for the Bush administration to finally depose Hussein and gain access for the oil companies chomping at the bit to get at Iraq's oil. If they could attack Iran, they'd do the same there. The Saudis remained close to the American leaders for this very reason. They were easily the most brutal regime in the Middle East, but there was no drumbeat to attack them and depose the monarchy since the Saudis were more than happy to sell the world their oil.

Cody knew all this from Zak, The Daily Show, and his own reading and research. The more it became clear the Iraq war was based on lies, the angrier Cody grew.

"I think a lot about those two guys I killed. When I did it, there was a reason, at least in my head. They were definitely trying to kill me. Shit, they killed two of my buddies right next to me. We just did what we were trained to do. But now I'm out, and I'm learning all this stuff about the Bush lies...I'm just not dealing with my anger very well."

"Is there anything specific you need to tell me about this anger? Have you done anything you shouldn't have?" Dr. Drexel leveled his gaze at Cody, but his voice remained soft and non-judgmental.

Cody didn't want to hesitate after that question, but the murder in California caused him to think slightly longer than he'd wished to before finally saying, "No, nothing specific. But I'm getting angrier the more I learn."

"I see. And do you think you'll act on this anger?"

"Who knows? That's why I'm here. I need you to tell me what to do about it." Cody's voice grew steadily more agitated. "Tell me why I shouldn't be angry. Give me a reason why we needed to attack Iraq!"

"I can't do that, Cody. I agree with you. I do want to help you deal with the anger, though. My job is to help you readjust to civilian life and get beyond your experiences over there. I can give you tools to help deal with..."

"I don't need tools, doc, I need to know why I killed those two guys!" Cody's hands were starting to shake, his face had become flushed. Drexel had seen this behavior a lot. Cody did not seem dangerous to him—not like some vets who'd come through his office. Some of them were scary as hell.

"I can prescribe some medicine that'll allow you to handle your anger better. It won't help with the reason for the anger, but it should help you deal with it." The doctor pulled out a pad and handed Cody a prescription for an anti-depressant.

"Thanks, Bill," Cody said. "I know you care, but if this is all the VA can do for us, well I suspect there'll be more vets coming in when we start the next war."

"Sadly, you're probably right. Come back in three months and see me again, OK? And here's my card. Call any time you feel the need to talk."

Cody nodded and left.

He filled the prescription at the VA before riding his bike home. It was almost dark when he arrived to find Zak at home reading.

"Hey, man, how was the VA? Any help?"

"Not much, just some anti-depressants. The doc was nice, and he agreed with a lot of the stuff I was complaining about, but yeah, not a lot of help. We'll see what these pills do. Think they're better than the evil weed?" He smiled at Zak who was already filling his bong.

"Nothing's better than this shit, man! Here, take a hit. It's a sativa called Sour Diesel."

Cody took the bong and sparked it up. While he was holding the smoke in, Zak held up a book he'd just purchased. "If you think the war pissed you off, wait until you read this!" The book was *Merchants of Doubt* by Erik Conway and Naomi Oreskes. "I'm about halfway through and getting madder by the minute. You know how we suspect the mofos who run the world lie to get their way? Well, these guys have documented the shit out of it.

"They start with the tobacco companies in the '50s, when they were noticing a lot of medical studies linking cancer to tobacco use. The companies studied these links themselves, and even they found links between their products and cancer! They figured there'd be legislation coming to curtail their profitable businesses, so they hired PR firms like Hill & Knowlton and some fake doctors and scientists to come up with other reasons for the cancer. Then they spent millions spreading the results of these fake studies in the media to convince the public that maybe cigarettes weren't the reason for the cancer. Stinking, fucking lies to fool the public and Washington. It worked, too! Like a goddamned charm. There wasn't any legislation passed against cigarettes until the Surgeon General came out in '64 saying cigarettes cause cancer."

"Goddamned bastards!" Cody said as he blew smoke toward the ceiling. "Tobacco killed both my grandparents."

"It's the same shit they did to get us in the war, and it's the same shit they're doing to stop us from doing anything about climate change. Lies! Fucking lies. And people die by the thousands. Hell, millions! I'm so pissed right now. Gimme that bong!"

As Zak took his turn, Cody picked up the book and read its back cover. "Can I have this when you're done?"

"Sure. I'll leave it here with a bookmark, and you can start reading it whenever you want. Just don't lose my place. Hey, are you cooking tonight? It's your turn, right?"

"Yeah, anything special you want, or is spaghetti OK?"

"It's called pasta. Didn't your momma teach you foodie talk?" Zak laughed at his own lame joke. That's what pot will do to you.

Over the next few weeks, Zak and Cody read the book. Cody was even more upset than Zak. By the time he'd finished, the book was dog-eared and marked-up throughout. He'd highlighted individuals responsible for much of the subterfuge. When Cody was about halfway through, Zak noticed his bookmark had changed to a piece of paper with names and page numbers scribbled on it.

"Who're these people you're writing down?" Zak inquired.

"Um, just the people who are the worst of the worst. Some of them have been lying for corporations for a long time. They're guns for hire. I don't know what I'll do with the list—maybe look them up to see if any of them live around here. I'd sure like to ask them what the fuck they were thinking when they took money for lying. Don't they know people are being killed in wars for oil? Shit, climate change is going to kill millions. These assholes are responsible for that."

"Partially responsible!" Zak interrupted. "Ultimate responsibility lies with the people using dirty energy in the first place."

"What alternatives do they have? You drive an EV. But how many people can, or will go to the trouble of converting a car like you did? A few hundred? Maybe a thousand? Shit, we've got 250 million cars in this country. Where are all of them going to get an EV?"

"Remember when we watched 'Who Killed the Electric Car?' " Zak asked.

"Yeah, well that's true," Cody replied. "We could've had lots more of them if they hadn't crushed those things, but still...that makes my point. Corporatists decided to kill the EV. California's government forced them to make them in the first place."

"All I'm saying is people have to share the blame. They need to be proactive, not be so stupid and accepting of everything they read and hear."

"Yeah, I'm with you there. Gimme one more toke, and I'll go make spaghetti." Both of them were getting hungry.

As Cody toked up, Zak said, "Hey, I was talking to Mel this afternoon, and he tells me Nissan and Chevy are going to have some actual EVs for sale soon. Maybe by January. I guess we'll see whether people will do the right thing, or keep listening to those fuckin' merchants of doubt."

Mel had been following the EV world closely. Even though his car was built for racing, he understood the need for everyday commuting cars to be non-polluting. Years ago, in 2008, he sponsored a screening of "Who Killed the Electric Car?" and invited the director, Chris Paine, and some of the people in the film to come for a panel discussion. The event had been well received with a full house and a rousing Q&A. One of the people from the film, Marc Nicholes, was especially hardcore about letting people know that EVs were coming to market soon.

Now that 2011 was nearing, EV enthusiasts were anxious to get one. Zak had been driving a clunker he and Mel had converted, but it was an old car with lots of problems unrelated to its electric drive train. Mel had convinced Zak to sign up for one of the Nissan LEAFs so he could have a proper, reliable electric car.

Zak got his LEAF in the summer of 2011 and Cody was there to greet him when he drove it home.

"Nice color! I like the shiny black!" Cody said as Zak got out of the car. "Can I have a ride?"

"Sure, let's get some pie to celebrate! But you drive. I want you to experience this thing. You're gonna love it!"

Cody got behind the wheel, pushed the start button, and heard the chime indicating the car was on. Zak showed him how to slip it into reverse and watched as Cody responded to the new technology.

"Whoa! Love that back-up camera. What's that dinging?"

"That's the chime to warn people when you're backing up. The car's really quiet, so they built in artificial noise to warn pedestrians."

Zak also showed Cody the eco mode that increased the regenerative braking, essentially recapturing energy while the car was braking. Everything about the car was efficient, and it had great power when needed.

At a light, Zak indicated a BMW to their right and told Cody to punch it when the signal turned green.

"Damn! Holy shit, that was fun!" Cody was impressed with the acceleration. The BMW wasn't racing, of course, but nevertheless, its driver had to have been impressed at this silent car zipping away from him without any apparent effort.

Arriving home with a fresh strawberry-rhubarb pie, Cody eased into the garage and parked close to the new charge station Zak had installed a couple weeks earlier.

"OK, pull the lever next to your left knee. That opens the charge port," Zak told Cody as he was getting out. "Take the connector out and open the orange port. Now stick it in until you hear it make a beep. I think it beeps a couple times." Zak was relaying what he'd been told at the dealership.

The car beeped three times, and a blue light on the dash confirmed it was now charging. "See how easy that is? Much easier than going to a goddamn gas station and pumping poison into your car."

"Man, I think everyone's gonna want one of these," Cody said. "Mom and dad have to get one. They're gonna love it."

The release of the Volt and LEAF buoyed most environmentalists—especially those who were paying attention to the electrification of transportation. It gave them hope that maybe the big fight against climate change could take a turn for the better.

The grid mix in Seattle, the sources supplying Seattle City Light its electricity, was pretty clean already, but Zak had previously taken the further step of signing up for 100% clean, renewable energy to run his house on non-polluting power. Now, his new car would be running on that same power, just like his conversion EV had.

"What're you going to do with the old EV?"

"I have a friend who teaches an eco class at North Seattle. It's that community college across I-5 from Northgate. He wanted a work project for his students, and man, is that car going to be a work project! It's going to be so nice having a car that can go a hundred miles without charging. And I got bluetooth and a back up camera."

"Next thing I'm going do is install solar on the roof. I got a flyer from SolarCity, one of Elon Musk's companies. I want to support anyone ballsy enough to start a rocket company and an electric car company at the same fucking time."

"I heard he's got a really cool luxury EV coming out soon," Cody added. They call it Model S, I think."

"Yeah, it's an awesome car! The car companies are gonna shit when that thing hits the market."

"You think we're really going to switch everyone over to electric?"

"I dunno. There's a lot of ignorance out there, and the established industry isn't going to roll over for these upstarts." Zak, while enthusiastic over EVs, was wise enough to know the enemies of positive change were powerful and entrenched.

"But people have to know this is better!" Cody said. "It's so goddamned clear. No tailpipe, no noise, 100% domestic energy you can make from sunlight falling on your roof. Jeez, what more do you want?"

"Well, we'll see," Zak replied.

"After that fucking oil spill in the Gulf last year, I don't know how anyone who gives a shit about the environment can still burn gas. I mean, what are they thinking?" Cody was building to a full-blown rant.

"Shit, Americans are brain dead when it comes to doing the right thing. They'll tell you they care about the environment, but when push comes to shove, they're just mouthing meaningless words. Mostly they're selfish and greedy. 'Murica!'"

Sure enough, even though Nissan and GM began offering well-built plug-in cars that garnered high marks from NHTSA and allowed for oil-free driving, most Americans didn't really care.

To be fair, millions of people didn't have easy access to electricity where they parked their cars, and landlords and condo associations were not readily approving requests to install charging stations. Some states, Hawaii and California specifically, remedied this problem by passing legislation allowing an EV driver to install charging where they parked as long as they met a few reasonable requirements. A big push to install charge points at workplaces also got underway.

In fact, long-time advocates for EVs and renewable energy around the world were encouraged by the growing ranks of EV owners. In June of 2012, Musk introduced the much anticipated Tesla Model S, which immediately became the most desired car in the world. Once production ramped up, and more people were allowed to drive or ride in this amazing car, word got out to the performance-car world that this was the future of automobiles.

But not all was rosy. The auto industry initially scoffed at Tesla and Musk's ambitions. Industry leaders like Bob Lutz were downright dismissive of this Silicon Valley upstart who thought he could waltz in and just start making cars. Tesla's near-death experiences, and there were several, lent false credence to industry denigration of Tesla.

The oil industry was paying close attention, too. Since the first modern attempt to bring EVs to market in the mid '90s and early 2000s, the industry had been hiring PR firms to lie about EVs to stem the technology's growth. Sadly, they were quite successful. In 2003, the California law that mandated a small number of EVs be made available to the public was rescinded in favor of fuel-cell cars. The auto industry used their own merchant of doubt techniques that had worked for the tobacco industry in decades past. These techniques worked beautifully in 2003 as the auto industry made false claims about the viability of EVs while speaking positively about how their new fuel-cell cars would solve the problems associated with using oil.

Based on these lies, the California Air Resources Board, arguably the most powerful environmental regulatory agency after the federal EPA, reversed its position on battery electrics in favor of fuel cells.

The movie "Who Killed the Electric Car?" detailed this mendacious move, and after Cody and Zak read *Merchants of Doubt*, they better understood the hows and whys of what went down. The book helped them spot this pernicious effort across a broad spectrum of national and global issues. The money-people were hard at work deceiving the public about their dangerous products and the effects some had on the environment, public health, and our predilection to go to war over oil.

Chapter 12

Cody's frugal lifestyle, and his investments in Apple, SolarCity, and Tesla gave him financial security beyond what he needed. He put a lot of the excess into the animal shelter, making sure the animals had enough food, medicine, and other necessities. Heather was extremely grateful. He also treated everyone, volunteers and staff, to bimonthly office parties that helped create a healthy and happy workplace.

His work in the visual effects world was beginning to bear fruit, as well. As the years went by, he became a regular VFX contractor working for ad agencies in Portland and Seattle, and he spent quite a bit of time in Vancouver and Los Angeles working on commercial and film projects.

Though his professional life was on an even keel, emotionally, he was unstable. Cody felt that everything seemed to be heading for a cliff in terms of the climate, and few people outside the hardcore environmental movement were paying attention.

He noticed that all the science pointed to one inescapable conclusion: global temperatures would continue to warm, sea levels would rise, and an increasingly energetic atmosphere would generate ever-more powerful storms which would wreak havoc. The costs were already in the hundreds of billions per year, and would soon be in the trillions.

The political scene was again heating up as President Obama in 2012 ran for his second term against Mitt Romney, a businessman with strong ties to industries willing to fund him with millions. The 2009 Citizens United decision allowing unlimited dark money in political races opened the floodgates for the richest Americans and corporations to affect the outcome of important races.

Scientists from around the world were nervously watching the US election, knowing that if Obama lost, the work he'd done to fight climate change would be reversed. Senator James Inhofe, one of the more conservative legislators from the deep red state of Oklahoma, was on record as saying "climate change is the biggest hoax ever perpetrated on the American people." He was the quintessential example of how the oil industry controlled Congress.

Cody and Zak were both reading a lot online and adding their own views to various political and environmental posts. Facebook was turning out to be a great venue for finding good articles and sharing them. Both men learned to work the social-media world to become informed about and disseminate information.

The more they learned, the more they understood that dirty energy, defined as carbon-based energy from coal, oil, and natural gas, was at the root of much of the world's problems. From wars over oil, to criteria pollutants that were killing millions, to money polluting politics, and ultimately the warming of our climate, dirty energy was killing people and the planet.

Cody grew especially agitated at how progress was slowed by Republicans in Congress who seemed hell-bent on stopping Obama from any success, even if it meant killing legislation that helped veterans or first responders who'd risked their lives on 9/11.

Their hypocrisy was stupendous, he felt. Very few of them had served in the armed forces or had children serving, but they were eager to start wars with countries flush with oil and then refuse to pay for the wars—or pay for the care of wounded soldiers or families of those killed in the wars.

Zak was getting used to hearing Cody screaming epithets upstairs in his third-floor room when he'd read something particularly bad, or when the two of them would watch The Daily Show or Colbert Report. The Daily Show in particular pioneered the art of catching people lying, but these people were teflon-coated personalities whose followers were brain-dead, so they didn't care.

With the Tesla Model S debut in June, and LEAF and Volt sales growing quickly, Cody had some reason for optimism. However, Wall Street crooks were hammering Tesla by shorting its stock so they could make money when the price dropped.

All manner of bad press was trotted out about Tesla, mostly things made up by merchant-of -doubt types paid to lie. Over a five-week period, three Tesla Model S cars were involved in fires when they hit road obstructions that punctured their battery packs. In one case, a driver speeding over 100 mph crashed into a wall. In all three cases, the drivers emerged with nothing more than minor injuries. The cars caught fire a few minutes later, and the fire department quickly extinguished the flames. The press ate this up! Major news outlets ran sensational stories on the fires and, predictably, the stock was hammered.

During these same five weeks, several thousand internal-combustion cars caught fire, resulting in severe injury and death, but media didn't cover any of that because internal combustion cars catch fire all the time. Musk managed to contain the damage by immediately re-engineering the shield protecting the battery pack to withstand the punctures that damaged his first two Teslas.

At this point, only a few people were knowledgeable about EVs, so Cody kept seeing the same names providing positive, truthful statements about the technology. Online forums, however, were rife with trolls vigorously denigrating Tesla and, by extension, all EVs. Cody and Mel spent a lot of time responding to these lies, as did Plug In America members who had been using EVs and solar energy for a decade or more. Cody and Zak had become experts and over time, they noticed that dozens and eventually hundreds of Tesla, LEAF, and Volt drivers were contributing to the forums. As other manufacturers began offering plug-ins, the growth of EV drivers accelerated and quickly surpassed 100,000 nationwide.

Still, for those hoping EVs would mitigate the worst effects of climate change, the technology was being adopted too slowly. You could buy EVs in California, but only a few states had copied their clean transportation laws, so most of the cars just weren't offered in much of the country.

Cody watched a video from Media Matters, a watchdog of conservative media, in which Fox News' Neil Cavuto repeatedly made laughable and bogus claims about EVs. Given Fox's popularity in red states, this sort of thing also seriously reduced EV sales. More merchants of doubt!

This kind of thing enraged Cody. He began to think dark thoughts about these people,fantasizing about choosing one per day who would die in their sleep at night. Never wake up. No violence involved—they'd just pass from natural causes. When his anger got really bad, he'd think of names for a list. Over the next few years, his list grew long.

After Obama's 2012 reelection, the right wing licked their considerable wounds and doubled down on stopping the president.

Red states enacted changes designed to create obstacles to voting, especially in minority districts. Disenfranchising these voters by enacting voter ID laws and gerrymandering would ensure minimal turnout. Their goal was to take back the Senate and increase conservatives' hold of the House. Between filibusters in the former and foot dragging in the latter, they could block progress at will.

The year had been the hottest on record, and Hurricane Sandy had destroyed a good portion of the northeast U.S. If environmentalists thought that would flip the climate deniers, they were sadly mistaken. While the storm did elevate the issue in the media, little was done to mitigate the underlying cause: carbon-based energy.

The more Zak and Cody read, the more they were convinced dirty energy was the lynchpin. It wasn't the whole problem, but it touched on many of the bigger problems. Climate change was the biggest, of course, but money in politics had to be fixed before anyone could address it. This being the first presidential election since Citizens United, money spent on the 2012 race easily reached a new record. Cody read that the oil industry had poured $147 million into Congressional races alone. As a consequence, no rational energy legislation would be passed.

He discovered a RAND study documenting non-war-related military expenditures for protecting access to the world's oil. The costs totaled some $80 billion per year. In addition, the Iraq war cost about three trillion, and the VA would spend another trillion caring for its 200,000 wounded soldiers.

Mountaintop removal, coal-ash disposal, and criteria pollutants from coal meant that using that source of dirty electricity harmed the environment and human health well beyond climate change alone. Similarly, natural gas was being acquired more and more from fracking.

Electricity generated by those two filthy sources was, by definition, dirty electricity.

Cody read that every year Americans were spending close to a trillion dollars for this dirty energy. He knew this money didn't take into account the external costs from military, health, or environmental sectors. Those costs were "paid" by the dead and wounded soldiers and their families, people who got sick and died from pollution, and the planet's poisoned flora and fauna. Economists called these costs "externalities."

Cody dreamt of how the economy would improve when renewable electricity powered all transportation. He and Zak were coming to an inescapable conclusion. The world would have to transition to this clean energy and run as much as possible off of that energy. The use of dirty energy worldwide had to be stopped.

Cody saw his country being run by bullies intent on maintaining the status quo. But these bullies weren't inflicting black eyes and broken teeth, they were bombing cities, killing people by the tens of thousands, letting children starve to death and displacing millions. These self-appointed leaders and megalomaniacal corporate titans were willing to do whatever it took to make as much money and gain as much power as possible.

These global bullies have no known enemy. Cody knew that evolution ensured an animal without a predator would grow unsustainably until resources ran out. Eventually something would happen to stop the growth. Food sources are over consumed, diseases decimate populations, and wars brutally eliminate thousands every month. Neither of the first two will affect these prosperous bullies. Only violence stands a chance of stopping them—either in a global war, or a targeted war.

Do societies evolve like species? Maybe.

A single human, relative to the 7.5 billion alive today, is analogous to a single cell relative to the whole human body. Just as a cell mutation can result in a better and more resilient human, a single human with persistent intention can help a better society evolve.

Some individuals are able to grasp simple physics and basic economics such that they can see major future trends. Cody could see that clean energy was already cheaper when all costs were considered. The entire world would eventually have to switch to this cleaner alternative. Cody also knew that the only reason our country, and much of the world, didn't readily see it the same way was because of money polluting the political process. This understanding compelled Cody to try to prevent the worst of the damage.

Mitigation. Triage. When these terms are applied to billions of people, the level of misery is impossible to imagine.

Cody felt that if he could somehow alter the minds of enough people with the right knowledge, an evolutionary change could take place. It would have to be something big, though. Really big.

Cody began to agree with Zak about the complicity of the masses in the problem. Fox News, and all the other EV haters in the media deserved their share of the blame for still-paltry EV sales. Millions of Americans who professed to be environmentalists also did nothing to reduce their contributions to climate change. They seemed unwilling to make any adjustments to their lifestyles.

This particularly bothered Cody. Zak, being older and more jaded, had come to terms with the idea that most people just weren't very good—that without something big happening to get their attention, the world would just keep getting hotter and crazier.

Cody felt that plenty of information existed online and in mainstream media about EVs and clean power, but the vast majority didn't care enough to even look for it. He met these people all the time in Seattle. In June of 2015, a big protest broke out over a Shell drilling rig being towed out of port on its way to explore for Arctic oil. Hundreds of kayakers surrounded the rig with the intent to stop it, but were only able to delay its departure a few hours. The protesters then paddled back to shore and loaded their kayaks onto gas-burning cars and SUVs. Some, no doubt, stopped at gas stations on the way home and gave money to the very industry they'd just protested.

If self-professed environmentalists like these were unwilling to take steps to reduce, or eliminate, their use of dirty energy, what chance did we have of encouraging middle America to do so?

There was some good news. California had passed laws back in the '60s and '70s to combat the atrocious air pollution from millions of heavily polluting cars and industry. These laws predated the advent of the EPA and gave California the right to pass laws stronger than federal EPA standards. Since the environmental lobby in California was strong, and elected leaders were mostly Democrats, they created the California Air Resources Board (CARB) to write and enact regulations to mitigate air pollution.

CARB created the so-called zero-emission vehicle mandate. Written in 1990, this law said that California's six highest selling car companies had to make one percent of cars sold in the state zero-emission cars. They had eight years to bring these cars to market.

GM's entry was their EV1. Its prototype had been built as a test project by a team GM hired to create a solar-powered car for a race across Australia. When CARB administrators saw this vehicle, they realized electric cars had become viable, so they mandated that the car industry build them in small numbers to start, and gradually increase the numbers over time.

The car makers hated being told what to manufacture, so they instructed their engineers to build an EV to comply with the rules, but simultaneously ordered their lobbyists to get rid of the law. Both teams succeeded. Engineers built several very good EVs, but after 5,000 of them had been leased or sold, the lobbyists overturned the law. When that happened, car makers began taking back the leased cars and crushing them. This is what the group Plug In America fought, and what the documentary "Who Killed the Electric Car?" was all about.

Because of that film, and especially because of Tesla's entry into the market, other car companies began thinking about EVs again. Nissan and GM led the way. The EV crowd hailed Nissan's LEAF and GM's Volt as the beginning of the end of internal combustion.

They were naive. The oil-company funded-merchants of doubt made sure the market for these cars would be tiny for many years to come.

It wasn't just the cars that bothered Cody. He saw merchants of doubt everywhere now. They'd honed their craft in the tobacco wars, improved their lying skills during the fights over the ozone hole and Reagan's "Star Wars" boondoggle. Now, the oil industry was paying them big to lie about climate change.

In October of 2015, the LA Times published a story about how Exxon had been studying climate change since the '60s. Internal memos proved their own scientists concluded that humans were causing the phenomenon primarily by burning fossil fuels. Exxon then hired merchants of doubt to lie about the reality of climate change and the seriousness of the problems it would cause.

In February of the same year, Wei-Hock Soon, a Smithsonian researcher who'd been publishing papers critical of established climate science, was outed as a merchant of doubt. He'd been on several oil and gas companies' payrolls, including Exxon, but had not disclosed this. His papers were lies intended to create doubt about climate change. This disclosure is what prompted the Times' reporters to look into Exxon's involvement in climate change to begin with.

Around the same time, Zak brought home *The Sixth Extinction*. Written by acclaimed New Yorker science writer Elizabeth Kolbert, the book detailed how human activity was causing thousands of species to go extinct every year. Most were in the oceans, where the acidity of the sea water was rising at an alarming rate due to the super absorption of CO2. For billions of years, the oceans had absorbed the gas, but since humans were burning so much oil, coal, and natural gas, the steep increase in CO2 caused the water's acidity to rapidly increase.

All species evolve over millennia. When conditions change rapidly, few can adapt quickly enough to survive.

Coral reefs were the canary in the coal mine. The book detailed how they were dying off—"bleaching"—in many parts of the ocean. Small life forms living among the coral were the base of the food chain, so as they died off, many larger fish began to run out of food. This, combined with mechanized trawler fishing around the world, meant the oceans were quickly becoming devoid of sufficient fish stocks to sustain a global-fishing industry.

The Sixth Extinction was an incredible eye opener for Cody. He could feel his blood pressure rising with every page. Kolbert's research was impeccable. Humans were creating an earth that wouldn't sustain the billions of humans alive today, much less billions more that demographers expected in the coming decades.

This book was a huge red flag. Why wasn't it being discussed on the nightly news? At the UN?

Even as the world was quickly becoming inhospitable to humans, most people just turned up their air conditioners rather than figure out how to turn down the source of the heat.

Chapter 13

Cody made monthly trips back to Eatonville to visit his parents. In the fall of 2015, he arrived with copies of *Merchants of Doubt* and *The Sixth Extinction* for Mark and Debra. Over dinner, he told them the gist of the two books and railed against the corporations and individuals who were responsible for the damage.

Debra glanced at Mark, indicating concern over her son's hardened stance. Their well-mannered little boy was now a ranting Iraq war veteran with PTSD and a growing hatred of some powerful people.

"Cody, honey, we know you're concerned about the world. We are, too. But you might want to take a breath here. There are solutions to every problem. You just have to look for them."

Mark chimed in. "Have you read *This Changes Everything*? It's by Naomi Klein, who wrote *The Shock Doctrine*. You read that one, remember? This new book is all about solutions to climate change. Reading it made me feel better. Some people are having success fighting these bastards. I loaned my copy to a friend at work, or I'd give it to you."

"What were Klein's solutions?" Cody's sounded hopeful for the first time that night.

"It's mostly about people fighting the oil and coal companies—the earth rapists." Decades of environmental activism had colored Mark's vocabulary. "There are some native tribes in Canada who were able to stop the tar sands from expanding, and some couple in Montana stopped a coal company from digging up their ranch. Oh, and some people in Greece stopped a gold-mining operation there."

"How did they stop these people? Are they no longer digging in the tar sands? I haven't heard this."

"No, they weren't able to stop them entirely—but they were able to slow them down and some places were saved a little. You should read the book."

Cody ordered the book right there at the kitchen table.

"Are you guys going to get another dog?" Cody asked.

"We're going to foster for that new rescue group," Debra said, happy the subject had changed to something more pleasant. "They have lots of dogs and cats needing homes, so we'll help with that for a while, and if one of them clicks, we'll adopt it."

"Yeah, we have a whole network of foster homes in Seattle," Cody added. "They really help a lot. Working there keeps me sane. I just want the pain in the world to stop." Cody dropped his head and stared at his lap. For some reason, he thought of Jazzie. Maybe it was talking about animals, since she'd been so close to Cooper, and she loved cats and dogs as much as he did. Thoughts of her flooded Cody's mind so often these days. He always ended up weeping.

Standing at their doorway watching Cody leave that night, Debra leaned into Mark and said, "I feel so bad about how things worked out for him. Jazzie would've made such a wonderful partner in life. I really miss her."

Mark held Debra tight and whispered, "Yeah, me too."

A few days later, Cody's copy of *This Changes Everything* arrived. He was in between VFX jobs, so he decided to buckle down and read quickly. It took him four days to finish. In the end, he wasn't satisfied. The solutions Klein offered were fine, but her examples were marginal, at best—mostly people organizing against corporations, with some having success in slowing, but not stopping, the raping. Extrapolating to the larger community, he just didn't see enough people being active to the extent needed.

More importantly, the book included virtually nothing about the two solutions he knew would be effective on the scale required: electrifying everything and cleaning the grid. Why would Klein omit these?

Sure, getting a majority of Americans to quit driving gas-burning cars would be tough, but it was already happening. That year, 350,000 Americans were driving on electricity. Solar was now cheaper than grid power in most of the U.S., and SolarCity was installing a new solar system, on average, every three minutes. Some people were definitely getting it.

"Hey, Zak, when you have the time, would you read this book? I wanna know what you think of Klein leaving out EVs and clean electricity."

"I already read it. I didn't mention it, because I wasn't impressed."

"Yeah, how could anyone think protests alone would work?"

"Why don't you ask her? They shot a documentary about the book, and it's screening in Seattle next week. She's going to do a Q&A. You could ask her then. I'll go with. It'll be fun." Zak grinned knowingly. He'd seen Cody ask pointed questions before and relished the idea of putting Klein on the spot.

The following Saturday, they drove Zak's LEAF to the Grand Illusion Cinema, a local art house. In spite of a heavy rain, the theater was packed.

The film was reasonably good. It showed protests from the book, along with compelling interviews with protestors. Again: Cody thought these solutions were marginal. So few would take on the herculean task of fighting the dirty energy industry when it meant taking time off work to spend hours or days camped out blockading a road in some forest. But other than a brief segment about solar installations on an Indian reservation, there was nothing about the electrification of transportation and solar energy.

After the credits rolled, the house lights came up and Klein and director Avi Lewis walked to the stage. The audience erupted in applause.

The couple spent about ten minutes discussing their reasons for making the documentary, and some of the troubles they had getting interviews when police or private-security teams were harassing them. They then opened the discussion for questions.

Cody waited to hear a couple of questions before raising his hand. Lots of people were eager to compliment Klein and Lewis for making the film but didn't ask hard questions about the content. Some asked how they could help stop Keystone, or some other oil-related calamity.

Cody was getting nervous that Klein wouldn't call on him before the Q&A ended. Finally, after saying she'd take one more question, she did.

"Ms. Klein, I appreciate you writing the book and making the documentary. I'm all about solutions to stop the planet's destruction. I wondered, however, why you didn't present in either the book or this film anything about electric cars or solar. It seems to me that, for the average American, switching to cars that run on clean electricity, and using clean electricity in our homes, would eliminate most of the pollution for which we're responsible. I've even read that it could be as much as a 90 percent reduction. Would you please address this?"

"Well, you might have missed it," Klein responded, "but I did talk about Tesla in the book."

Her dismissive tone bothered Cody.

"Yes, I remember the reference, but I expected more, given how effective it is to stop buying and burning gas. Eliminating dirty energy to power our cars and homes is by far the most we can do as individuals. Also, when we stop buying dirty energy, we stop funding these bastards. How do you expect to beat these guys when most of the people reading your book and watching your film drive gas-burning cars and use dirty electricity? How many people came here in an EV?"

Looking around, no one but Zak had raised a hand.

Cody's tone had become accusatory, and Klein wasn't interested in hearing any more. She said, "I'm sure you believe that, but you've had your say and they're kicking us out, so we've got to go."

Cody couldn't believe she was shining him on. He killed two men in a war for oil and she was dismissing him as some radical.

Cody, raising his voice, asked, "What kind of car do you drive?"

"I drive a hybrid!" Klein sniffed.

"So you're still polluting the environment and giving money to our enemies!" Cody shouted as people started to leave. "How do you expect to beat the enemy when you pay them money for their filthy oil?"

All eyes were on Cody.

Klein and Lewis ignored his question and walked briskly off the stage into the lobby. Cody received a smattering of groans and boos. Ignoring them, he looked at Zak. "What the hell? I'm getting booed for expecting a leading environmental author to walk the walk? Incredible!"

Zak just chuckled. "Troublemaker! You think these people really care? You saw how many raised their hands when you asked who drove an EV here? They burn gas, man, but they all think they're doing everything they can. We gotta engage and educate them. Maybe they don't know about EVs yet. C'mon, let's go to the lobby and make more trouble."

When the two of them entered the lobby, a crowd had gathered around Klein and Lewis. and people were getting copies of her book signed, taking selfies with her, and generally gushing.

Cody and Zak stood off to the side waiting to engage people in a fruitful discussion. A tall woman recognized Cody and approached him, stridently accusing him of badgering Klein. She was loud enough that the crowd took notice.

"Who do you think you are, talking to Naomi like that? What gives you the right to criticize her choice of a car?"

Cody responded calmly. "I read her book hoping to find solutions, but those I found were marginal, at best. I wanted to know why she hadn't included EVs and solar—things the average person could do to make a significant difference. She essentially dismissed the question, which is why I asked what she drove."

The military had taught Cody how to efficiently state facts.

"Not everyone can afford an expensive EV," the tall woman said. "My landlord won't let me charge an EV, so I can't own one."

"Well, maybe you could charge it at work, or lobby the state to pass a law like California has. Their law mandates that landlords let you install a charger."

"Yeah, like I have the time to lobby!" the woman said.

"Besides," Cody continued, "I think Naomi can afford any car she wants." He said this loud enough that the crowd, as well as the author herself, could hear. "I'd also ask if she's got solar on her roof. As a successful writer, she clearly has the funds to do both."

Klein was listening. Some around her were noticeably upset.

Cody was angry at everyone's quiescence when it came to taking any action that would potentially limit their profligate lifestyles. Heaven forbid they couldn't drive up into the mountains on a whim, that they'd have to actually plan for such a trip.

Zak stood back observing Cody in action. He liked what he saw.

Cody was about done. No one was engaging him on the merits of his points—just the tall woman who only offered excuses.

His voice cracking, he reiterated loudly, "How do you people expect to beat the oil companies if you pay them for their filthy energy? You're giving them money and demanding they fill your tank. And then you expect them to stop drilling in the arctic, or digging up the tar sands? If you aren't willing to take simple measures to eliminate dirty energy from your lives, then there's no chance we'll win. The oil companies own all of you!"

Cody now had everyone's command. "I killed two men in Iraq for fucking oil! This shit's changing the goddamned climate! Why the hell isn't this a top priority? Stop buying their freakin' oil, and things will change!"

He slowly scanned the room. He was more sad than angry. He turned and walked out.

Zak loved the spectacle of this young veteran schooling the do-little liberals. The snobby elitists who talked a good talk, but didn't give a rat's ass about their impact on the world. Zak stayed to see what people said after Cody left. He sidled up to the group around Klein and heard a few of her acolytes say how rude that guy was, etc.

Not hearing anyone addressing Cody's words, Zak said to the group, "He's right you know."

Everyone stopped talking and looked at the large bearded man. "You can't beat the oil companies while giving them your money." Zak stood with his arms outstretched and his shoulders hunched, his eyes wide: it was the universal look of, "What the fuck did you think would happen?"

As a child, Zak had harbored visions of grandeur, imagining himself a comedian of some talent. He'd stand on stage before a crowd and wow them with his wit.

This was not that. No one could argue with his point, and none did. But, their icy stares told him everything he needed to know. He left, finding Cody waiting outside. It was still pouring rain and quite cold. Pulling out his small pipe, he said, "C'mon. Let's spark this baby up and go get some food."

When they got in car, Cody waited for Zak to load up the pipe and hit it with flame, sucking in a long deep toke before passing it to Cody. Cody took his turn, holding in a lung-full before slowly expelling the smoke. Zak intuited Cody needed some space and stayed silent.

They listened to news from KUOW, their local NPR station, and waited for the delicious warmth of the heated seats to infuse their spines.

Zak turned the radio down and tried to gauge his friend's mood. After a couple minutes, they were both feeling the pot, along with radiant heat flowing into the car's cabin. The warmth felt good. Cody stuck both hands up to the heater vent rubbing them together.

"That didn't go so well, huh?"

Zak just laughed and laughed. "Well, that depends on what you expected to happen. Most progressives are almost as bad as the fucking Republicans. They can't be bothered to change their lifestyle even a little. You saw how they were fawning over Naomi. They just wanted selfies and her signature in their books."

"But why didn't they at least ask me questions?"

"They were scared of you, man. You had the balls to stand up and call the emperor naked."

As they sat in the car, they watched people leave the theater and get into their cars. All were gas-burners.

"There they go, spewing goddamn pollution out their fucking tailpipes," Zak observed.

"Let's go eat. I'm starved." Cody's anger was getting the better of him in spite of the pot. "I want Thai. Let's go to Kwanjai. I love that place."

Zak carefully pulled into the evening's light traffic. Stoned, he took surface streets to reduce the chances of making a mistake.

At Kwanjai, they got Thai iced tea and were waiting for their food when a woman from the adjacent table asked, "Aren't you the guys from the Naomi Klein movie just now?" She was probably in her 50s, as was her husband. Typical Seattle-ites, they were dressed in their REI finest, looking like the nice liberal Democrats they were.

Cody braced himself for an unpleasant conversation. "Um, yeah, that was me—or us. You were there?"

"Yes, and I wanted to tell you you were right to call those people out for not taking action. You made some very good points."

Her husband nodded vigorously. "We were thinking the same thing, but you put it into words that made sense. We don't have an EV yet, but we're getting a used one soon. A friend in LA says we can get a used LEAF for less than $10,000! We couldn't swing a new one, but for that price, we're gonna jump on it. Do you guys have an EV? I imagine you do, given what you said."

"Yep, got a black one out there in the parking lot," Zak said. "It's a great car. You'll love it."

Cody was curious. "Why do you think Naomi and all those people were upset I brought this subject up?"

"I think most people are just comfortable living their lives," the woman replied, "and they're used to the way cars have always been. They're scared to try something new."

Her husband added, "Most in that audience are likely to switch to EVs eventually, just as we are, but there're reasons, some good, some not so good, for their reluctance to pull the trigger."

Remembering Cody's comment about killing two men, the man instantly regretted his word choice, but Cody didn't outwardly respond.

"Have you guys read *The Sixth Extinction*?

"No," the woman said.

"I highly recommend it. It's by Elizabeth Kolbert, the science writer for the New Yorker. She's awesome! But the book is pretty depressing. I read it before reading Klein's book. It's about how people are creating the sixth extinction. There've been five great extinctions since life evolved. The last one was when meteors killed the dinosaurs 65 million years ago. The only mammals that survived were some small rodents. We, of course, evolved from them."

Cody's attitude was improving fast. They'd found kindred souls. Their food arrived at about the same time, so they pushed their tables together and shared their dishes. By the time they left, all four were friends. Zak promised to contact them about going solar, and help them install a charger for their EV. When Cody found out they were fosters for a rescue group, he practically fell in love with them.

As they prepared to leave, the man reached into his shirt pocket and pulled out a folded piece of paper. "Here, Cody, you should have this. I printed out a quote from Naomi when she spoke this summer at the Vatican. They invited her there to a talk in preparation of the COP21 in Paris. This is so pertinent to what you said in the theater."

The man unfolded the paper and read: "In a world where profit is consistently put before both people and the planet, climate economics has everything to do with ethics and morality. Because if we agree that endangering life on earth is a moral crisis, then it is incumbent on us to act like it."

He continued, "But she drives a gas burner!" He threw up his hands and shrugged much like Zak had when he departed the theater.

"Vindicated!" hollered Zak as they all shook hands.

Cody wasn't as morose as he had been, but he was still in a funk. He didn't open up to Zak about it.

In his room that night, he second guessed his decision to drink that Thai tea so late in the evening. He was restless and jittery. He kept replaying his argument with Klein's fans in the lobby, wondering if he could've been more effective by maybe using different words. His anger grew at the self-identifying environmentalists for not understanding how they contributed to the problem.

The next few days were a whirlwind of violence. Mass shootings had been in the news all year with the Charlie Hebdo attacks in Paris, the white supremacist who killed nine African Americans in a South Carolina church, and then, in quick succession, the Paris massacre, the murder in the Colorado Planned Parenthood office, and the San Bernardino mass killing. All were terrorist related, either Christian or Muslim, and the pro-gun versus anti-gun lobbies were at each other's throats. The one constant was the corporate message: "Stay scared all the time."

The corporate-controlled media offered little rational discussion about climate change. The Paris COP21 conference was filled with impassioned pleas for reductions in CO2 and methane, but the media was more interested in explosions and gunshots that killed dozens rather than pollution and climate change that killed millions.

He was scanning stories about COP21 when an LA Times article popped up: "Brown Readies for Close-up on Global Climate."

California Governor Jerry Brown was considered pretty hardcore on the subject. He was a fourth-term governor who'd been derisively labeled "Governor Moonbeam" in the '70s and '80s, during his first two terms, for his liberal views on the environment and certain social issues. He was one of the youngest governors in California history then. And when he ran again in 2010, he became the oldest, as well as the longest-serving governor in the state's history. He was very popular with enviros for his positions on climate change and his efforts to curtail California's use of dirty energy.

Due to Congress' intransigence on environmental issues, Brown was doing everything he could as the governor of the wealthiest state—the state with the most cars and the technology center of the world—to push his clean energy agenda. He was a good guy, a rarity in the political world.

The Times article mentioned his attempts to get a solar array installed on his ranch in northern California, but the last paragraph was what really got Cody's attention. It disclosed that Brown's car was a Crown Victoria—a car primarily known for its use as a taxi and sometimes as a police car. It was grossly inefficient and burned gasoline! When asked why he drove this car, he told the reporter, "Part of me wants to drive it until it drops."

"Wow," thought Cody, "it's Naomi Klein all over again! Even Governor Moonbeam doesn't get it."

What would get these people's attention? What would make them understand you can't win a fight against powerful enemies while simultaneously funding their efforts?

Brown had lost a big fight with the oil companies just months earlier over legislation that would've reduced California's oil consumption by half. Big Oil fought this hard—using merchant of doubt tactics—and their money won the day as the 50-percent oil reduction provision was deleted, although the rest of the bill passed with some decent environmental protections.

Brown was angry at the oil industry for their lies and misinformation campaigns, but again, he was paying for their filthy product. Was he a hypocrite, or just ignorant of why driving an old gas burner "until it drops" was a bad idea?

Cody wanted to believe the latter, but being ignorant was getting harder these days with Google and all.

Since environmental leaders like Brown and Klein didn't get it, no wonder the public was clueless. But there wasn't time to hold their hands one by one and point out the fallacy of their beliefs. Something needed to be done to get their attention—to get everyone's attention. Something big.

Cody tried writing a letter to the LA Times, hoping to convince Brown to ditch the Crown Vic in favor of an EV. There was no reason he shouldn't get one, and preferably a Tesla since it was a California company.

"Please Gov. Brown, we love your green credibility, but you have to ditch the Crown Victoria to stay true to your own words: 'Waste is never good.' Internal combustion engines are incredibly inefficient. Only about a quarter of gasoline's energy moves the car; the rest is wasted. When asked about the car, you said, 'Part of me wants to drive it until it drops.' Don't listen to that part of you! Listen to the part that says waste is never good."

Cody clicked send. At least he'd done something.

The letter wasn't published, and the news out of Paris reflected growing global concern over climate change. However, the American congressional response, backed by the energy industry's merchants of doubt, were busy arguing against Obama's and Brown's proposals for reducing pollution.

This news, combined with the crazy pro-gun/anti-gun fight and the insane spectacle of candidate Trump filling the media, consumed Cody. He took solace in working at the shelter, bringing joy to abandoned animals. The lives they saved, and the animals' responses to being cared for, helped Cody cope, but it didn't mitigate his growing sense of doom.

Cody's Google alerts, meanwhile, were flowing with post after post about the Paris COP21 conference. One essay stopped Cody cold. It was by Michael Brune, the executive director of the Sierra Club, and Bill McKibben, the founder of 350.org. They reported about a push by Senate Republicans, as well as some Democrats, to end the oil export ban. This would increase oil production and pollution, and even more money would fatten the industry's coffers while weakening the national economy. It would also tell the world the U.S. was not serious about dealing with the most dangerous experiment humans had ever devised, the warming of the planet.

Cody was certain the bad guys would succeed. Sitting at his desk, he decided he was going to act. He needed to do something that would both stop the bastards from perpetrating climate change and send a signal to those who would follow their lead.

Murder. Assassination. It sickened Cody, but he couldn't think of anything that would get the perpetrators' and the public's attention like a good old-fashioned political assassination.

It was so clear. The media covered mass murders. Front-page stories, whole sections of the newspaper were devoted to people killing people. These shooters were generally ideologically driven, mostly religion-based. Some were psychopaths, or deranged. Their targets were mostly innocent civilians.

"Why don't these killers shoot the real bad guys?" Cody thought. "The fuckers perpetrating climate change deserve to die. Shit, they could at least go shoot up a gun store or an NRA convention."

It was mid-December 2015, a cold and rainy morning in Seattle. Zak was in court, so Cody had the place to himself. He was conflicted. Too much aggression, fueled by caffeine, flowed through his body. Dangerous thoughts of taking more lives, this time lives of importance, were coursing through his mind. Cody opened the drawer and pulled out his pipe. Taking a small bud from his stash, he dropped in into the bowl and hit it with his Bic. He drew in a deep lung full of the sweet-smelling smoke and let it settle into his bloodstream. His kitty, Dilly, startled him when she jumped on his lap. Stroking her fur helped calm him as the THC mellowed his jittery body.

However, he kept thinking about killing.

Chapter 14

Who would be worthy of death? Would it really make a difference? How many of them needed to be killed to do any good? How could he do this alone?

He couldn't share his thoughts with anyone, and certainly not the VA doc who was treating his PTSD. No, whatever he did would have to be done without anyone knowing anything. Except maybe Dilly. She heard all of his thoughts. Talking to her helped.

Cody felt he should make a list of people deserving death for the parts they'd played in perpetrating climate change. He opened a new email and addressed it to himself. In the subject line, he typed, "People DD." Then he deleted "People." He was thinking he'd just print this out later and delete it.

Who would be first on the list? There were many, many choices.

The Koch brothers for sure, he thought. He wrote "Koch brothers."

"Hmmm...James fucking Inhofe! That motherfucker has to go!"

Fox News had a whole staff carrying water for the dirty energy industry. "God, who do I start with there? Pretty much all of them," he thought. He wrote "Fox News on-air people."

"Rush Limbaugh!" he shouted to himself. "Got to silence that gas bag!"

Cody pulled out his copies of *Merchants of Doubt*, *The Sixth Extinction*, and *This Changes Everything*. Pouring over the books, he found a trove of people who deserved to die. He added all their names to his list.

As the list grew to two pages, then three, he realized the task's enormity. How could he kill all these people? He couldn't do it alone. He'd have to prioritize and just pick the most deserving—and those he could easily kill. He knew after the first one or two, it would get much harder given that security would ramp up.

He wasn't a particularly great marksman, but he wasn't bad, either. Unless he could come up with a better method, he'd use the Winchester.

Scanning the web for stories on his targets, one caught his attention: "Drone Shot Down at Oklahoma Senator's Controversial Fundraiser." Reading on, Cody learned that Senator Inhofe was holding a fundraiser at a ranch in southern Oklahoma, at which tame, banded pigeons were thrown into the air so they could be shot by people who'd paid money to his campaign. Cody thought the man was not only a huge climate-change denier, but a fucker who makes money killing animals for sport. The fundraiser was just over a week away. Inhofe would be target number one.

Cody found the ranch on Google Maps. It was about 150 miles southwest of Oklahoma City on Lake Altus in sparsely populated Kiowa County. Scanning the satellite image, he studied the features of the landscape for high ground and cover as he'd been taught in the Army. He found a good location within easy rifle shot of the site's main parking lot. His old hunting rifle, the same gun he used to kill the dog-fighting piece of garbage, would work fine for this job.

He sat back, staring at his favorite picture of Jazzie. She was dressed in her skimpy green running singlet and shorts. She was in full stride at the finish of a cross country race and the photographer had caught her in perfect form. He thought of the two of them on long runs through the woods, his furtive glances at her bobbing breasts, his insatiable lust for her...

Cody felt overwhelmingly sad. He longed for his youth—before he knew of climate change, before the war and the horrors he'd witnessed there. Before he knew how brutal some could be toward others, not to mention how mean people could be to the poor animals. He thought of the planet with its evolving biosphere and devolving society.

Cody considered his actions evolutionary. It was distasteful assassinating corrupt political, business, and media people, however the circumstances demanded it if the larger population, and its environmental surroundings, were to survive.

****

Cody began planning his trip. After Inhofe, he'd go after Rush Limbaugh, who he found to be particularly noxious. Limbaugh lived in Palm Beach, Florida, so this was going to be a long trip. He'd need to have an alibi for being gone so long, and the news he was going to make would break before his return, so he needed to have an airtight story.

For the first time in a long time, Cody felt full of purpose.

The next day broke clear and cold. Filled with enthusiasm for the task at hand, Cody bounded down the stairs to find Zak making coffee. "Hey, old man, what's your day like? Going to sue the shit outta some assholes?"

"Ha! I wish. Just filing papers down at the courthouse and taking care of some mundane legal stuff. I've got another gas station accused of dumping. My success with the last one got people watching for others and the calls are coming in. This is going to be a good year!"

"Cool, man. Say, I might be going to LA for a few weeks on a job with DD. It's a good gig, some secret film that needs a lot of cleanup work. I should know by this afternoon. If I go, you OK taking care of Dilly?"

"Sure, how long you think you'll be?"

"They tell me it could be two to three weeks. I'll try to find out and let you know. Might be a play-it-by-ear thing."

"Got it," Zak said, indicating the coffee. "I made it extra strong this morning, so you might want to add some extra half and half. I'll be home around 6, so if you know any details, let me know then."

After Zak left, Cody went online to find a rental van. He began making a list of everything he thought he'd need: good bedding, his bike, the rifle and ammo, cold-weather clothes, food, computer and phone, and lots of cash. He didn't want to use his debit card for anything other than the van and that was only because the rental company required it.

Planning took his mind off what he was actually going to do. By the end of the day, he'd packed everything into the van and parked it in the driveway. He called Heather and told her he was off for a few weeks on a job, and then he called home.

"Hey, mom, how's it going?"

"Hi, Mr. Never-Comes-Over-Anymore. Are you coming down? We miss you!" Debra's voice was happier than usual. "We have a surprise. We got a puppy! You have to see her. She's cra-zy cute! We haven't even named her yet. Come help us give her a good one."

"Awww. That's great, mom, but I'm going to LA for a few weeks. Gonna work on some big secret studio picture. I have to leave early in the morning. Send me pics, or video. Yeah, send some video! What kind of doggy is she? Anything like Cooper?"

"I miss Cooper so much," Debra responded. "She looks like a mix of lab, shepherd, definitely some pit, and who knows what else. She's already housebroken, and whoever had her for the first couple of months took good care of her. She's got no fear issues, loves everyone—even the cat. She loves the cat!"

"Fantastic! How's dad? You guys all good?" Cody tried to sound as normal as possible, but he was getting fidgety and wanted to end the call as his thoughts returned to what he was going to do.

"Your father's great. He's thinking of running the LA Marathon this year, so training is pretty heavy. He's in a new age-group now that he's 60 and wants to get a good time while he's still healthy. You know your dad, always looking at the clock on those runs. We'll get an Airbnb in Santa Monica where it ends. Are you going to be in Santa Monica? Can you look for a place that's close to the finish line?"

Cody was already thinking of other things by now and managed to mumble, "Um, sure," before begging off the call.

Chapter 15

Zak was due home soon, so Cody's military training compelled him to run a last-minute check. All seemed to be in place. He grabbed his bong and filled it in anticipation of Zak's arrival. Right on schedule, he heard the front door open.

Zak walked in with a young, attractive woman in tow. He hollered upstairs for Cody. "Yo, Cody! Come down here. I got someone you should meet."

Zak rarely brought anyone home, but this woman was the new client suing her neighborhood Exxon station for dumping waste oil.

She'd secretly taken pictures on two occasions and, also using her iPhone, conducted a surreptitious interview, asking the owner why he was polluting the water with the oil. The owner dismissed her with a sexist comment about her looks. When Zak saw the evidence, and how the guy acted toward her, he clapped his hands with glee, knowing he'd win a big judgment against the asshole. He brought the client home to meet Cody, thinking the two might get along. Cody hadn't had a girlfriend since Jazzie, and this woman seemed like a decent fit for him, and vice versa.

Cody's first impression was, Wow! She was similar to Jazzie in size, and her top-of-the-line Nikes confirmed her potential as a runner. She had jet black hair, but her face struck him most. She was beautiful! Even prettier than Jazzie. He felt a tinge of guilt for even thinking such a thing.

As he walked up to her, hand extended, he stared at her clear blue eyes and incredibly sweet smile revealing perfect teeth.

"Hi, I'm Cody."

"Hey, Cody, Victoria. Very pleased to meet you. Zak says some nice things about you." Her eyes sparkled. She didn't want to turn away, and neither did Cody. The handshake lasted a beat longer than it should have, but nobody in the room was going to file a complaint.

"Victoria's my new client. Wait'll you hear what she did!" And with that, Zak ushered them into the living room, talking a mile a minute about how Victoria spied on the gas station after smelling a strong petroleum odor coming from the street grate in front of her house. When he got to the part about her recording the conversation, he was practically shouting.

"Victoria, show him the video! Wait'll you see what this guy said to her."

Victoria pulled her phone out. It was the latest iPhone 6 with a turquoise Hello Kitty cover, but this Hello Kitty was sporting Ninja clothes and a big sword. Cody smiled. This Victoria was one tough cookie!

As she played the video, Cody moved in close, so that their arms were touching. He could feel her warmth through the thin fabric.

Zak had seen the video, so he excused himself and bounded up the stairs to get the bong. Finding it pre-loaded, he was back downstairs in time to hear Cody exclaim, "Holy shit! He said that to you?"

Victoria said, "Yeah! After he made the crack about my boobs, he told me to 'get the fuck outta his sight!' " She pushed play again to show Cody. The man's language was coarse and his face was flushed red.

Zak offered up the bong to Victoria asking, "You imbibe?"

"Well, now that it's legal, sure," she said, simultaneously rolling her eyes and reaching for the pot. Legality had nothing to do with it.

After the bong made its way around to Zak, he took his turn and excused himself to go make dinner. "Everyone OK with pasta? I hope so, cuz that's what I'm making." Zak was in a great mood. He had a new client who was gorgeous and smart and maybe a good fit for his roomie.

Cody said, "You must be a runner with those shoes and that body." He was hoping mentioning her body wouldn't put her off. He didn't need to worry.

"Yeah, I ran track in high school, tried out for the Husky team, but didn't quite make the cut. I still train, though."

She's clearly a runner, thought Cody admiringly. Runners train, joggers jog. "What was your event? I ran middle distance at Eatonville High."

"I was decent at the 1,500, but didn't have the speed. I ended up running 5Ks and 10Ks mostly. Endurance is my strong suit."

"What's your 10K PR?" Cody figured she must be decent to have tried out for the University of Washington Huskies.

"I can still get under 40 easy enough, but my PR is 38:05. I'd love to get under 38 some day. I need to do more hills and speed work, though. It's tough running alone. I used to run with some friends, but they moved away, and I just haven't found another group that runs my pace."

"Those are pretty good times. I'll run with you, if you like. I haven't been training much lately, but this'll give me a reason to get back into it. Where do you live?"

He liked where this was heading.

Dinner was fantastic. Zak used a great pesto from Eugene that was the rage in the Pacific Northwest. Just dipping bread into the sauce was heavenly. Victoria couldn't stop raving about the flavor of everything. Zak and Cody knew the pot had a lot to do with it, but both enjoyed the beautiful woman's presence and her enthusiasm.

As the pot began to wear off, Cody's mind turned to less happy thoughts. He was mere hours from leaving on a trip that would change his life—and the lives of many—forever. But this amazing, gorgeous woman had just walked into his life. She was giving him second thoughts. He believed he was being selfless by working to rid the world of evil, knowing his life would be on the line the instant he pulled the trigger. Was he willing to throw his life away on this quest, especially since he now had a chance to have a relationship with this woman? A chance for a normal life?

"So when are we going to go running? Yo, Cody, anybody home?" Victoria waved her hand in front of Cody's face to snap him out of his trance.

Cody came to, startled and a little embarrassed. "Sorry, I was thinking about my trip tomorrow. What'd you say?"

"I just asked when we could get together for a run, but it sounds like you're leaving tomorrow?"

"Yeah, I've got some VFX work on a film in LA. Probably be there a few weeks."

"VFX?"

"Visual effects. It's like special effects—explosions and various effects that are shot on camera, only our stuff is all done with computers. We composite, or marry, our images with the live stuff. I mostly do mundane clean-up work like removing power lines, replacing skies, adding buildings or erasing buildings, things like that. It pays well and allows me time to volunteer at the animal shelter."

"I'm learning more about you all the time! Tell me about your animal work. I've been fostering kitties and doggies for a few years now and really love it. I finally adopted a couple kittens a few months ago, so I might not be fostering anymore. Depends on how they get along with my guys."

Whoa. Another reason to like Victoria, he thought. "What do you do for work?" Cody asked. "Are you in the legal field?"

"Ha! Not my cup of tea, but I'm glad that people like Zak are there when I need them. I run a small business." She said it with a dollop of pride.

"What's your small business?"

"Take It Off!"

"Say what? Take off what?"

"It's the name of the company, a lingerie company. We sell sexy panties and such." She said this with a great big smile. She knew how this news affected men. They all thought about what she was wearing underneath. She did not discourage their fantasies. It was part of the allure.

Zak exhaled a low whistle, excused himself, and cleaned the table. They could hear him washing dishes in the kitchen.

Cody was having such a good time. He couldn't remember when he'd felt so happy.

And then, he remembered. He was with Jazzie. Over 12 years had passed since she'd been murdered. He'd never get over that feeling of hearing those words from his mother, the unbelievable horror as the god-awful news sunk in. His world came crashing down like nothing he'd ever felt.

Cody hadn't had sex in years. He'd had a few girlfriends after he got out of the service, but none had lasted past the first few dates. His PTSD didn't help. He could get edgy and quite opinionated when conversations turned to politics, a trait he picked up at home and that blossomed in the Army. But after the war, after killing people, he'd lost some of the humanity he'd had as a child. Women sensed this. And they all gave up on him before he could give up on them. He was nice looking, he was fit, but he was broken.

Victoria was the first woman who made him excited to be a partner again. He found himself wanting to drink her in. He wondered what she felt like, what she looked like in various states of undress. He was getting aroused.

It wasn't late, only about 9 pm, but they'd been talking nonstop for over an hour. Zak disappeared after cleaning up, and they suddenly realized he'd been gone all that time. The conversation lulled, and they found themselves staring at each other. Both were thinking the same thing. The pause extended. Cody's brow furrowed ever so slightly.

Victoria noticed, taking the gesture for the question it was. Before he even knew he was asking, she said, "Yes!"

"Yes?" Cody said.

"Yes, I want to...I want to fuck you." Her broad smile made the words sound even sexier than her use of the crude "fuck." "I want to take off all of your clothes...." Cody's finger shushed her lips, and his own big grin told her all she needed to know. He led her upstairs to his room, suddenly feeling conflicted. He was 12 hours away from launching his deadly mission. But he was delirious.

In the middle of the night, as the couple satisfied their mutual lust, a high pressure system moved across the Pacific Northwest. And as they slept the sleep of exhausted lovers, the clouds moved to the east, leaving a clear night sky with stars sparkling like diamonds.

Cody's fantasies about Victoria had come true beyond expectation. She clearly liked sex and was an athletic partner in bed. Her petite, hard body was incredibly sexy.

Sunlight poked through the thick, opaque curtains and cut brightly across the bed. They lay motionless, entwined, as the narrow beam moved ever so slowly across their naked bodies. Cody awoke first. The urge to pee usually got him up. This morning was no different, although it was as different a morning as he'd experienced since coming home from the war.

Before he left the bed, he quietly stared at this beautiful sleeping woman, taking in the parts of her body not covered by the bed spread. Her body was as close to Jazzie's as any could be. He couldn't believe his good fortune at having met her. Reluctantly, he swung his legs over the edge of the bed and got up slowly so as not to disturb her.

When he came back, she was awake, but still under the covers. "Mmmmm...you were so good to me last night! How're you feeling this morning?"

Cody stopped at the foot of the bed and smiled. Standing there naked, he was now the object of Victoria's stares. He liked it. The covers exposed her breasts, small with erect nipples. He was getting aroused again. It felt as good in his head as in his stiffening penis. Victoria couldn't help but notice. She got up, and gave the now hard organ a gentle tug. She kissed him on the lips and whispered, "Get back under the covers. I'll be right back." She pushed him onto the bed and left for her own pee break.

Morning-after sex is often better than the night before, and this was no exception. Zak was making coffee and the noise from these two made him grin. He'd been right about Victoria, and he felt happy for his friend.

Zak was on his second cup when the two lovers bounded down the stairs.

"Coffee!" they both shouted, beaming, happy.

"Glad to see you two so giddy. I guess the conversation went well after I left." Zak wasn't into sex so much, but he enjoyed the thought of these two doing it in his house. As an onanist, he was content to listen to others going at it and take care of himself.

"I made a full pot, help yourself."

"Thank you for inviting me over," Victoria smiled at Zak. "Cody is amazing!" She looked at Cody, who planted a loving peck on her cheek. "I just wish he wasn't leaving."

Cody smiled back, just a smidge weaker than he wished. So much was going on in his head! The endorphin rush of hot sex, his incredible infatuation with this gorgeous woman who seemed to personify everything he wanted in a mate.

But he was leaving within the hour to change the world.

He thought about backing out—forget everything and just get on with life. But he knew that was impossible. He thought of all the books, articles, and talks he'd attended, the films he'd seen. All the scientific evidence piled up and pointed to certain calamity. He'd come to this conclusion months before for valid reasons. There was no turning back.

Cody finally managed to respond to Victoria. "I'll be back soon enough. We can talk, text, and email. By the time I return, we'll be old friends...with incredible benefits!" She grabbed his face with both hands and kissed him hard on the lips. The kiss lingered.

Zak laughed. "I had fun hearing you guys go at it, but I don't know if I'm ready to watch."

"Don't worry, I gotta go," Victoria said. "I just wanted one more kiss to hold me over." She sighed as she pulled away from Cody, never taking her eyes off his.

At the front door, with Victoria's Uber driver waiting at the curb, they double checked email and phone numbers before embracing once more with a long a deep kiss.

Zak was leaving as Cody walked back in. They hugged, and Zak told him, "Keep me posted, OK?"

Cody called after him, "Zak, thanks again for introducing me to Victoria. She's awesome! Seriously, I'm on cloud nine."

Chuckling, Zak replied, "I got my jollies, too." Then he burst out laughing, turned, and walked away.

Chapter 16

Cody instantly changed moods. It was time to act. He had to shower, pack his daily needs, and double check everything in the van. He didn't lose the grin, however. He'd keep that for most of the long drive.

Leaning against his loaded vehicle, he stared up at his bedroom window. He recalled seeing Victoria's body as she removed various articles of clothing, including some very nice lingerie, until her petite hard body was naked in his arms. His eyes closed as the memory engulfed him.

A lumbering, growling garbage truck turned the corner, it's mechanical arm reaching out to grab cans placed along the curb. The noise shook him from his nice little dream, and he got into the driver's seat thinking he couldn't wait until they made those things electric.

His first day would be easy. He planned on driving down I-5 to Eugene. Over the years, he'd made the trip many times for track meets with family. It was a straight shot down through Portland and then another hundred or so miles to Pre's town.

Throughout the entire drive, he thought of Victoria. Why couldn't the world be perfect so he could fall in love and live a normal life? Why did the fucking bullies get in the way all the time and screw everything up?

It was well after dark when he pulled into Alton Baker Park. Alton Baker was a large, sprawling park on the north side of the Willamette River, which flows east to west through Eugene. The park was a venue for numerous races.

Cody parked in a far corner of the empty lot, hoping to make it through the night without being hassled. He needed a break from sitting all day, so he changed into shorts and a sweatshirt, threw on a light jacket to keep out the chill air, and set out for an easy run.

The moon was waxing full on this crisp, damp night. It was always damp in the winter in Eugene, even when skies were clear. The park was mostly empty, just a few homeless souls who couldn't get out of town before winter and had to make do in the cold and wet. When spring came, with its warmer, lengthening days, the city would become a homeless haven.

Cody's stride was effortless along the soft wood-chip trail. He recognized the large open field where cross country races started and finished, and remembered watching his sister in her senior season, the top high school runner in Washington State, pushing to catch four runners who had the misfortune of being in her sights. She had unleashed her famous kick, reeling them in one by one for the win. He remembered how, on the ride home, the family could barely talk because they were hoarse from screaming so hard.

He'd raced there twice in his junior and senior years. Both times, Jazzie rode down with his family to watch. She'd competed her senior year, just a couple months before she was killed.

Once he began thinking of Jazzie, he found it hard to stop. He ran harder, hoping the pain of the effort would supplant the pain of his memories.

By the time he got back to the van, he was exhausted. He'd pushed pretty hard for the shape he was in. Running in the dark, on unfamiliar trails and at near race pace, was asking for a turned ankle, but he'd been lucky. Breathing hard, with sweat soaking his shirt, he walked up to the van just as a shadowy figure appeared from the other side. The parking lot's lone light backlit Cody, giving him a good view of the man. Dressed in filthy rags, he was clearly one of the homeless.

"Who are you?" Cody demanded, his fight-or-flight receptors fully engaged.

"Nobody, man, just looking for food." The man was not intimidating. If anything, he'd been beaten down by life. Cody allowed his body to stand down. "You got anything you can spare, man?"

"What's your name, buddy?" Cody was beginning to feel sorry for the guy. It couldn't be too pleasant living in a cold, wet park for the winter.

"I'm Ray, Raymond Wilson from Alabama."

Cody detected a faint southern accent. "Cody, from Seattle." He reached out to shake Ray's hand. "I got some sandwich stuff. Hang on, let me get it out." Cody went to open the side door to retrieve his ice chest, hefting it out of the van. He hadn't eaten much since leaving that morning, and now he found himself hungry as hell.

Ray helped him lug the ice chest to the nearest picnic table, where they both sat down. Cody pulled out a small flashlight and set it up so they could see what they were preparing. He figured peanut butter and banana would give them both nutrition and energy. He grabbed a couple of Gatorades from the chest and handed one to Ray.

"I hope you like bananas and peanut butter." Cody handed Ray a sandwich.

"Oh, man, you kiddin'? This is great stuff! God, I haven't eaten in two full days. Winter sucks here, man. I gotta get back to Alabama where it's fuckin' warm, man."

Cody figured he was a little older than Ray, but not much. "Why'd you come here in the winter, Ray? Didn't you know it was cold?"

"I came for the country fair back in July. That was cool as shit, man. You ever been?"

"No, but I've heard about it. It's famous up in Seattle as the last great hippy fair in the country."

"You got that right!" Ray responded. "That place was like magic. I wanted it to go on forever. I want to live in that world, man."

"What kind of world is that, Ray?"

"Where everyone's nice. Everyone's beautiful, man. Even the ugly people are beautiful. Know what I mean?"

"I think so, yeah. Why do you think they're so nice there?"

"The drugs, man!" Ray snorted a laugh. "There's lots of good drugs at the country fair! Lots of drugs! When I got out of the Army, life got weird. People where I lived were hungry for more war. Everyone I met wanted us to keep fighting in Iraq and Afghanistan. I fought in both those places and can tell you this: it was no picnic. The shit I saw..."

"I fought in Iraq, too. Where were you?"

"Falluja. We got hammered in a big fight, but we kicked their asses. God, I don't even want to think about that shit! On my second tour, I was sent to Abu Ghraib in '05. It was a shitty time, especially when they attacked us in April. That was worse than Falluja if you can imagine, man."

"I can. I saw some shit, too. Can't ever get it out of my head."

"PTSD?"

"Yeah, most def. Not that the VA is helping."

"You use drugs?"

"I like marijuana. It helps."

"Yeah, me, too."

"Wait here."

Cody went to the van and returned with a pipe and a small stash.

"Alright! You're a helluva guy, man!" Ray exclaimed as Cody passed him the loaded pipe and a lighter.

They talked for over an hour about their respective war experiences, about why they were sent there to fight, and even a little bit about women. Ray didn't seem to have anyone in his life he could call a close friend, and he'd become estranged from his family after his PTSD manifested in behavior they couldn't handle.

Cody had not packed too much extra in the way of clothes, but he did have a second jacket that would fit Ray pretty well. He was walking back to the van to retrieve it when headlights from a car turning into the lot silently raked across the area. Ray and Cody watched as the police car slowly rolled up to them.

The officer in the car said, "The park is closed after dark. You folks need to move on out."

Cody hadn't realized the park had closed, but it instantly made sense: this was why the place had been empty when he arrived.

"Sorry, officer, I'm passing through and wanted to find a place to sleep. My budget doesn't allow for motels. Is there a legal place I can park the van overnight? I'll be leaving in the morning."

"Well, most all our streets are legal parking, so you shouldn't have trouble finding someplace. It's going to get cold tonight though. Sure you can't afford a motel?" Eyeing Ray, the cop said, "You two together?"

Ray was about to speak, but Cody beat him to it. "Yeah, we're traveling to LA together. Looking for work."

In his job, the officer ran into some pretty unfortunate people, but he'd learned to differentiate between those who were psychotic, those in temporary difficulty, and those just beat into the ground by an uncaring, dysfunctional society. Cody's firm diction and cordial manner indicated he was only temporarily down and out, and therefore probably OK.

"OK, guys. Stay safe and try to keep warm."

Ray was already walking to the van as the officer drove away. "Appreciate the quick thinking there, Cody! Can you drop me off someplace safe?"

"I know a good place. Throw your stuff in the back and hop in. I used to run track here in high school. I think I can find it..."

Cody had never driven in Eugene, since his parents always drove when they were here for track meets, but he sort of knew how to get back to Hayward Field at the U of O. It was the best track stadium in the U.S. He'd run there twice, and his sister had run there three times in high school, and many more times running for her college team, the Oregon Ducks.

He used his iPhone to get to the university, and from there he drove up the hill to Pre's Rock. On the way, he told Ray the legend of Pre.

"This place we're going is where Pre died in his MG after leaving a party the night of his last big meet in May of '75. He was the best American runner, certainly of his era, and arguably of all time. The man had heart! He fought the assholes who ran the AAU back then, and if he hadn't died, he'd be a fucking senator or governor now. He was a political animal to the core. Didn't take shit, know what I mean?"

"Sounds like a cool dude. They should make a movie about the guy."

Cody laughed. "They did. Two of them, plus a documentary. When you get someplace where you can watch some videos, look for anything on Steve Prefontaine. You won't be disappointed."

They drove past Hayward Field and turned left, heading uphill to Hendrick's Park, which was famous for its rhododendrons blooming in spring. A couple blocks later, near the top of the hill, a neighborhood of nice homes was tucked away among a forest of towering Douglas fir. Cody pulled over near a rock outcropping.

"This is the rock Pre hit in his car. The story is, he was a little drunk when he left the party, and when he came around that curve, there was a car coming toward him. He swerved into the rock, his MG overturned, and he was pinned under the car. The crash didn't kill him, but the car's weight on his chest kept him from being able to breathe, and he was asphyxiated. Supreme irony!"

"Huh, what do you mean?"

"Pre had one of the strongest cardiovascular systems ever measured. His lungs could bring in oxygen at a higher rate than almost anyone, and his heart could pump his super-oxygenated blood more efficiently than other hearts. That's why he could run so damn fast. To die because he couldn't get oxygen into his lungs is the irony."

They both looked at the rock in the weak moonlight. Ray said, "You're pretty smart, Cody. That was a good explanation. Sad as hell, though. It sounds like this Pre guy was a popular dude."

"You have no idea. The entire state mourned his death. You gotta see "Fire on the Track," the documentary they did on him. If you want to know Pre, that's the show."

"Is this where you're going to drop me off?"

"No, you can't really sleep here. We'll go back to the park where there's a shelter."

Cody drove a few blocks to another part of the forested park and pulled into a secluded spot hidden enough that they might not be seen.

It was near freezing, so Cody suggested Ray stay in the van with him for the night. Ray was ecstatic and began to praise Cody's kindness, but Cody shushed him. "Look, we're both vets. We need to help each other. You stretch out up front, and I'll take the back. Let's get some shut eye."

The next morning broke bright and sunny, although only a bare sliver of direct sunlight sliced through the trees to illuminate the frost on the windshield. Ray woke to these intricate patterns and stayed still, not wanting to wake his host, and marveled at the fractal patterns' beauty.

Cody woke soon after, and they both exited the van to relieve themselves. They got back in and drove down the hill past the university to the YMCA. Pulling up to the curb, Cody handed Ray a slip of paper with his email address and a $20 bill.

"I hope you find what you're looking for, man. Life's too short to waste on things that don't matter. This is a good Y. They got showers and a nice, hot jacuzzi. Last time I was here it only cost $5. Use the rest for a good breakfast. And take care of yourself."

Cody noticed Ray tearing up. "We both saw some bad shit in the war, Ray. It changed us. You need to take care of yourself. This is just a small bit to help you get started. It's the least I can do."

Ray accepted the money. "Most people just look down on me like I'm some piece of garbage. I'm going to try to fix myself, Cody. You take care, man, and thank you. Seriously, thank you! I'll let you know how it goes."

Cody pulled away from the curb and headed toward I-5 south. He stopped at a Starbucks for coffee and a muffin. He caught a whiff of himself standing in line and realized he'd driven all day yesterday then run several miles without taking a shower. He felt bad imposing his stink on others, but he didn't want to waste time with a shower just yet.

He did, however, want to check his email in case Victoria had written, so he grabbed an open table in the corner. Not one to obsessively check email, he hadn't seen that she'd written yesterday around noon.

"Hey, good looking, I can't get you out of my mind! What are we gonna do about that? Just letting you know you had an impact on me last night, and I don't just mean the sex. :~) :~)

When you get the time, let me know your feelings, OK?

V"

Cody quickly responded.

"Victoria! You're constantly on my mind. Driving down I-5 can be a bore, so I've had lots of time to think about us. I'm already dreaming about my return and our first run together. I made it to Eugene last night and ran in the park where I ran cross country back in school. It was cold and dark but clear enough: the moonlight lit the trail.

I met a homeless vet there and we shared stories most of the night. He was a troubled soul.

I'll call tonight around 8.

Cody"

****

His drive that day proved more enjoyable, given he was anticipating his call with Victoria, and was able to fantasize about sex with her, a pleasant distraction from the long stretches of freeway. He also had spectacular views of southern Oregon's mountains, and shortly after entering California, he could see magnificent Mt. Shasta.

Just north of Sacramento, his GPS showed a shortcut to I-80 east by taking Hwy 99 south out of Red Bluff, CA. The road was slower, but more scenic than the freeway. He made it all the way to the I-80 junction before stopping for the night at a rest area. After a quick meal, he called his new honey.

"Hey big boy!" she answered cheerily. Her enthusiasm instantly made Cody happy.

Visualizing her, Cody settled in for a long conversation. Cody didn't know she was into swing dancing in addition to being a runner. That made her even sexier. He promised he'd take lessons when he returned.

Also her side profession—freelance writer—surprised him. She had a journalism degree from Columbia and had briefly worked for a small newspaper before starting her lingerie business. That she'd recorded the gas station owner's verbal assault now made sense to him. She told Cody she was writing up the story for the Seattle Times and would finish it after Zak worked his magic in the courtroom.

Cody smiled. He thought he had a Pulitzer-worthy story if ever there was one, but then his mood changed as he realized they'd probably never get to see each other after that. He'd either be spending life in prison, or he'd be dead.

"Cody, you OK?" she asked.

"Yeah, it's just been a long drive, and I'm getting sleepy."

"Let's call it a night, then. I'm tired, too, and I have a long run with friends in the morning. Let me know when you're there and settled in."

"Sure, will do. Victoria?"

"Yes?"

"Um, thanks for, uh...Aw, man, I'm being lame. I like you. You're the best thing to happen to me in a long, long time. I'm glad I met you. Really, really glad."

"Oh, you're so sweet, baby. The feeling is quite mutual. I've been on cloud nine since we met. I can't wait for you to get back....Sleep well."

Sharing his feelings with Victoria felt good. He had been trying to ignore the reality of his situation—that he was planning to murder a sitting senator—but after he hung up, it was all he could think about. He still had several days of driving ahead, and then some scouting.

Cody connected his remote WiFi device so he could research the fundraiser site online. It was scheduled for the following week, and was all over the local news due to controversy over the pigeon shoot.

He figured three more days of driving and then he'd find a place to camp in the van without drawing notice. He needed to be within reasonable distance of the ranch so he could use his bike to scout it. He'd look like any long-distance biker out for a training ride—probably not a common sight in that part of Oklahoma, but it was the best he could do.

He used Google Earth to examine the small rocky hill he'd chosen. The resolution was limited, but it looked like the rocks were big enough to afford him seclusion. He'd need some luck, however, to get a clean shot at the senator, since there might be a lot of people around him. If he wasn't able to get a clean shot right away, he'd have to try during the actual pigeon shoot. But he had no idea where that would be conducted. He had to make Inhofe's assassination work in the parking lot.

"They fucking kill birds for entertainment," Cody thought. "Jesus fucking Christ! On top of everything else, the motherfucker needs to die for that!"

Right now, the birds were undoubtedly headed toward the same destination, tightly caged in the darkness of a truck's trailer. How would it feel to be released into the light, only to be blasted out of the sky seconds later? Cody laughed bitterly as he pictured shooting Inhofe after his own car ride; he knew exactly what it would feel like.

For all of this to work, of course, he was going to have to keep lying to Victoria. What else could he do? He had his priorities straight, but lying to his new love felt horrible. That he might only have a few days, weeks, or months left to be with her made him profoundly sad.

He thought about Gary Cheney, the dog-fighter scum, and the men he had killed in Iraq. When had he not been fighting some kind of war? The old, toxic brew of sadness over lost love and rage over the brutality of men swelled up in him again, refueling the righteous anger toward his target.

PART THREE

EXECUTION OF THE MISSION

Chapter 17

Driving a U-Haul through the prairie after having assassinated a senator felt surreal—Cody was too preoccupied to drive safely on the interstate. He wanted to keep to a reasonable 55–60 mph, so he stuck to secondary highways and farm roads, working his way south and east. Even at those slow speeds, he managed to get into Texas and most of the way to Dallas before pulling over at a rest stop outside of Decatur. The drive had been through really boring land, and for this, Cody was grateful.

He had stopped in Wichita Falls for gas and found a grocery store where he stocked up on food and drink. While there, he watched to see if people were acting differently or talking about the event. Nothing. It seemed as though life were completely normal. Life was decidedly not normal for Cody. He felt as if the people around him existed in a separate reality.

At the rest area that night, he began scanning the news for updates. Nothing new from the FBI or police about suspects or evidence. Cody assumed they'd spot his bike's tire marks and follow them across the dry cove and onto the trail. He knew they'd interview every resident on that route to learn if they'd seen someone on a bicycle. Recalling how he hadn't seen a soul outside, he felt confident that wouldn't result in anything useful.

After listening to the news for over an hour and hearing nothing new, Cody called Victoria.

"Hey, Victoria, how's my new girlfriend?" He was genuinely happy to talk to her but had to make sure he sounded that way.

"Hi, sweetie! How're you? How's the work going? You making some fun movie magic?"

"Ha! I'm making Toronto skylines look like New York. It's boring magic."

"Did you hear the news? James Inhofe was assassinated this morning! Holy shit, who would've thought one of the bad guys would be taken out? It's usually the good ones who get killed."

"What? I haven't been online all day. What happened?"

"They said he was shot in the head while at some fundraiser in Oklahoma. No one knows who did it yet. Pretty exciting, huh?"

"Well, if anyone deserved death, he'd be high on the list." Cody relished the ability to speak the truth without her understanding just how true it was. "But I'm sure those Okies'll send another one back to the Senate just as bad as him."

"Maybe so, but at least he's gone. Good riddance, too. He's the guy who said climate change was a big fucking hoax. Remember last year when he brought a snowball to the Senate floor? What an asshole!" Victoria didn't mince words.

"Hell yes. What else is new? Zak helping you with that gas station guy?"

"Oh, yeah, talked to Zak today. He was ecstatic over the Inhofe thing, by the way. I've never seen him so happy. And we're going to sue the gas station for damages to the local waterway. Zak says state and federal laws are involved, so he might need to take on some help since it could get complicated. Exxon owns the station, so they're bringing some legal muscle to the fight. It's gonna get ugly, but he's confident we'll win."

Cody needed to chill out, so he dug his pipe out and loaded it while she was talking.

"I can't wait to get home and help you guys with this fight. I can't say VFX is really boring, but it pales by comparison to beating up on polluters. That's the work I want to do. Scuse me, gonna take a hit."

He sparked up the bowl, sucked the sweet smoke into his lungs and held it.

Victoria's sultry voice was like magic to Cody. "How I wish I was there with you right now. I keep replaying our one night together. You were so hot!"

He felt himself getting hard at the memory of their great sex. He craved her touch. Exhaling the smoke, he replied, "Me, too, babe. I can't wait to see you again. We'll have so much to talk about. I want to know everything about you."

"Awww, you're so sweet! Speaking of that, when are you coming home?"

Cody thought for a second. "They keep giving me more shots, so it'll be at least another week, maybe two. I'm banking the money and living as frugally as I can. They have food at the studio, and I work so late there's no time for spending money beyond renting a room. LA can be boring when all you do is work."

He hated the lies.

"Got it. I can hold out for two more weeks, but I gotta warn you, I'm going to ravage you when I get you in my arms!" Her voice had a dirty, devilish flavor that strengthened Cody's erection. Oh, man, he wanted to be home bad!

"Well now, you've gone and given me a hard on! Whatever will I do with it?"

"I know what I'd do with it, but I think you'll have to take care of that yourself, big boy. I'm sure you know what to do."

"I'll be thinking of you the whole time."

"Hmmm...that sounds like fun. Maybe I'll do the same. This'll be fun!"

"Alright, sweetie, have a good time. We can compare notes next time we talk."

"Good night, Cody. Sleep tight."

Cody slept soundly considering the circumstances. Traffic woke him the next day around sunrise, when an 18-wheeler pulled in next to his van. He went to the restroom and washed his hands when the trucker, a bulky, 50ish man with a huge beard, came in reeking of cigarettes. Hating the smell, Cody hurriedly dried his hands and left.

The sun was peaking over the horizon, and Cody could see his breath, but he expected the day to warm. His goal was to drive into the Dallas/Fort Worth metro area and find a place to get a good breakfast and a newspaper. He cranked over the van's engine and turned the heater on high. Then he found NPR on his phone and listened for a report on Inhofe.

It wasn't long before the lead story came on. By now, the FBI had taken over the investigation, with the state police assisting them. The NPR correspondent, Dina Temple-Raston, asked the FBI representative, agent Gavin Washington, what they knew so far.

Temple-Raston: "I'm speaking with Agent Gavin Washington of the FBI. Agent Washington, what do you know so far about who shot the senator?"

Washington: "We're operating on the assumption that the perpetrator was a skilled marksman. The shot was taken from a hillside just over 200 meters distant from the parking lot where Senator Inhofe was being greeted by event participants. No one reported hearing gunfire, which leads us to believe the gunman used a suppressor. We're still waiting on ballistics to determine what type of rifle was used."

Temple-Raston: "Do you have any suspects at this time?"

Washington: "No, it's too soon to speculate about who might've done this. It'll take some time to conduct forensics and gather evidence. I will say there's very little evidence so far. We located tire tracks from a bicycle that the shooter may have used to escape.

Cody thought, "Good luck with that."

Temple Raston: "Is Homeland Security involved in the investigation?"

Washington: "They're being kept apprised, but for now, the FBI and Oklahoma state police are leading the investigation. Homeland Security is heading up the enhanced security for Congress and other potential targets."

"Bingo!" exclaimed Cody.

Temple-Raston: "Other targets? Are you saying this person might be targeting other members of Congress?"

Washington: "We don't know anything about the person who committed this crime. But when a member of Congress is assassinated, we consider every option and act accordingly."

A shock jolted Cody's body. He'd just listened to an NPR interview with an FBI agent talking about catching him. The seriousness of what he'd done began to sink in.

****

Cody passed through most of Dallas/Fort Worth before exiting the highway for food. He was hungry for something other than energy bars and sandwiches and in dire need of a shower. His choices were typical American freeway fare: IHOP, Denny's, Carl's Jr., and Dairy Queen. He picked IHOP since he figured he could get a meatless meal without too much trouble.

As he walked in, he grabbed a copy of the Dallas Morning News from the stand by the door. The place was half empty, but instead of taking a table, he headed straight for the bathroom. He figured he could clean up a bit using the sink and paper towels—enough to tamp down the stink.

After sitting down and ordering waffles, he stared at the paper's headline: "Senator James Inhofe Assassinated." Three stories covered the event itself, how the FBI was investigating it, and what Republican strategists and political operatives thought. All the lunatic GOP presidential candidates were bloviating about how we needed to spend more money on Homeland Security and the Department of Defense. Never mind that this had nothing to do with national defense. These right-wingers would use any excuse to throw more money to their pals in the defense industry. A perfect example of the "shock doctrine" described in Naomi Klein's book of the same name.

Cody devoured all three stories while downing his waffles. He lingered over a third coffee while checking email. Zak had sent one the night before, around the time he had been talking to Victoria, celebrating Inhofe's death. He included links to several Facebook stories about radical environmentalists who were ecstatic about the assassination. This news brightened Cody's mood considerably. One of the stories even compared Inhofe's work to Hitler's, which was a stretch in Cody's mind, but he understood the analogy. To Cody, there were many Hitlers out there, all of them deserving to die.

He quickly wrote to Zak. "Re: Inhofe, an amazing turn of events! We'll have lots to discuss when I return. Gotta get back to work..."

Back on the road, Cody spent the next four days driving no faster than the speed limit along the blue highways of Texas, Louisiana, Mississippi, Alabama, and into Florida. His destination: 306 Farthington Ave., Palm Beach, FL. A simple Google search had located the home address of Rush Limbaugh, the "big fat idiot," as former comedian and now senator, Al Franken, once labeled him.

Since he was taking his time, he stopped often to rest and check email and Facebook. He wasn't a big Facebook user, having only about 20 friends, but it was a great place to find stories about Inhofe. He decided not to post or like any of these stories, however. No need to tempt fate.

When driving, he preferred listening to KCRW, both for the music and news, but he felt compelled to seek out Limbaugh's radio broadcast to hear what he had to say about Inhofe, if for no other reason than to generate some fresh hatred for the fat pig. He was not disappointed. Rush was at his finest casting aspersions right and left—but mostly left. He was a font of conspiracy theories, blaming everyone from MoveOn.org to animal-rights activists to climate activists (right on!) to Obama.

Security for Congress was on high alert, but there was no talk of security for other right-wingers. Cody was counting on that.

The South depressed Cody. Avoiding the interstate, he drove through some of the most economically disadvantaged towns he'd ever seen. The people he encountered at gas stations, grocery stores, and restaurants seemed to be dispirited, and on the few occasions he spoke with them, he sensed they weren't very well educated.

Cody remembered his parents talking about conservatives' decades-long effort to defund public education. They suspected the reasons were to create a population who'd believe whatever crap they were told. Fox News, Rush Limbaugh, and the right-wing lying machine: they easily manipulated these people to vote against their own interests. The results were evident to anyone who cared to look.

And in case some were aware enough to vote for their interests—better education, more jobs, higher minimum wage, etc.—they were stymied by efforts to keep them from voting. Gerrymandering and voter suppression kept Democrats from voting and reduced the impact of Democrats who managed to get elected.

By the time Cody entered Florida, he was again ready to do battle with these merchants of doubt. Florida's panhandle was even worse than much of Alabama and Mississippi. Poverty, ugliness, and a sense of defeat permeated every little town he passed through.

It was well after dark by the time Cody entered the endless string of cities stretching from Miami in the south to Jupiter in the north. Palm Beach was just a few miles south of Jupiter, but it was as wealthy as the other towns were poor. In that sense Palm Beach was as far away as the planet Jupiter.

Just before midnight he pulled into a large shopping center parking lot and pulled off to the side near a few RVs. Their owners were trying to find a safe place to sleep, too, and would leave before stores opened the next day. There were lots of these people, essentially homeless except for their car, van, or, if lucky, an old lumbering RV with a bathroom, kitchen, and a lumpy bed.

In preceding decades, homelessness had grown to epidemic proportions due to government mismanagement—Republicans mostly, but some Democrats were just as guilty.

The world's problems while large were solvable. But those who ruled the world didn't want to solve these problems, they wanted to profit from them.

The weather had been steadily improving as Cody drove south, and in Florida, it was downright balmy. When he awoke, the sun was already up and his neighbors were cranking their engines. He overheard someone talking about a guard coming around soon. This was all he needed to hear. He jumped up, quickly dressed, and drove away without talking to anyone.

Cody found the ubiquitous Starbucks signs welcoming. He liked their coffee and the WiFi always worked. He needed to find a laundromat, and he needed a YMCA to get cleaned up. A quick Google search found both within a few miles.

While at the coffee shop, he studied maps of Palm Beach. Limbaugh's palatial compound was at the north end of the island. This was going to be tough. He couldn't drive the van onto the island. There'd be cameras everywhere. He'd have to catch his target in public. He began Googling everything he could find on Limbaugh. He was beginning to worry whether he'd be able to find his target, when a small story from the local Palm Beach Daily News popped up.

"Rush Limbaugh to Play in Celebrity Golf Tournament This Saturday." It was a small blurb about a charity for blood diseases that Limbaugh sponsored. Today was Wednesday, so he had a couple days to figure this out.

"So the asshole gives to charity. I guess even the worst people have a positive side, but it's not gonna save his ass," Cody thought.

The tournament would be held at the Palm Beach Country Club, a posh place equidistant from Limbaugh's house and the bridge leading off the island. Zooming in on the map, Cody studied the square golf course packed tightly between North Lake Trail on the island's west side, and North Ocean Blvd. on the Atlantic side. There were no obvious places he could hide on the course. Access was only through a gate on the west side and the main entrance on the southeast corner. No doubt cameras covered both locations.

As Cody studied the map, he found one promising option. Bordering the north edge of the golf course was Bahama Lane, a one-block street with ten large homes and one empty lot. The lot was cared for and had some trees on its east side where, potentially, he could hide. He would scout it on the bike, but first he needed to get cleaned up.

Cody got back into the van and changed into his riding shorts and T-shirt. He drove over to the laundry and washed everything he had. When he arrived at the YMCA, he took a long shower, shaved, and tried to make himself look presentable.

He'd skipped breakfast and might be riding around that afternoon, so as he drove toward the bridge that connected the mainland to the island, he looked for a small mom and pop café or sandwich shop. He found just the place, the Vegan Café, right across the street from the public library. It was maybe a little nicer than he was looking for, but he was starving, and it was close to his destination.

From the restaurant's newspaper rack, the headline screamed at him. "Possible Break in Inhofe Case." He hadn't heard anything on the radio, nor had he seen anything online, so he bought a copy to read over lunch.

A friendly waitress named Zamira seated him in a booth next to a window. When she offered him a menu, he politely declined and asked, "What do you guys make that's gonna fill up a hungry traveler?" His big grin put her at ease, and she replied, "You like salad?" Her Cuban accent and big smile put Cody in a good place. He felt welcomed.

"Sure. I'm so hungry I'll eat almost anything. It's just gotta be good, healthy food."

"Our kale salad is the best in town. What do you think?"

"Sounds great! Can I have some bread, too? I'm starved."

"Sure, be right back." She turned on her heels and strode off. The encounter was efficient yet pleasant.

The newspaper story was front page, above the fold. The Inhofe assassination had been headline news for the first two days, but then the stories were bumped to the back pages. What was the big break in the case?

"Local animal-rights activist questioned for posting threatening messages against Inhofe," read the sub-head. The article explained that a local who'd been protesting the pigeon shoot at the Inhofe fundraiser rode a mountain bike with similar tires to those Cody's bike had. They matched the tracks on the hillside that ran across the dry cove.

Cody smiled, thinking they'd waste time going after this man but also hoping the poor guy didn't own a Winchester. He also felt bad an animal-rights activist would suffer through an inquisition over something he had no part in. Hopefully, it'd be short and not harm his reputation. He would certainly be exonerated. At the very least, the activist had to be pleased about the reason for being detained.

Zamira walked up with Cody's salad, a giant plate heaping with kale and other veggies and slathered with a creamy dressing. Cody smiled at the pretty woman and thought about calling Victoria. He'd call tonight when he was safely ensconced in the van.

He finished the article while eating, but there was nothing more of interest. The man was pissed off he'd been detained for questioning. He was even quoted as saying "Inhofe got what he deserved! I didn't do it, but I'm happy someone did."

"Bingo, again!" Cody thought. That wouldn't help him with the locals, hard-right conservatives who revered the senator. But he felt good knowing others shared his feelings about the climate-denying politico. The son-of-a-bitch had needed to be stopped.

He left Zamira a big tip and walked out to the van.

The Flagler Memorial Bridge was a few blocks away, but Cody needed to find a quiet secluded place to leave his van. He went back to Google maps, where he saw a railroad track running north/south nearby. Several blocks to the north, 11th Street dead ended at the tracks. He drove over to check it out.

The street was quiet except when the trains rolled by. No one who could afford to live elsewhere would live near the train tracks, so no security guards would be investigating a rental van parked on the street. Thieves were another matter. With no security, his van could easily be broken into, so he couldn't leave it for long.

It was almost 1 pm as he parked on the street next to a vacant lot. He sat quietly and observed. There was virtually no traffic—just the occasional car or truck turning off Railroad Avenue, another quiet street paralleling the tracks and ending at 11th. After making sure no one was watching, Cody pulled out his bike and secured the van. He quickly rode off.

It took less than two minutes to get to the bridge and one more to get across it. Cody was timing everything so he'd know how long it would take to get back to the van riding at a recreational pace.

The island was like another world. This was one of the country's wealthiest enclaves. Only about 8,000 people lived there full time, and their names included some of the most successful people in sports, entertainment, industry, and technology.

He turned left on Bradley Place and rode a few blocks until it turned into N. Lake Way. Traffic was light, mostly landscaper trucks, the occasional security car, and of course a smattering of luxury vehicles. Cody wondered who was in these limos and Mercedes. Was his target among them? He knew Limbaugh had to get off the island now and then, so maybe.

There were other cyclists, individuals and couples tooling along. Everyone was riding at a leisurely speed. Cody was pleased to see he fit in, even if his bike was a bit more worn out than most.

Riding past the mansions hidden behind tall hedges, Cody felt their privacy afforded him some as well. He passed a gate, and made sure to turn his head away from any cameras that might be trained on the entrance. He'd need to disguise himself more, and the bike, too. His helmet and sunglasses hid his face pretty well, but if any of his close friends in Seattle saw a security-camera image of him, they'd be able to ID him.

He was getting paranoid about the cameras. He knew the FBI would review every video on the island and he'd definitely show up. How long before they'd link the bike at the Inhofe assassination and this bike riding through Palm Beach? Seeing all the other bikes made him feel better, but still. And there was the matter of his gun if it were strapped to the bike.

North Lake Way ended at Country Club Road, which bordered the golf course on the south. Cody turned right. With its high wall and surrounding shrubs, he couldn't see the golf course at all, but within a minute, he arrived at the property's main entrance. On his right was the ocean and a clean, white-sand beach. It was beautiful, but Cody could never live in a place of such wealth. The rich ruined everything with their walls, hedges, and security cameras.

Arriving at the north end of the golf course, Cody could see his destination around the bend: Bahama Lane. But first, he wanted to ride by Limbaugh's house for fun. Continuing north, the ocean was now obscured by a row of massive homes. He was now getting into the richest part of Palm Beach.

The pavement was flat and smooth—everything was perfectly maintained. He could feel the wealth. So much money! What did they do with it all? Cody knew many wealthy people donated to help the less fortunate, but seeing this level of excess, he wondered if they were giving enough.

For a stretch, the houses were smaller, and Cody could once again see the ocean. But after half a mile, the road curved left again, and he knew he was getting close. He stopped to check his map to confirm how many properties he'd pass before getting to Limbaugh's house. His was the sixth one up. The hedges and trees along this part of the road were substantial. You couldn't see anything on the property at all. Seashell Road bordered the property on the north and Cody noticed the heavy steel gate with at least two visible cameras pointed at the entrance. This sent a chill down his spine. How far back in time would they check the cameras? Would he be recognizable from this distance?

He rode on Seashell Road for only half a block before he turned left on N. Ocean Way. Cody meandered through the leafy streets, looping around the island's north end before going south.

He decided to check the empty lot on Bahama Lane, but instead of tempting fate by returning along the same route, Cody rode west a block to N. Lake Way. He knew from the map it would connect to Bahama in about a mile. It was mid-afternoon and the late winter sun was strong even though it was low in the sky. A couple of teenagers, probably playing hooky, rode past.

There were only eleven lots on Bahama Lane, but the street was almost three football fields long. Turning left, Cody found the third lot empty. There was no gate, nothing to stop him from riding right onto the lot. A thick group of trees grew in the southeast corner. Only a fence separated the lot from the golf course, but the trees looked like they would offer enough cover.

Cody rode right past, not wanting to be seen trespassing. Riding to the end of the street, he turned and rode past the lot once more. It sure looked like it would work. So now he needed to time how long it would take to ride at normal speeds back to the van. The total distance was only 2.5 miles, and riding time worked out to 15 minutes.

Once back at the van, Cody stashed the bike in the back and, glancing around to see if anyone was watching, drove slowly away. He found a large shopping center a few miles away where it would be safe to park.

Cody settled in for a restless night.

****

Friday dawned clear and warm. Cody would spend the day prepping for the big event— and his escape. He needed to plan carefully for any and all contingencies. Timing was crucial. Assuming no one heard the shot, and no one saw him leaving the empty lot on his bike, he'd have maybe 10 minutes to fasten the gun to the bike and ride to the bridge. Once he was over the bridge, he'd be free and clear, but anyone on the island when the police arrived would be suspect. Especially someone on a bike with something long protruding in front of the frame.

A lot depended on where Limbaugh would be when Cody shot him. The map showed several potential locations on the golf course's north side, where, if he got a clean shot, Limbaugh would be a good distance from the course's entrance and any first responders would take some time to reach him, allowing extra time for Cody's escape. He'd have to play it by ear, there were several holes within easy range of his Winchester, so he'd have multiple opportunities.

Much would have to go right for Cody to make a clean escape. His helmet and sunglasses should obscure his face, but his bike would be pretty easy to trace if a camera got a good view of it. After some thought, Cody drove to a crafts store and bought masking tape, rolls of red, white and blue crepe paper, and, on a whim, a small American flag.

Back in the van, he wrapped most of the bike's frame with crepe paper, obscuring the brand name and other identifying markings. He then strapped the towel-wrapped rifle to the frame, adjusting it to reduce the length of barrel that was protruding. As a final touch, he stuck the flag's dowel into the barrel and taped it securely so it looked like his bike was in a Fourth of July parade.

Cody wasn't sure if this would draw him undue attention—it wasn't July—or if people would just assume he was a patriot flying his colors. It was a toss up, but he liked how the rifle was no longer a problem. It was now part of his disguise.

He had one more thing to add, a T-shirt with an American-flag theme. He Googled Goodwill and found they had a super store on Okeechobee Blvd. just a few miles away. There he found several shirts that would fit the bill, picking one with an American flag *and* an eagle.

Exiting the Goodwill, he noticed that a remote corner of its lot abutted a freeway. It looked like a safe place to spend his last night in Palm Beach. Cody figured he would leave the Goodwill lot by 5 am the next day and drive to the 11th St. location, where he'd leave the van and ride his bike to Bahama Lane. He'd have plenty of time to nestle himself in the bushes before any morning walkers were around. From there, he'd have to wait several hours and hope like hell no one found him.

Now all he had left to do was gas up the van and get dinner.

He returned to the Vegan Café so he would not have to settle for some limp salad at a meat-serving establishment. The place closed at 5 pm, however, and it was getting late. He rushed over in time to order another kale salad, to go. Zamira remembered him with a nice smile as she handed over the food. "I hope you're gonna be one of our regulars. You've got good taste in healthy food!"

"I wish I could, but I'm only in town for a few days. If I come back, I'll definitely stop by." He gave Zamira a friendly smile. She was the kind of person everyone should emulate: friendly, helpful, empathic, and, from what he could sense, probably passionate. He hoped she had a loving partner.

Zamira triggered a daydream about Victoria. He didn't want to think about the soul-crushing karmic repercussions that killing a vile human would bring. He wanted to think about spending days, weeks, months, and maybe years with this smart, sexy, incredibly gorgeous woman he'd only seen for about 12 hours—although it was an incredible 12 hours.

Cody drove to the corner of a run-down shopping center where he listened to KCRW and ate his salad. The hot afternoon sun gradually sank behind the shopping mall, providing a modicum of relief from its direct rays. The evening proved somewhat less muggy as twilight's shade settled in. A light breeze granted more relief, Cody's sweat evaporating as fast as his body secreted it.

He watched as overweight and undernourished people carried to their cars plastic bags bulging with stuff they probably didn't need. But their poor education in underfunded schools didn't provide them with the critical-thinking skills they needed to understand how marketing and advertising was manipulating them into buying so much crap.

Cody was suddenly overcome with an overwhelming sense of dread. Watching these people saddened him. What had happened to the United States? Where did all the good people go? These people seemed barely able to care for themselves, their intellect dulled by moronic media, drugs, and alcohol. They didn't care about the world, only their little piece of it. They were perfect fodder for the corporate machine enticing them to vote against their own interests, and their inadequate education ensured they didn't understand reality—only the Fox News version of it.

Cody began to doubt his mission. Was taking a human life, and enduring that unbearable knowledge for the rest of his life, worth it? He'd already killed four men: two in war, the dog-fighting monster, and now Senator Inhofe, a monster in his own right.

But his doubt didn't linger. He hadn't started this trip on a whim. For years, he'd been bombarded with story after story of corporate malfeasance on a global scale, some of it bordering on genocide. The effects of climate change will be worse than all the genocides ever perpetrated on humanity. That's what the science said.

These poor people he was observing were merely unwitting victims of this machine. The more he thought about it, the angrier he became.

He was putting his life on the line to rid the planet of merchants of doubt and the politicians and corporatists who funded them. Cody thought of children who were starving, or being raped, shot, and mutilated by those who sought after oil; he thought of the tens of millions who'd be uprooted from delta land farmed for millennia and forced to find new homes amid the teeming masses already dealing with food shortages caused by climate change.

He thought of all the reports he'd read about assholes pushing their agendas, financed by monied interests to game the system against average hard-working people.

No, there were no doubts in his head now, nor would there be anymore. He'd stepped off the cliff and gravity would ensure he'd follow through on his mission. He started the van and drove to the Goodwill parking lot for the night.

****

Cody jerked awake at the sound of his phone's alarm. Dressing quickly and downing the first of several Red Bulls, he got into mission mode. It had rained during the night, but the temperature was already 74 degrees and would climb past 80. Local news was reporting mostly clear skies all day. This was good. He'd been worried about getting rained out.

The bike was ready to go, but Cody looked it over for any possible problems. He didn't know how long he'd be hiding in the bushes waiting for Limbaugh but figured it could be several hours, so he packed a handful of power bars and a banana.

It was pushing 5:20 and Cody was pretty much ready. Dawn was still a good hour away, so he sat quietly for a few minutes and reviewed his plan. It was pretty simple. The main thing was to avoid being seen going into the vacant lot and hiding in the bushes. He hoped no one would come onto the lot and snoop around. The shrubs and trees didn't look like they'd afford much cover if anyone got too close.

He held out his hand in the dome light's dim glare and watched as it shook slightly. His whole body trembled. That feeling, similar to how he'd felt before he killed Inhofe, was also akin to how he felt before leaving for a dangerous patrol in Iraq. Heightened awareness and high energy.

Cody cranked the engine, startling a murder of crows to flight from an old mature oak. He pulled slowly away and carefully drove the two miles to 11th Street, pulling up to stop at 5:45. He killed the engine, turned off the lights and just sat for a moment. There was no noise other than light traffic on Palm Beach Lakes Blvd., a little over a block to the north.

Cody was grateful for the warm temps, if not the humidity. He wondered how it would feel when the temperature got over 90. Couldn't be very pleasant.

He pulled out another cold Red Bull and downed it before sliding open the door and rolling out the heavy bike. His Trek Top Fuel was light, but the Winchester lent it some heft. Without turning on the light, Cody rode off at a leisurely pace. He saw no hint of humans awake in the vicinity.

Hardly anyone was on the roads—only a few delivery trucks and early risers. Cody rode over the Flagler bridge to the island. Once he got on the busier streets, he turned on his light.

When he got to Country Club Road on the golf course's south end, he turned left and followed it to North Lake Trail, which bordered the course's west side. Dawn was barely breaking with just a hint of light to the east. He rode a bit harder. It took less than two minutes to get to Bahama Lane and mere seconds more to the vacant lot.

He'd seen only one car since crossing the bridge, and no one seemed to be out yet on Bahama, although some houses had lights on. These people clearly liked to sleep in on Saturday morning, which was fine by Cody.

He pulled onto the lot and rode straight back to its southeast corner. Now that he was closer, he could see the bushes were not very thick. Trees bordered the house next door, which was also separated by a formidable wall of about seven feet. While the shrubs didn't offer much cover, the tree trunks were large enough that he could park the Trek against the wall and the trees would hide it from the street fairly well. Cody would have to sit tight against the wall for the trees to hide him, too. A casual observer on the street would not see him. As long as no one came onto the lot, he'd be fine.

No wall separated the lot from the golf course. Nothing but a chain link fence and a thick row of shrubs. All the other houses had walls, but it appeared whoever owned this lot hadn't bothered to build one. Cody was surprised the golf course didn't build a wall itself.

He felt he was hidden enough from the road, but just barely. He was trespassing, and if someone called the police, it could get very ugly, especially if they discovered his rifle.

The sun was still over the horizon, but it was light enough to read. An elderly couple walked by the lot, never looking in Cody's direction.

Cody spent the next several hours in a hyper-aware state. A third Red Bull set his teeth grinding and his ears ringing. He kept checking his phone for news of the Inhofe killing, but nothing new was coming up. While this comforted him, he knew today's assassination would change that dramatically.

As the sun rose, he saw the first players amble out on the course, foursomes mostly, one group after another. The charity event would begin at 10, and it was close to that when the early players stopped coming through. Cody figured the club was prepping for the charity group. It occurred to him that other celebrities would be there and that security might be tighter than he'd expected. Regardless, guards would be at the entrance—and maybe one or two on the course itself.

He thought to try the shot from further away to decrease the chance it would be heard. His suppressor was effective, but depending on how quiet the course was, the sound could carry and security could radio ahead to first responders about the shot's origins. He couldn't take that risk.

The three Red Bulls really wanted out of his body. Cody's military training had prepared him for all contingencies, and he'd brought an empty water bottle for this purpose. No way he would leave any bodily fluids on the ground for forensics people to find. DNA would be a solid lead. He'd been careful to avoid leaving anything at the Inhofe site, and this one would be similarly clean. The water bottle was filled well over half, which concerned Cody, since he knew he'd have to go again in a couple hours. He cut off all fluid intake just in case, sealing the water bottle and stashing it in his pack.

Something seemed to be happening. No players had been on the course for almost half an hour, but a security golf cart with two uniformed officers was now speeding across the grass from the east. At first, Cody was concerned he'd been spotted, that they were coming for him, but the golf cart passed and headed back south. They were checking the course for any stragglers in preparation for the main group coming through.

Cody retrieved his rifle from the bike. He kept an eye on the street and made sure to keep close to the neighbor's wall just in case. He found he could lie prone, with the rifle barrel stuck through the fence, and still see through the scope. He scanned the north east corner of the course and discovered he had decent visibility. The bushes on the golf course side of the fence provided more cover but also obscured much of the course's far areas. All Cody needed was for Limbaugh to stand still and he could take the shot.

Moments later, two men in suits walked the course. Clearly guards. They both stopped at the green and looked around, then turned to watch a large group that was moving toward them, five golf carts with three to four people in each. They pulled up and stopped near the green.

Cody unlocked the safety.

Scanning the group with his scope, he quickly found the big fat idiot. There were maybe 20 people in the immediate vicinity. He watched as they took turns tapping their balls toward the little hole.

Cody hated golf. He'd been chased off courses as a young runner and held a grudge. He also knew how much water and fertilizer these courses used. But it was golfers he hated the most. They trended Republican, and Cody knew that around the world business and political deals were conducted on golf courses, and not the kind that helped society at large. Some, he imagined, were good people, but for the most part, they were an exclusive club of evil bastards.

And one of the most evil bastards of all was in his rifle's sight right now, puffing on his fat cigar. In his head Cody could hear Rush Limbaugh frothing at the mouth about some imaginary crime by the left. Cody was antsy to end this monster's tirades once and for all.

The distance was a bit under 300 meters, well within range, but it would take a steady hand to make the shot. He waited for Limbaugh to take his turn with the putter. He knew that would be when the asshole would stand still for a few seconds.

After half the group had taken their turn, Limbaugh waddled over to the green with his putter and stood over his ball. It was his turn now. His turn to get his just deserts.

Cody took a deep breath and relaxed his body. His finger tightened on the trigger as his scope zeroed in on Limbaugh's head. Holding steady, he fired. Limbaugh had just drawn back his putter when those around him heard the thump of the bullet hitting his left shoulder, knocking him to the ground. Cody had missed the headshot, but had still done severe damage. Most of the people surrounding Limbaugh couldn't figure out what had happened. The guards had not heard the shot, but were scanning in all directions, looking for the shooter.

Cody fired twice more in quick succession, both bullets hitting the now prostrate Limbaugh. The first hit his upper spine, severing the spinal cord before ripping through his black heart. He died within moments. The second passed through a man's leg before entering Limbaugh's lower back. The man had bent over to assist Limbaugh.

Everyone was scattering. The two guards drew their weapons. They were looking wildly for any sight of an assailant.

Cody put the safety on and calmly but quickly got up and wrapped the towel around the rifle before strapping it to the bike frame.

He reinserted the American flag into the barrel and used tape to secure it. He mounted his Trek, fastened his helmet, put on his sunglasses, and rode out of the vacant lot, turning left on Bahama Lane. One car had just pulled out of a driveway, but was going in the opposite direction, so the driver most likely didn't see Cody at all.

He pedaled steadily—a little fast, but not so fast as to arouse suspicion.

The guards had immediately called for back up, causing two police officers on site to jump into golf carts and speed across the course. An ambulance left the Palm Beach Town Hall and raced up North County Road toward the golf course two and a half miles distant. Two police cars left their station moments later and passed the ambulance with their sirens and lights blazing.

Cody was half way down North Lake Way when he heard the sirens. Three screaming emergency vehicles would wake anyone still sleeping in. Cody had guessed correctly that the first responders would take the shortest route from their headquarters to the golf course. Shooting Limbaugh while he was on the course's northeast corner drew all the responders to the opposite side of the island from where Cody was, giving him time to make it to the bridge before anyone would think to check for people leaving the island.

It was 11:32 on a sunny Saturday and lots of cars were driving in both directions over Flagler bridge. The bridge had a bike and walking path on its north side, and a drawbridge in the middle for tall-masted boats. One such boat was very close, so the lights began to flash, indicating traffic must stop to allow the bridge to open.

Cody freaked out. He had to get over that bridge now!

Sirens from the other side of the bridge were growing louder. Cody didn't know that police from off the island were on their way; word was getting out about what had happened and who the victim was.

The lights stopping traffic on both sides of the bridge were flashing red and cross arms had come down. Two police cars with their lights ablaze were stuck in the clog of cars on the other side of the bridge. Cody began pedaling for all he was worth. He got to the cross arm and jumped off the bike, ducked under the cross arm, and pulled his bike after him. The bridge had not started to rise, so Cody jumped back on his Trek and booked it across, ensuring his escape from the island.

The two patrol cars didn't even notice him. They were frustrated hearing the radio crackle about Rush Limbaugh's assassination. Only those near the front saw what Cody did, and didn't care aside from thinking he was reckless.

Cody only cared about getting to the van and getting the hell out of town. Pedaling hard off the bridge, he took a right on Flagler Dr., riding full speed the half mile up to 11th, and then turned left. Only a few blocks to go.

When he arrived, breathing as though he'd finished a 5K full out, two African American kids were riding bikes in the street, jumping off a crude ramp they'd constructed from cinder blocks and plywood. Cody ignored them and dismounted from his bike, unlocking the van and lifting the bike inside. The boys watched, unsure of who he was, and curious about this guy with the strange bundle strapped to his ride. He was an unusual sight in their neighborhood, but they wouldn't connect him with news about the shooting that would soon break. That was on the rich island to the east of them, a place they were not welcome because of long-standing racism that, while not as openly expressed as it had been decades earlier, still kept certain populations from enjoying the same beaches as wealthy white folk.

Cody avoided eye contact with the kids, and left his helmet and sunglasses on until he was in the van with the windows rolled up. He started the engine, took off the helmet, and drove slowly away.

He immediately turned on the radio to listen for initial reports. Nothing yet.

Chapter 18

A couple of left turns put Cody on Palm Beach Lakes Blvd. heading west. Within two miles, he took the entrance to I-95 north, and for the first time that morning, he could breathe easy. He was still sweating, and he had to pee like a racehorse, but he wanted to put some distance between himself and Palm Beach first. The gross excesses of the filthy rich gnawed at him. That, and he'd just committed murder - again.

Cody rolled his window down letting the wind pour over his face in hopes it would purge his essence of the violence he'd committed. He longed for the clean fresh air of his beloved Pacific Northwest. He couldn't stand the oppressive humidity of southern Florida. Heat and humidity that kept you damp from dawn to dusk, a wet wind that did not cleanse.

Wanting to get off the interstate, he took the 710 Highway, a two-lane blue highway also known as the "Beeline." There wasn't a bend or bump for 64 miles.

After he'd driven well past any sign of human habitation, he turned north on a little dirt road that disappeared into low-growing xeromorphic scrub oaks and sandy pines. It was pushing 1 pm and the temperature was inching toward 80 degrees.

With both windows down to let in the country air, Cody breathed deep.

Now that he was out of town and away from traffic, the air smelled clean with just a hint of pine. Sandy pines native to the area smelled different from the giant 150-foot Ponderosa pines and Douglas fir where he lived. And this air was heavy with heat and humidity, while Cascade mountain air was cool and dry.

The smell of pines reminded him of a time 20 years earlier when he and Jennifer raced each other through a forest on the eastern slopes of Mt. Rainier. It was during a family camping trip on a warm summer day, which felt something like this winter day in Florida.

But a tailwind brought his vehicle's pollution into the van, snapping him back from his daydream. The stench instantly reminded him of his own contribution to the pollution killing the planet. He duly noted the irony.

Cody stopped and jumped out of the van to pee. The sense of release practically shook him to his knees. His penis in hand guiding the stream away from his shoes, the relaxation of his sphincter, which he'd been clenching since pulling the trigger, let loose all the tension from the previous hour. His whole body trembled before settling into a blissful state. He heard only the breeze and the far off chatter of a kestrel. The sound reminded him of Cooper chomping on a squeaky toy.

The thought of Cooper took him to a good place, a place where he wanted to stay. Other memories, good memories flooded his mind and he thought again of the woods back in Washington and the impromptu race with his sister. He was 10 and she was 12. Jennifer was already showing prowess as a runner, yet Cody was keeping up with her as they sprinted hard through the open spaces between the tall trees. Cody could not recall ever feeling better than he did at that moment.

He cried, realizing he'd never feel that good again. It wasn't because he was older and his health was in decline, but because people had done unfathomable things to him, to others, and to the planet. And now, in retaliation, he'd killed people. Five people were dead, and he had to kill more. Many more. He couldn't bear the thought. What had he done? What kind of life had he made for himself? He hated what had happened to him—hated it, hated it, hated it! He was so pissed at what these assholes had done to him and to the world.

But killing Inhofe and Limbaugh had infused him with purpose—to seek revenge for those already dead and those who were yet to die. He could cite dozens of studies showing that thousands died every single day from dirty energy worldwide. Cancer, lung, or heart disease squeezed from them their final breath.

He worried his killing wouldn't really change anything, that the assholes he'd assassinated would be replaced by more assholes. But at least he'd begun, and his hatred ensured he'd continue.

Pulling back on the highway, the local AM station interrupted its broadcast with a special bulletin.

"We have breaking news...Police at the Palm Beach Country Club are reporting that radio host Rush Limbaugh was shot to death this morning while playing golf at a private charity event. There are no suspects at this time, but preliminary reports indicate the shooting is similar to the recent assassination of Senator James Inhofe. More on this breaking story as reports come in."

Cody remained in a foul mood as he drove for miles in a daze along the long, straight, flat road. He didn't want to stop and interact with anyone, but hunger pangs compelled him to find a grocery store in Okeechobee and stock up on food and drink.

Before leaving town, he pulled into a gas station to top off. To avoid heavier traffic on the coasts, he'd follow the blue highways through the central part of the state. He wanted to get to the 10 Freeway and into the panhandle before calling it a night. He hoped his attitude would improve before he spoke with Victoria. The thought of talking to her gave him a warm feeling. He settled in for more long, boring miles punctuated only by updated news reports.

Cody scanned the AM dial for Limbaugh's show. There were a lot of them in Florida and they were on fire with angry ditto-heads screaming about a left-wing assassination conspiracy. All were shouting over the murder of their beloved fat pig. It all made Cody smile. As the miles passed, and details about the assassination were reported, Cody's attitude continued to improve.

After a good hour of listening to the enemy, Cody switched over to KCRW, which was airing an hour-long special linking the Limbaugh murder and the Inhofe assassination—even if they weren't calling Limbaugh's killing an assassination yet. Cody wondered how the media determined whether a murder warranted the label "assassination." No matter, the fat pig was dead, and there would be much figurative dancing in the streets in some liberal enclaves.

Other media were connecting the two killings—the method was the same, and once ballistics were run, it would be confirmed.

Some reports called the perpetrator a killer. Perhaps unrealistic, but that hurt Cody. He'd always thought killers were exceptionally bad people. They killed without reason. Cody had a very good reason. He was killing "Hitlers"—people who, by their actions, were causing the death of millions. If left unchecked, they'd cause the death of billions.

NPR's Dina Temple-Raston was interviewing FBI agent Gavin Washington again.

Temple-Raston: "Agent Washington, in light of Rush Limbaugh's murder this morning, do you believe there's connection to the Inhofe assassination?"

Washington: "The circumstances are similar enough that we believe there could be a connection. Once we get a ballistics report, we'll know more."

Temple-Raston: "Is there anything else leading you to think there might be a connection?"

Washington: "Both were high profile conservatives. And both were shot from a distance without anyone hearing anything. Based on those two facts, there is speculation that the same person, or people, are involved."

Temple-Raston: "Do you suspect more than one person is involved? Could this be related to terrorist activity?"

Washington: "We're considering everything at this time. An FBI forensics team will hopefully find something to give us an idea who did this."

Temple-Raston: "Thank you, Agent Washington. We'll report more on this important story as it unfolds."

"Unfolds." The word struck Cody as apt. The FBI would find clues and report them, peeling away the grey layers of ignorance to get at the truth inside.

"Good luck with that!" thought Cody.

He thought of Victoria and wondered, briefly, if he should call her. He decided it was too crazy to talk while driving. His head was swimming. He needed to keep cool and consider his options. He'd call her later that night. Talking to her about the news also raised flags, but he only needed to stay sharp and not say anything too revealing. He had to feign ignorance.

He practiced his responses out loud to reduce the chances he'd slip up. This helped pass the time and keep him awake. Cody hated driving long distances. Especially in a van. Especially after killing people.

Still, he made good time on central Florida's quiet, two-lane highways. The Red Bull jitters had worn off by late afternoon, allowing him to relax a bit and get into the groove of the long boring drive. He began to think about next steps. Maybe he'd get away clean from both of these murders and be able to strike again. He thought about how far he could take this before getting caught. What was his end game? He hadn't thought it all the way through. Victoria being in the picture changed things, too.

He was pretty close to the 10 Freeway on Highway 90, which ran parallel through the Florida panhandle. It was well after dark when he stopped in Live Oak to get gas. While there, he checked his map for a place to stay the night. He found a quiet dirt road just west of town that led to an illegal dump site. Perfect.

He didn't like the vibe from the people at the gas station. They all looked and sounded like Limbaugh ditto heads. When he went in to pay, three of them were talking about the killing. They sounded about as ignorant as the typical ditto head, and they were mean as hell. One of them bragged about how he and some friends had "beat up some hippies" over in Jacksonville for the crime of having long hair.

The military was full of men like these. They hated anything having to do with the environment, social issues, or basic human rights. These were the people the right-wing machine used to intimidate progressives at political rallies, Planned Parenthood clinics, or any place where good people were trying to effect progressive policies. They all had guns and loved killing. Many of them joined the military, not for patriotic reasons, but so they could legally kill humans. They were America's version of ISIS soldiers.

Cody paid for his gas and left. He kept his eyes on the rearview mirror as he drove away to make sure no one followed him. Those people scared him.

"Mean fucking morons," he said to himself.

Back in the van, Cody drove about ten miles until he found the dirt road. There was no one in front of or behind him, so he turned and followed along until it ended at a big pile of household garbage mixed with tires, white goods, and other typical human detritus.

"The pigs can't even pay for garbage service," Cody thought. "The world will be better when they're all gone."

After positioning the van for a quick getaway, he sat in the driver's seat staring into the blackness. The sky was clouded, but it was still warm. He rolled down the window, feeling the soft breeze blow through the stuffy van. Luckily, he was upwind of the garbage. All he could smell was the fragrance of sandy pines.

He needed to get the anger out of his system before calling Victoria, so he got in the back to stretch out on his makeshift bed. Rummaging through his pack, he found his stash and loaded the pipe with a tiny piece of bud. He added another for good measure and then laid down, closed his eyes, and waited for the cannabinoids to do their thing.

Within two minutes he was feeling pretty good. He tapped the KCRW app on his phone, chose their Eclectic 24 music channel, popped in his ear buds, and let the music carry him away. He thought of Victoria's face, her body, and the feeling of holding her tight after their athletic sex. After twenty minutes, he was ready to make the call.

"Hey, sexy girl, what's up?"

"Oooohh...baby, you called just in time. I was thinking of hitting the sack soon, but now I'm wide awake. You do that to me, ya know?"

"Sorry it's so late, but the film biz doesn't care about my schedule—only its own. How was your day?"

"Good! Zak and I met with the Exxon attorney, and they sound like they'll settle. The video seemed to have an impact, if you know what I mean. Ha! You should've seen the bastard's look when he saw it. And speaking of bastards...did you hear about Rush? Holy shit! Two of the worst of the worst are dead! Man, who would've thought this would happen?"

"I did hear about it. Everyone at work was buzzing. He was probably the most hated man on the right. Wonder who'll replace him."

"Whoever it is, they gotta be wondering if the same thing will happen to them. Shit, whoever is killing these assholes is going to be a hero to the left. Already is a hero in my mind."

Cody smiled to himself.

"I wonder who it is, too. Probably ex-military. What did Zak say?"

"Zak was euphoric," she giggled. "We went out for a drink after the Exxon thing, and heard about it on the way to the bar. Zak was hooping and hollering like crazy. We got into a great talk with a couple of guys at the bar and took turns guessing who'd be next. It was great fun!"

"Based on the first two, the guy's going for the big ones. Speaking of big ones, how're your two doing?"

"Ha! They're as small as they were last night, but wait...the little nipples seem to be getting bigger! Lemme see...Yep, mmmm..."

Phone sex was better than no sex, but it left Cody longing for more. He fell asleep to the sounds of a million harmonizing crickets, while Victoria nodded off to the steady thrumming of a cold Seattle rain. Both dreamed of the other's embrace.

Cody awoke Sunday morning to a gray sky. It wasn't raining, but it looked as if it might start at any time. Before driving off, he pulled out a sandwich and checked his email. He had a note from his chess coach.

"Hey, Cody,

Long time, buddy! I hope this finds you well. I've been keeping up with you through Zak; maybe he told you. Anyway, he says you're coming back from LA soon, and I thought it would be good to catch up when you get home. Shoot me some times when you can handle a visit and maybe a few games of chess.

Your old pal,

Mel

PS: Amazing about Inhofe and Limbaugh! But don't good things come in threes?"

****

Reading the email filled Cody with happiness. He had such fond memories of his time with Mel. The chess lessons were great fun. And learning about EVs and efficiency, and racing around in his White Zombie. Cody knew Mel was the source of Zak's love of efficiency and clean energy, too.

The world needs more Mels and fewer Rushs, he thought. Well, at least we have one less Rush.

He wrote Mel a quick reply, saying he was a week away from returning home, and any time after that would work.

Back on the road, he thought about how far he had to drive and when he wanted to get home. His desire for Victoria was growing by the hour. He decided to pick up the pace and got on the freeway.

The mission was accomplished—for now. All he could think of was getting back to a normal life, but was that now impossible? He felt conflicted. He'd accomplished something big, but would it really result in positive change in Congress? In the Media? Did he have to go after someone in industry, too? Would he have to keep killing people until they understood what he wanted them to do?

That was the problem.

Cody was very clear in his head that those who were most responsible for climate change, either through political obstruction, media collaboration, or the industries directly responsible, would be targets. But no one else knew why these men were killed. Would it help if he could somehow let people know why this was happening? How would he do that without tipping his hand?

He scanned the dial for Rush reports. The AM stations were spewing hate and indignation. Their hero was gone, felled by an assassin. Many of them wanted revenge, but against who? Speculation was all over the map. The poor animal-rights guy who'd been detained by the FBI clearly wasn't guilty of the Limbaugh killing, but they kept him in custody anyway—just to give the impression they were doing their job. The guy didn't even own a gun and was an avowed pacifist.

Cody was halfway across the country having driven for two full days. Interstate 10 got him out of Florida and through Alabama and Mississippi. But after Louisiana and east Texas, he was tired of the deep south and took an alternative route further north. He kept cruise control on for most of the trip, sticking to the speed limit and driving in the trucker's lane, since this was the safest way to avoid accidents or speeding tickets. Red Bull and coffee allowed for long days behind the wheel, and long conversations with Victoria were now a nightly event. Cody made sure to find a quiet place to park so there wouldn't be traffic noise in the background. He felt awful keeping the truth from her.

Four days after Cody shot Limbaugh, FBI Agent Washington reported that ballistics confirmed both assassinations used the same rifle, a Winchester 70. The man being held in Oklahoma was released.

They found the spot from where Cody shot Limbaugh, but forensics found nothing of value, not so much as a loose hair. No witnesses saw anyone coming or going to the lot that morning. The FBI announced that the assassin was likely a pro, and they considered him to be highly dangerous and likely to strike again. Considering who he'd killed already, they were profiling him as a radical left-wing terrorist.

Cody thought it was all true, but they were missing the connection of the killings to the environment. If they didn't know, there would be no change in policy.

"I'm just going to have to tell them," Cody said to himself. He was about halfway across New Mexico, just past Albuquerque. The sky was a blazing blue, the air crisp and clean, and Cody suddenly knew he'd have to write a manifesto explaining why he'd killed these two men and why he would kill more.

The idea consumed him all afternoon. He outlined the piece in his head while driving. He was conflicted about wanting to get home and wanting to get this down in his computer. As the sun began to set, Cody started looking for a place to camp for the night. He'd never been in this part of the country and was blown away by its beauty. He wondered why people couldn't see such beautiful land as worth saving.

Several miles west of Gallup, New Mexico, just across the Arizona border, he found what seemed to be a safe place to stop. He'd been driving steeply uphill for over a mile, and when he turned around to position his van for his exit the next morning, Cody saw a stunning twilight glow over the distant mountains. He was enchanted to the point of euphoria. He clamored out to stretch his legs and stared at the jagged, backlit edge of a remote mountain range. Looking straight up, he saw the Milky Way, right there! A powdery frosting of light born of a billion stars. He'd only seen it in photographs and they just didn't compare to the real thing. Cody drank in the view. The cold air was crisp and the stiff breeze assured he would only get colder, so, not being dressed for it, he returned to the warm van.

It was time to write!

Chapter 19

Climbing into the passenger seat, Cody pulled open his laptop, his hands shaking from the cold and excitement, and began to write furiously.

DESERVING DEATH

A Manifesto for Correcting the Great Imbalance.

I killed James Inhofe and Rush Limbaugh. I intend to kill many more. Ironically, I am killing to stop the killing. My intent is to reduce the slaughter of millions, and eventually billions of humans due to climate change.

Scientists tell us the Earth's climate is warming because we burn carbon-based energy—oil, coal, and natural gas. The effects are already being felt, and while alarm bells are ringing all over the world, the industries responsible for this problem deny its very existence. The science is clear, however. If we continue on our current trajectory, we risk billions of lives, and there is a remote possibility that our planet could be rendered inhospitable to the human species.

It's that serious.

I didn't enter this world of death on a whim. I've seen cruelty on an industrial scale first hand. You don't see it because your media won't show it, but it's happening, and it will get much worse.

I'm well versed on the stranglehold corporations have over our government, in large part because of Citizens United and McCutcheon. Allowing unlimited dark money in politics and dumbing down our public-education system ensures that the 1% will be in power forever. Those at Fox News, Brietbart, and Drudge know they are mouthpieces for dirty-energy industries currying favor from our government. These monied interests have taken over most of our media.

Given this, it's clear there is no political solution.

I've watched with horror as local police forces armored up with military equipment and use this power to "control" civilians with legitimate complaints against our government. Corruption is everywhere and many good people seem to have given up fighting it.

I've been following the climate debate for years—and I know that solutions exist.

Three books have galvanized my position. Elizabeth Kolbert's *The Sixth Extinction* describes how thousands of species are going extinct every year due to our warming planet. These extinctions, and thousands more to come, are going to have devastating impacts on human life as populations grow and food supplies dwindle.

In the second book, *This Changes Everything*, Naomi Klein describes several attempts to stop the oil and mining industries from destroying nature. These efforts have had minimal success. Her book was meant to show how we can win against these powerful entities, but all it did was show how powerless we really are.

The third book, *Merchants of Doubt*, confirms that the liars with all the money will dominate our political process forever. The following quote says it all:

"And make no mistake, spewing hate has a significant impact upon society. It's the equivalent of modern-day propaganda: our population is barraged with a stream of consistent messaging. As ordinary people go about their daily lives, they're exposed repeatedly to the same ideas. Pretty soon, these notions begin to sink in and take effect. The audience begins to adopt a worldview consistent with these messages, regardless of whether they're true. It's a remarkable phenomenon.

"From Nazi Germany in the 1930s to Bosnia and Rwanda in the 1990s, history is replete with examples of propaganda's effectiveness in shaping public opinion. Many people are susceptible to it and can be swayed by it, especially the less educated.

In America today, right-wing media is engaged in this very same activity through Fox News and extremist talk radio. This network is constantly barraging its audience with a stream of consistent messaging. And this messaging is overwhelmingly negative and destructive."

Cody Cain http://bit.ly/1WhRjPi

I encourage everyone to read these books so you'll understand how serious the problems are.

We no longer have time to wait for a political solution. Overturning Citizens United and McCutcheon may eventually happen, and I encourage those working on this problem to keep fighting, but at least a decade will pass before any meaningful solution can come to pass, if at all. From what I've read, this may be too late.

So, after much thought, I've decided I have to kill Hitler. As the philosophical question goes, if you could go back to 1933 Germany and kill Hitler, knowing what he'd do in a few short years, would you do it, even if it meant you'd die in the process? Most people would say yes.

Taking another life in order to save millions of lives is, in the end, the right thing to do.

Polluters are turning our world into a "greenhouse gas chamber" that will cause the deaths of many orders of magnitude more people than Hitler ever killed. If you would kill Hitler, then you understand why these people need to die, too.

Those perpetrating climate change walk among us. Their numbers are now diminished by two.

I have drawn up a list of others who merit assassination. They include leaders in dirty-energy corporations. I'll not target those who work for these companies, although I can't promise there won't be collateral damage.

I'm also targeting those who, through their writing or speaking, engage in lies to maintain the status quo. Everyone on air at Fox News is a target. The right-wing bloggers, Fox wannabes—all merchants of doubt. The more prolific you are, the more effective you are, the more I will hunt you. Bjorn Lomborg—the "skeptical environmentalist"—and Marc Morano are paid mouthpieces for the fossil fuel industry. Morano's organization, Committee for a Constructive Tomorrow (CFACT), is full of these assholes. Watch him in the documentary *Merchants of Doubt*, and you'll want to strangle the guy. He's a huge soft target.

Also on my list:

The Center for the Study of Carbon Dioxide and Global Change, which calls carbon emissions an "elixir of life"; the George C. Marshall Institute, which claims there is not "the slightest evidence that more CO_2 has caused more extreme weather or accelerated sea level rise"; and Wei-Hock Soon, a researcher who has received over $1.2 million in funding from the fossil-fuel industry. All liars!

I expect to get caught eventually, perhaps soon. My hope is that others with more lethal skills and better weapons will step up and join the fight.

The Bush administration employed the "shock doctrine" after the attacks of 9/11 and invaded Iraq under false premises, murdering at least 100,000 civilians in the process. Thousands of our own soldiers died and hundreds of thousands were wounded. According to our VA, over 20 soldiers commit suicide every day. The Republicans refuse to properly fund the VA to take care of these men and women who volunteered to fight what they were told was a just war. But it was a war for oil prosecuted so that rich bastards running those oil companies could get even richer.

Despondent over what they did and what they saw, many of these soldiers are now killing themselves in greater numbers than we lost while fighting the war.

While many of our soldiers subscribe to the right-wing philosophy of Dominionism and are a big part of the problem, others are thoughtful, good people who believed they were doing the right thing by joining the military and fighting for their country. They now know they were lied to, that their buddies were killed for corporate profits, and they're royally pissed about it.

I encourage these soldiers to take up arms—not against your country, but against those corporatists and media lackeys who've destroyed true democracy, who start wars and send thousands to their death, and who will eventually cause the death of billions.

These people need to die. The sooner the better.

We'll not stop this madness by ourselves. I hope the assassinations we carry out will result in action on climate change. If we get a carbon tax from our efforts, that will be progress. If we get Congress to enact legislation removing money from politics, that will be a huge win! Only then will the people's voice be heard above the merchant of doubt lies.

So far, scientists and environmental activists seem to be speaking only to themselves. The right-wing machine has marginalized them. This is why Rush Limbaugh is dead, and every one of the Fox News talking heads is a target.

Security will be tighter, but this gives us a golden opportunity to infiltrate their security apparatus. Since many who seek jobs as security guards have military training, some of you might be able to get positions guarding these high-value targets. This would give you the opportunity to kill them with ease. Of course, that would mean giving up your life or getting captured and spending the rest of your days in prison. At least you'll know you did a good thing for society.

It's important to select only targets with the most blood on their hands. Remember, you signed up to fight for our country, but you ended up killing for corporations instead. The heads of those corporations are the highest-value targets. All of the oil, coal, and natural gas companies are targets. Anyone above mid-management level, including all members of boards of directors, are targets. Many of these are soft targets. They don't have security—at least not yet.

Anyone associated with pipelines, refineries, or oil extraction are targets. Anyone involved with the Western States Petroleum Association, the Interstate Oil and Gas Compact Commission, or the American Petroleum Institute is a target.

Corporate heads of military contractors are targets. The military-industrial complex Eisenhower warned about is as powerful as the energy sector. Many of these corporations share members on their boards. Most are public companies, so their names are a matter of public record. KBR and Halliburton are two good examples. A simple Google search will identify others. Who makes the tanks, the guns, the warships and bombers? Those are the people pushing for more wars. Seek them out and kill them.

Tobacco company executives are targets. They invented the merchants of doubt and their industry kills more people every year than any outside of dirty energy. Watch this: https://www.youtube.com/watch?v=e_ZDQKq2F08. All of them are targets.

Any politician taking dirty-energy money is a target. James Inhofe is example number one. Most are Republicans, but some are Democrats. Look at the state level, too. The energy people fund locally as well as nationally.

Anyone associated with the Drudge Report, Breitbart, or Michelle Malkin are targets. I got lucky with Rush Limbaugh, but now security has gotten tight, so others might be harder to hit.

These are particularly important targets: Glenn Beck, Ann Coulter, Laura Ingraham, Ben Shapiro, Dana Loesch, Bill O'Reilly, Sean Hannity, Grover Norquist, Mark Levin and Alex Jones. Evil people, every one.

Anyone associated with the right-wing organization, ALEC, is a target. Also the American Enterprise Institute, Americans for Prosperity, and the Heartland Institute.

There are many more, including
http://www.desmogblog.com/committee-constructive-tomorrow

http://www.desmogblog.com/2016/04/11/iogcc-oil-gas-fracking-stealth-lobby

****

"When plunder becomes a way of life for a group of men in our society, over the course of time they create for themselves a legal system that authorizes it, and a moral code that glorifies it."

-Frederick Bastiac

****

"WAR is a racket. It always has been.

It is possibly the oldest, easily the most profitable, surely the most vicious. It is the only one international in scope. It is the only one in which the profits are reckoned in dollars and the losses in lives.

-Major General Smedley Butler

****

In our country, too many innocent people are being killed by guns. Most of the killings are murders for no good reason. The NRA is complicit in these deaths through its lobbying of Congress. Its headquarters is in Fairfax, VA. If you feel the need to kill, there are people who have a huge negative impact on the Earth and our society. If they were dead, the world would be a better place. Some good would come from your action.

We need many changes to fix this world, but the two I'm most concerned with are making those who use dirty energy pay the full cost, and getting money out of politics.

One: Internalizing the external costs of dirty energy will hasten the transition to a clean and sustainable future—one that will have a positive impact on the environment, reduce military spending, improve citizens' health, and ensure our continued existence on this planet.

Two: Installing a limit on how much money can be spent on our elections and lobbying our representatives will give us our democracy back.

We need to overturn Citizens United, and we need to impose a stiff carbon tax on all forms of dirty energy. Those who cause harm must pay!

Our political problems stem from the willful ignorance and laziness of the American people. While many of you are conservative, most are not. That progressives do not control the government is on the shoulders of those who do not vote at the ballot box and those who do not vote with their dollars.

You want proof?
http://www.bostonglobe.com/metro/2015/10/31/environmental-group-goes-door-door-search-non-voters/splEps90zjSHrD1mimvNIM/story.html

"Earlier this year, researchers for the group found that nearly 16 million people who identify as environmentalists did not vote in the 2010 national elections."

We've managed to pass good legislation that will begin leveling the playing field for renewable energy and electric cars, but most Americans who could easily avail themselves of these options continue to use dirty energy instead. They do this even though many of them consider themselves "environmentalists."

Let me be clear: you cannot be an environmentalist if you continue to use dirty energy when viable options are readily available. You cannot hope to beat your political and strategic enemies while simultaneously purchasing their filthy products and funding their operations.

Merchants of doubt have filled millions of minds with lies. It's up to you to discern truth from these lies.

Only science is real. "Beliefs" are not.

We are at war with the corporatists who have stolen our country. We'll succeed in killing some of them, but if the millions of you who want a clean environment and a political process not controlled by the 1% do not vote and take actions to reduce or eliminate your use of dirty energy, then we cannot win.

Stop buying dirty energy, stop polluting, and VOTE.

I'll leave you with this:

When you die, if the world is a better place because you lived, you succeeded. If the world is not better because of your existence, you failed. It's that simple. You know right from wrong, good from bad. Act accordingly.

REVEAL CHECK MOTHERFUCKERS!

Gambit

****

Cody felt satisfied with the draft, but figured he'd sleep on it. He threw on a jacket and jumped outside to once more take in the magnificent night sky before his shivering body finally forced him back into the van.

The relief he felt completing the manifesto produced a serenity he hadn't experienced in years. It read like a rant, but it seemed he'd articulated the whole of the problem. It felt good. Cody's entreaty to disgruntled vets was something his enemies would have to deal with, potentially for a long time. This was the meaning of the chess term, "reveal check."

The phone rang just as he opened the door to his van. Victoria's number glowed on the screen, and he thought for a brief moment he'd let it go to voicemail, but at the last second, he picked up.

"Oh, baby, I'm so glad you called. I just finished wri...working on a tough shot, the last of the day. I'm so done with this job. I might get to leave tomorrow, definitely by the next day. I want to see your pretty face. I'm so sorry I didn't take a picture of you before I left. All I have is this great memory, nice as it is, but I want to see you. And hold you. Kiss you. And, you know, that other stuff."

They both giggled. This call would end up with another hot session of mutual self-gratification, but both of them were jonesing for the real thing.

****

Morning. Cold. An incredibly bright sunbeam penetrated the driver's side window, filling the van with light. Cody crawled out of his sleeping bag and turned on NPR. Expecting to hear an update on Inhofe and Limbaugh, he was surprised to hear another name instead.

"Supreme Court Justice Antonin Scalia was found dead this morning in Texas. No foul play is indicated, but in light of the recent assassinations of Senator Inhofe and talk-show host Rush Limbaugh, local police and the FBI are not discussing the cause of death until an autopsy is performed."

Cody sat up straight. He was now wide awake.

This was huge news on many levels. How would it play in the media? Would the FBI spend time looking for clues that didn't exist? Would this make his work harder or easier?

Within minutes of the announcement, Mitch McConnell announced that the Senate would block anyone President Obama nominated to the court.

"Fuckers!" Cody screamed, noting how short his temper had become.

The Republicans claimed to be strict Constitutionalists, but here they were trying to block a sitting president from carrying out his duties as they are clearly outlined in the Constitution.

"Fuck those bastards!"

He downed his last Red Bull and carefully made his way back down the dirt road to the freeway. With the powerful desert sun in his side mirror fueling his growing anger, Cody headed west across Arizona toward home.

He thought how their side would stop at nothing to win. Killing people was just a consequence of doing business. Like other good people pushed too far, Cody felt compelled to take what he thought to be the only viable action that would fix the problem. He began to perceive of himself as an evolutionary abnormality set in motion by a power beyond his control.

Cody knew the reality of the issues at hand. The physics and economics were clear and simple, and the money so massive that the most powerful people on the planet would stop at nothing to keep and expand their status quo. But to do this, they needed buy-in from the public. As long as there were no alternatives, that would be easy. Now that solar and wind were cheaper than coal and gas, and EVs were better and cheaper than internal combustion vehicles, some of these powerful people understood that transitioning to renewable electricity and electric transportation was inevitable.

And this scared the shit out of them.

Americans spend close to two trillion dollars every year for dirty energy. Its producers didn't want any of that money going toward clean alternatives. But they knew the best they could do was slow the transition. The proverbial cat had gotten out of the bag.

Tesla was delivering tens of thousands of the best cars ever made to celebrities, car enthusiasts, and thought-leaders. Contracts for solar and wind energy were selling for less than coal. Word was getting out that better alternatives were here now.

Energy and transportation was only part of it. Pharmaceuticals, agriculture, media, banking, and of course, defense, were all sectors where money spent on lobbyists and political races earned astronomical returns.

Need to sell more weapons? Start another war.

"Good god!" Cody thought, "They've got it all tied up so nice and neat."

He knew there was no easy fix. He'd seen too many Facebook posts where people complained about the world's problems. Then they'd go right out and buy gasoline and dirty electricity. It didn't occur to them that they were the problem. Cody hoped his manifesto would change that.

****

Cody needed to get his manifesto to the media. He'd collected email addresses of political writers at the NY Times, LA Times, Washington Post, and lots of left-leaning bloggers, but he couldn't just email the document to them from his laptop at a Starbucks.

He knew enough about computers to know that all documents contained metadata that could be traced back to the computer on which it was written. But he figured if he printed the manifesto, then scanned its pages into a PDF, he should be able to find a library and send it to all these editors at once without being traced.

He hoped he was right about this since he didn't have a good alternative.

Stopping for lunch in Winslow, AZ, Cody found a copy shop where he printed the document. He deleted the file from the printer cache before leaving to look for a library with a scanner and computers.

The copy shop was safe, since he was just printing and no one would ever know he stopped there, but FBI would swarm the library pretty quickly once they traced the email to the computer that had sent it. He should wear a disguise and be careful with his fingerprints.

Before he left Winslow, he stopped at a second-hand store to buy a hat and a pair of old jeans. He also found a long-haired wig he would wear under the hat.

He hoped using a small-town library in Arizona or southern California would throw off those who'd search for him.

He drove for hours until reaching Kingman, AZ, around 4 pm, which gave him plenty of time. The Mohave County Library was located just a couple blocks off the freeway and a block away from a Walmart. He parked in the store's lot instead of the library in case cameras were monitoring its exterior.

He grabbed a canvas grocery bag and threw in his laptop, the copy of the manifesto, some paper napkins, a small bottle of rubbing alcohol, and a notepad with a black sharpie. Donning the wig, sunglasses, the old jeans, a nondescript white t-shirt and a floppy hat, he looked in the van's mirror to gauge whether someone looking at security footage would be able to recognize him. He felt it would be tough for even Zak to tell it was him.

Stepping out into the sunlight, he felt the heat. It had to be almost 90. As he approached the library, he picked up a small pebble and stuck it in his right shoe. This gave him a slight limp, enough so his walk wouldn't look familiar.

There were no cameras in the parking lot, nor any at the library's entrance. The building's air conditioner was on full blast, chilling Cody in the light T-shirt.

He walked past the front desk without acknowledging the young woman tending to a small child's question. With purpose, he marched over to the far side of the large main room, laying his bag on a table. He chose a chair with its back to the wall so he could observe the whole room. After removing the sunglasses, he opened his laptop and pretended to read while glancing around for a computer, hoping he could find everything he needed without having to ask anyone.

There was a public computer not too far from the front desk. Two women were using it, so he walked over to the periodical section to look for a newspaper to read while waiting.

A New York Times headline caught his eye: "Scalia Death Ruled Natural: No Connection to Inhofe/Limbaugh Murders." He took the paper back to his table and sat down to read, careful not to touch anything with his fingers. The newspaper was OK, since they generally threw them out every day, and the FBI wouldn't be able to trace the location and arrive there until the next day.

While reading, he noticed an article about the billionaire Koch brothers plotting an assault on electric cars.

"What the hell?" Cody thought. "It's bad enough they use their money to stymie legislation, but now they're going to spend millions to convince people not to buy EVs. More merchants of doubt shit!"

His anger grew near the boiling point. He wished he'd named the Kochs in his manifesto, but it was too late. He did, however, decide to target them next, but he needed to go home first and plan the attack carefully. They wouldn't be an easy target, especially after his manifesto hit the media.

The two women finished with the computer and walked away. Cody glanced around and didn't see anyone else who looked like they were waiting, so he grabbed his bag, leaving the New York Times open to the Koch story, and sauntered over to the computer. He pulled out the notepad and sharpie. Naturally left handed, he wrote with his right: "THIS IS REAL. PLEASE TAKE IT SERIOUSLY."

There was an old scanner next to the computer, so Cody retrieved some paper napkins and with his back to the front desk, he raised the scanner cover with a napkin and placed the scrawled note on the glass. After scanning it, he scanned all five pages of the manifesto into a file, labeling it "Kingman Chess Club." He returned the documents to his bag.

Now he just needed to key in the journalists' addresses. This took quite a while since he had to watch for typos. He also need to create a compelling subject line. He settled on, "I Killed Inhofe & Limbaugh." There was no guarantee anyone would run with the story, but he felt certain someone would. He only needed one.

Once ready to hit send, Cody glanced around the room. No one was paying him any heed. He sat very still. This was as big a step as firing that round into Inhofe's head. Once he pushed send, a shit storm was sure to follow and he couldn't predict how it would end. He'd been very careful so far, but the FBI and NSA had formidable tools. Deep down, he knew his life was probably going to be cut short—either he'd die in a quick firefight, or he'd be captured and sentenced to life in prison.

Cody hit send.

The burden lifted, his pulse quickened. He deleted the file. Not that they wouldn't find it, but he might as well make them look for it.

He pulled out the small bottle of rubbing alcohol and, using another napkin, surreptitiously wiped the keyboard clean of his fingerprints. Next he checked to make sure everything he'd brought into the library was in his bag. He then limped casually into the bright February sunlight.

Once in the van, he took off the wig and hat and drove out of the Walmart parking lot.

As he covered the two blocks back to the freeway, a dozen or so journalists were clicking on a startling email. Their pulses quickened as they read. Most were on the phone a half page in. Before Cody had traveled two miles, alarm bells were ringing in newsrooms and bloggers' circles all over the country.

The New York Times was first to contact the FBI. A Buzzfeed blogger was first to run, with a quick teaser story online. Within 30 minutes, Cody heard NPR break into its live feed with correspondent Dina Temple-Raston, who'd immediately called Agent Washington of the FBI.

The NPR announcer said, "We're interrupting our program to go to Dina Temple-Raston who has a breaking story on the assassinations. Dina?"

Temple-Raston: "We at NPR have received an email from someone claiming responsibility for the deaths of Senator Inhofe and Rush Limbaugh. Other media outlets are reporting receiving the same document. I'm on the line with Agent Washington of the FBI. Agent Washington, can you tell us whether this manifesto is real?"

Cody looked at his watch, 5:17. This had happened quickly.

Washington: "The New York Times forwarded us the document just a few minutes ago, so we're just now looking it over. It reads as though it could be real, but it's too soon to say for certain."

Temple-Raston: "Do you think you have a better understanding of who this person is?"

Washington: "From our first read, the motivation seems to be based on the environment, climate change. Most troubling is his attempt to recruit veterans to his cause."

Temple-Raston: "In what way does he recruit veterans?"

Washington: "I'm not going to elaborate or speculate on that at this time. Our focus is on verifying this document, finding this man, and stopping him. He states that he'll continue. He even provided a list of potential targets."

Temple-Raston: "It's quite extensive."

Washington: "Yes, the list consists of people this person deems guilty of hurting the environment. Mostly it's a list of groups, but several individuals are named."

Temple-Raston: "Can you tell us who is—"

"Damn, that worked like a charm," Cody gleefully exclaimed as he looked for a Limbaugh station, tuning to KAAA 1230 out of Kingman right in the middle of a blathering tirade from Glenn Beck.

He sensed fear in Beck's angry voice. Most likely, this was all part of his act, but it could be genuine fear. Beck was a high profile talk-show host, second only to Rush in the conservative universe, and Cody had listed him as a target. Maybe he worried his bodyguard might pop him at close range. This was exactly the kind of reaction Cody had hoped for.

These radio stories buoyed Cody's attitude. He decided to drive straight across the Mojave in the cool of the night and get to Bakersfield. From there, it was a day and a half to Seattle.

Back at the library, the librarian was folding up all the newspapers, including the New York Times still open to the Koch brothers story—the one with Cody's fingerprints. She threw the papers into a recycle bin and a hard-working Latino man picked them up a few hours later on his paper-recycling route.

The FBI was already tracing the email to the library's computer, and an agent would fly in from Phoenix to meet the librarian at 11 pm. The poor woman would get little sleep that night. A forensics team would arrive in the morning.

Chapter 20

Cody pulled up in front of Zak's house mid-afternoon. It was an exhausting last few days. He parked at the curb, turned off the engine and then noticed the LEAF in the driveway plugged in and charging. "Damn!" he thought, "What'll I do?" He needed to get the rifle inside without Zak seeing it.

No telling what Zak was doing. When he was working, he tended to situate himself in his study, so maybe that's where Cody would find him.

He grabbed his computer and a few loose items and walked in. The front door was unlocked, so Zak was definitely home.

"Hey, Zak!" Cody hollered as he came in.

"Yo, Cody!" came a muffled reply from the study. Cody could hear Zak with each heavy footstep. Dilly scampered into the room from the kitchen and jumped on a chair next to Cody, pushing his head into Cody's arm to make sure he got his head scratched.

"Welcome home, roomie! How was the drive? Is your movie gonna win the Oscar? It better have some black people in it, or else."

That last comment went right over Cody's head. He had completely missed the Oscars.

"It rained like a mother in Eugene last night and this morning, but it cleared up before I hit Olympia. It's a long goddamn drive. Next time, I'll fly."

"We gotta talk about the killings, that manifesto, holy crap! Victoria tells me she's been keeping you up on things."

"Oh, she's got me 'up' all right. I can't thank you enough for bringing her home that night. She's making me dinner at her place, so you'll have to fend for yourself one more night."

"She's a dream client. Smart as hell, and I've never met a more committed enviro. You don't want to be on her hit list, I'll tell you that."

Cody thought about his own list. That was the list you didn't want to be on!

"She's incredibly sexy, both physically and mentally. It's her mind that makes me want her more than anything. I haven't felt this way since Jazzie."

"Damn, boy, I envy the shit out of you!" Zak slapped him on the back as he said this. "Man you stink! When's the last time you took a shower?"

Cody realized it had been days.

"Sorry, I let things go while I was finishing up the last few shots. I'm gonna empty the van and then shower. Maybe we can smoke a bit after and catch up before I go over to Victoria's."

"Sure, need some help with the van?"

"No, I got it. You don't want to get anywhere close to my clothes, man. If you think I smell bad..."

"Got it. I'm finishing up some stuff, so holler when you're fresh and clean."

"Will do."

At the van, Cody strapped the rifle in its towel to the bike frame. He then took an arm load of his dirty shirts and let them cover most of the bike such that the rifle wasn't visible. It would look like Cody was trying to save trips by carrying as much as possible at once. He got the bike and gun inside and, while Zak was busy in the study, carried everything upstairs, where he quickly unstrapped the rifle and stashed it in his clos-et.

Two more trips to the van and it was cleaned out. He'd return the van in the morning.

Dilly loved the pile of dirty clothes. She'd laid claim to it while Cody was getting the last of his stuff, her paws kneading the smelly garments infused with Cody's essence.

"Dilly girl, did you miss me?" Cody said as he picked her up and held her tight. "I really missed you. I did some crazy stuff while I was gone. Did you hear about it? I hope they don't take me away from you, baby."

After his shower, he carried Dilly downstairs where Zak was waiting in his office with a loaded bong.

"Here you go, Mr. big time movie guy. You probably didn't get too much of this down there, I bet."

"Ha! It's the film biz, man. They got pot in California, Zak. Lots of it. That war's been won." Cody took his turn with the bong.

While he was holding the smoke in, Zak asked, "Jeezus, what do you think about the assassinations? Rush and Inhofe both! And then Scalia dies, too! Trifecta!"

Blowing out the smoke, Cody replied, "I was working a lot and trying not to listen to the news, but everyone at the studio was buzzing over it, so yeah, we were pretty happy. Do you think it's more than one guy?"

"Didn't you hear about the manifesto?"

"Yeah, but I haven't seen it. You got a copy?"

"One sec," Zak said, turning to his computer to bring it up to print. "The guy who did it wrote this kick-ass manifesto admitting his role in the assassinations—Inhofe and Rush, but not Scalia. Scalia apparently died of a severe karmic reaction from all the bullshit he did on the court." Both laughed. "But the interesting thing was he killed them because of their involvement in climate change! Check it out." While the document was printing, he took his turn on the bong, handing the pages to Cody one at a time as they came out of the printer.

As he read, Cody said, "Oh man, this guy is a man after my own heart!"

"Wait until you get to the veterans part," Zak replied.

"Jeezus! He's recruiting suicidal vets to join his cause! Holy shit! That's gonna raise eyebrows in certain circles. Might make some of those targets reconsider their positions."

"That's his intent. Read the target list. It's a who's-who of the bad guys. He even threw in tobacco and military contractors. And some of the players from *6th Extinction* and *Merchants of Doubt*."

"Marc Moreno!" Cody exclaimed. "He's the guy in *Merchants of Doubt* wearing the blue shirt, right?"

"The one and only. Remember how pissed we were at him after seeing the film? We both wanted to strangle the guy."

"Yeah, he stood out in my mind, too. Man, this is amazing. Do you think they'll catch him?"

"Don't know. But if they do, he'll be a martyr to a lot of people. I'm mostly curious about whether any vets will join his movement. That'd scare the shit out of the bad guys. I wonder how they'll screen recruits for security teams now. They're going to need some good psychological profiling before they hire anyone. Even then, the targets' movements will be curtailed some."

"Maybe that's what he wanted," Cody said. "Who do you think is next on his list?"

"It's a long list," Zak said, "it could be a lot of people. I know who I'd like to see die. The Koch fucks. Did you see they're spending millions fighting EVs? EVs! I can't believe anyone would try to kill the EV again. I bet they've armored up their security already. You can bet they're scrutinizing their veterans like crazy."

"You're probably right." Cody was ready to move onto another subject. It was hard for him to keep up the ruse. "Sorry to put an end to this guessing game, but I have a beautiful woman waiting for me to come eat what she has to offer!"

Zak laughed and said, "Don't blame you for that. We can talk more tomorrow. Enjoy yourself!"

Cody bounded upstairs to get his bike. While there, he texted Victoria for her address and was pleased to see she lived less than two miles away.

Victoria met him at the door of her small bungalow dressed in jeans, running shoes, and a sheer red camisole with no bra. Her perfect breasts beckoned as she smiled. Cody looked at her from head to toe, finally staring into her eyes and seeing the same emotions mirrored back at him. They embraced tightly while Victoria reached around behind him to close the door.

"I missed you so much, Victoria. It's been a long three weeks. Your face is as beautiful as I remembered. So, so beautiful." He kissed her long and deep.

"Cody, I've never wanted someone as much as I want you. How did you do this to me after one freaking night?"

Holding her face in his hands as though it were a precious vase, he slowly brought her lips to his for a second kiss, holding this one longer than the first.

More than a minute passed, their tongues entwining. Victoria gently pushed away and, taking his hand, led him to her bedroom. She took off his jacket and two shirts, running her hands over his chest and caressing his neck. He then removed her silky camisole, revealing her small perky breasts and hard nipples.

Her two cats were unceremoniously bounced from their comfortable sleeping spots as Cody and Victoria crashed onto the bed. The warm spots where the cats had been sleeping felt good to Cody's back as Victoria quickly removed her jeans and climbed on top of him.

When it was over, Victoria had scored three orgasms, and Cody two. A first for him.

"I came twice, baby. Look what you did to me!"

"Three for me! I think we're compatible, no?"

They rolled around in bed for over half an hour, exploring each other's body and learning what each other liked, which was a lot.

Eventually, hunger conquered horny, so they got up and dressed just enough for dinner. When they left her bedroom, the kitties jumped back on the warm bed.

Victoria made a great lasagna served with the best French bread of Cody's life. A bottle of red wine completed the meal. Initially talking about Cody's adventures in LA, they segued to the assassinations and this unusual killer who was targeting bad guys. Victoria, like Zak, was strongly behind the ideas he communicated in his manifesto. While Gambit had been extraordinarily passionate and unrestrained in his appeal to the public at large, and veterans in particular, the underlying arguments were sound.

"What do you think his endgame is?" Victoria asked.

"Well, he wants a tax on carbon and money out of politics. That part's clear. Those are both great end games, but ... I dunno, you think it's possible he'll get either?"

"Ha! Not bloody likely! Those guys on his hit list are the most powerful people on the planet. They're not likely to give an inch. They'll protect themselves real good, and the FBI, NSA, and any number of intelligence agencies will eventually catch the poor guy. He'll be martyred for sure."

Cody's buoyant mood got knocked down a notch.

Sensing his mood drop, she offered, "But if his call for veterans to come to the fight works even a little, that changes everything. Can you imagine what the fuckers in oil company boardrooms would do if their own bodyguards started killing them?"

"Actually, yeah, I can. Wouldn't take more than one or two to really shake things up. And once the first one happens, it'll encourage others. Who knows how far that could go. But will they do it? Most of the guys I fought with were right-wing assholes who just liked to kill. But not all of them. There were a few like me who hated the war once they realized what a fucked-up place Iraq was. And when we realized the war was based on lies, that pissed us off something fierce. I could see some of 'em doing this. Not many, but some."

"Well, here's hoping something good comes from the killing." Victoria held up her wine glass for a toast. Cody saw a strange combination of sadness and hope in her face. Her beautiful, beautiful face.

Cody and Victoria spent their second night together in a physical and emotional bliss the likes of which neither had ever experienced. Cody woke up next to her as dawn was breaking. The two cats were asleep between them. He felt he was dreaming. All the crazy stuff he'd done was a nightmare, and now he was awake in the real world, lying in bed next to a wonderful woman. All that other stuff was merely a media story, something happening in a parallel existence.

He'd met Victoria a mere three weeks before, the night before he left on his road trip to kill. And already he was feeling this intense physical and emotional euphoria. What a crazy strange life, he thought.

He stared at her sleeping face in the dim light, so serene, so beautiful. He leaned close and smelled her skin: just a hint of plumeria, the Hawaiian flower of love, barely noticeable and very pleasant, like a warm island afternoon. He held tightly to this pleasant thought and gradually drifted back to sleep.

When he next awoke, Victoria was downstairs in the kitchen making coffee. On the radio, Donovan played: "Sunshine came softly through my window today..." Outside, the sky was blue, the ground wet. Pink and white crocuses covered with a soft rime frost lay scattered along the edges of her front yard glowing in the rimmed light of the low winter sun.

"Good morning, sunshine!" she said.

Cody had slept soundly. His eyes were barely open and he had bed head. He brightened at the sight of his love, cup in hand, smiling with those mesmerizing eyes. Oh, man, was he a lucky guy!

Thoughts of his horrible actions had been creeping back into his consciousness, but her presence vanquished the painful memory like fog in the desert. He wanted to stare at her forever.

"Morning, gorgeous!" he whispered. They kissed long and deep. Her warm, sexy body, enclosed within a soft layer of plumeria-scented skin, melded into his. He snuggled his chin into the crook of her neck and nuzzled like a purring cat. He didn't want to let her go. He felt that, as long as he held her tight, the memories would never return.

Through the bay window a bright, warm shaft of light played across the paisley cotton tablecloth. Victoria motioned for Cody to sit. As he slid into the booth, he just beamed at her. He was silly in love. Yet, his mind began roiling again with what he'd done.

He struggled to ignore the horrendous acts he'd committed, all while desperately trying to crawl back into the mind of his youth, to the innocence of the Cody who loved Jazzie.

Without knowing why, he began to tear up. Victoria noticed the glint of moisture in his eyes as she put the coffee down and slid in beside him.

"You OK, sweetie? What's up?"

He smiled a weak smile and looked down. He thought of Jazzie. He'd told her he loved her after their first time having sex and repeatedly until that terrible day she was killed. In the decade since, he'd never said, nor felt, this way toward another woman until now.

"I...I'm just so happy to be here with you. Right here, right now. It's been a long time since I felt this...this..." a tear fell. "It feels like love." He watched the sunshine through the window. "Too soon?"

Victoria had heard that word a lot in her years of dating, but it never had this ring of authenticity. She'd never been in love—not the real thing anyway. Lots of puppy love or lust, but not that "I'll do anything for you" kind of love we all deserve to experience at least once in our lives.

"Oh, Cody." Her face softened. "No one's excited me like you have. I love how you think, how you look, and your passion for all things good. You make me very, very happy, and you saying that thrills me to my core. I love you, too."

Cody was floating. He wanted to stay with Victoria forever and never go back out into the world, that god awful world.

Cody grasped her face in his hands for another slow kiss. He no longer wanted to be a killer of evil men. He only wanted to love Victoria and lead a normal life in a sane world.

If only he could.

Victoria would have to leave for work eventually, but she owned her own company, so she could go in late. More great sex was on the agenda...

Chapter 21

After a couple of weeks had passed, Cody sat scrolling through Twitter, checking for mentions of the manifesto, when he came across a video showing a Manhattan-size iceberg breaking up and melting into the ocean. The massive ice shelves were really moving; it was like watching a pack of chunky school children push past each other into a pool, but the scale of it, the sheer horrifying scale of it, was nauseating. Cody felt his guts tighten up; this horror show, yet another totally preventable atrocity, was the result of climate change, of course. He felt suddenly restless; why was he here playing house, when he should be out there, doing his work?

"You all right, hon?" Victoria said, noticing Cody's tensed shoulders and his frown.

"Yeah. No. I can't—I'm watching glaciers melt on my fucking phone, you know?"

"Let me see." She sat down next to him. Cody noticed her ass, the way he always did, but even it only offered a faint reprieve from his mood.

"Damn," Victoria murmured softly. She cupped his hand holding the phone with her own to continue watching the video. "Baby, you're shaking."

Cody stood up abruptly and dropped the phone on the table. "God, I hate stupid people. I hate them for what they're doing to this planet."

"I know, but you gotta calm down," she said. In her work as a journalist, Victoria had interviewed people from the entire socioeconomic and emotional spectrum: meth-heads, billionaires, prisoners and census takers. She had talked to a murderer on death row once for a story about recidivism; she remembered how, even through the plate glass window, she could feel the rattle of his hands, the judder of the prison's steel counter as he recounted how angry his victim had made him. Cody's hand had been shaking like that. Victoria swallowed and closed her robe around her.

"Calm down?" Cody shouted, and then seeing the look on her face, he breathed out heavily. She was right: why was he getting so angry? He felt love for her again, and suddenly the buzzing rage seemed distant, almost ridiculous. That wasn't who he was, or it wasn't who he had to be, not anymore. He was taking things into his own hands; he was solving problems.

But Victoria seemed less sure. "Are you having a flashback?"

"Flashback?" Cody said, with slightly more heat than he had intended. "More like a Flashnow! Look at this shit."

"I know you've been dealing with your PTSD really well lately, but you're not looking too great right now," Victoria said firmly. Cody both admired and was slightly frightened by her steeliness; it was the other side of the woman who paraded around in front of him in her favorite undies while cooking dinner. But it also annoyed him: she was misreading his signals, and he couldn't tell her the truth. All he wanted to do was be honest with her, but he couldn't.

"I'm not...it's not that," Cody spluttered. He pressed his palms into his eyes. "Christ."

"I think you should lie down."

"I don't want to lie down," he said as calmly as he could.

"So what is it?" She crossed her legs and Cody felt a spike of arousal shoot through him. "Why are you so angry?"

The choice was how to lie to her. He saw now that everything in this life he wanted and loved had always been temporary, would always be taken away from him. She was here now but a time would come when he would never see her again, never touch her. Every goddamn minute he spent angry with her was another minute he would not get back. He sighed.

"I think I am a little tired, and you're right, I should go lie down," he said finally.

"We don't have to go the party tonight if you don't feel like it," she said.

Ah, the party. After the initial court date and a few private meetings, the gas station had quickly decided to settle, and agreed to pay a sizable fine to the state for the environmental damage and a separate settlement to Victoria for her harassment charge. Zak had a big payday, too, so he planned a large party at his house to celebrate. He had invited all of his radical friends, attorneys, enviros, and drinking buddies. Cody had invited Heather and his friends at the shelter. And Victoria had invited a few of her friends—some from her running group, three of whom were models for her lingerie line.

"No, I'm really looking forward to it," Cody said. He managed to smile finally as he took Victoria's hands into his own. "Let me get a little sleep, get into the party mood."

Cody was still a little unsettled as they drove up to Zak's house later that night. He was hiding it well—a spontaneous lovemaking session post-nap had restored both of their spirits—but the underlying sense of urgency was still there. He felt split, as if he was watching himself climb out of the car, reach for the bottle of Johnny Walker Red, and knock powerfully on Zak's big wooden door.

"Amigos!" Zak shouted joyously as he threw open the door to the couple. "Come in, come in. I'm just telling everyone about that perjuring gas-station owner. Hey guys, you know Cody and Victoria!" The assembled, smiling and rosy-cheeked, saluted Cody and Victoria with glasses at varying levels of capacity before Zak, in full storytelling mode, cheerfully spoke over them. "The guy's attorney had to cover his face! Poor schmuck. Even Exxon's lawyers couldn't help his case. Almost felt bad, seeing all that corporate money go down the drain."

"Hey, Cody!" Heather grabbed him by the elbow, pulling him away from one of Victoria's lingerie model friends, who he had just introduced to one of his running buddies. "Look at you! Coupledom suits ya."

The story of Cody and Victoria's whirlwind romance had spread through the party. Heather smiled and pinched Cody's cheek, like an overly chummy aunt, and laughed at herself as Cody looked at her warmly. "Just wanted to say, she's beautiful. And I'm so happy for you. Now get back there." Heather pushed him away, past the now-flirting lingerie model and running buddy, and right next to Victoria. Cody finally felt his mood lift and luxuriated in the moment. He stuck close to Victoria as they meandered through the party, meeting friends of friends and making new ones. Most of the guys were envious of his good fortune: Victoria was gorgeous, fit, and had the balls to stand up to Exxon.

As the drinking and pot smoking turned everyone—even those not imbibing—into loud, wild partiers, the evening peaked. Things quieted down after some began to leave around midnight. Coffee was made, and those still there settled in the large living room, where discussion turned to the assassinations.

Virtually everyone thought the killings were a good thing, though a few people thought the murders were counterproductive. They were clearly in the minority, however, especially when talk turned to the manifesto: Cody's logic was solid. In the moment, however, he pretended to be stoned, taking an extreme interest in his coffee in order to avoid saying anything. Still, he was pleased to note that even those who found it counterproductive to kill agreed that the manifesto was solid.

Victoria then offered, "The problem is if someone assassinates right-wing assholes, progressives are also likely to be killed. The right has a tradition of assassination, killing abortion doctors for instance." Cody took note of this jarring comment, but didn't say anything. Others in the room murmured assent, however.

Zak said, "Even if Scalia wasn't killed by this guy, it's a clear win for us. Obama's nominee probably won't get confirmed, but either Clinton or Sanders will pick the next judge, and they might have a Democratic Senate to make it an easy confirmation. That's a huge win for our side!"

"True that," Heather added, "but I want to know who's next on Gambit's list. Good things come in threes, and I don't count Scalia as being number three."

Several people in the room shouted out names: "The Koch fucks!" "Bill O'Reilly" "The Kochs! They're the worst of the worst!" Consensus centered on the Kochs. There were any number of reasons, but their recent pledge to fight EVs was foremost on people's minds. Cody listened intently, and Heather's mention of things coming in threes reminded him he owed Mel a call.

"Did you all read what Gambit said about the people's responsibility in this mess?" Cody asked with as much innocence as he could muster. "What do you think about that?"

"Oh, you mean driving electric cars?" one of the rescue volunteers said.

Many in the room had already switched to electric cars, or no cars at all. Some, who had not yet switched, squirmed at Cody's question and vowed to do so soon. Victoria and her friends were among them and they then talked about the best available plug-ins.

Cody stated the nut of the problem as succinctly as he could. "Without some legislation taxing dirty energy, the transition to clean energy will take too long to mitigate the effects of climate change. As long as unlimited dark money is allowed in politics, there will be no political solution."

Victoria smiled at him with a mixture of pride and a flicker of something else; hesitation? Curiosity? He watched her watching him for a second, captivated by her beauty but also slightly wary. What did she see? What was she looking at exactly? Did she suspect?

"I know, right!" said Claire, one of the lingerie models. The spell between Victoria and Cody had been broken. "We spend all of our time complaining, but when do we actually do anything? Take some damn responsibility, already."

Her remark was met with the boisterous enthusiasm of an intoxicated party winding down. Cody felt their love for him, but he also felt a sense of helplessness. Were these just the convenient declarations of a pot-fogged evening, or would people take real action in the light of day? Most of the people in this room were as left-wing as you could get, and yet maybe only a half of them were going to actually fight climate change. What did that mean for the nation as a whole?

As Zak reunited everyone with their coats and purses, Cody gripped Victoria's hand. He knew now, perhaps even more so than before, that he had to continue his mission.

"Zak, babe, if you had an extra X chromosome, you best believe I'd be taking you home," Heather said mock-flirtatiously as she gave the attorney her card. "But I dig you, man. Let's hang out soon."

Zak hugged her tight. "So glad to meet you, lady. And let's strategize about those animal abusers you were talking about when I'm sober enough again to read twelve point."

Heather laughed and closed the door behind her.

Cody led Victoria upstairs to his room. They were both tired, but Victoria was elated to have met so many like-minded people and heartened by promises from those who hadn't yet acted to fight climate change to get on board. They were too tired for sex, so they snuggled under the covers to keep warm. Victoria fell asleep instantly, but Cody stayed awake well past dawn.

Chapter 22

The next morning, a steady cold rain was pattering on the window. Cody watched Victoria wake up. She smiled sleepily at him. He tucked a strand of hair behind her ear, then kissed her. "I'm going to try to see an old friend of mine named Mel today. It would be great if you could meet him. He emailed me while I was gone."

"Good morning to you too," Victoria said, but then yawned happily. "Is he coming here? Maybe he can come over for lunch?"

"I'll ask. I'm going to call him soon."

"Oh, wait. I have a photo shoot today. What time is it?" Victoria picked up her phone and winced at the display. "I need to make tracks."

As Victoria hopped in the shower, Cody picked up the bedside extension.

"Mel, long time, ol' man. How's your chess game these days?"

"Cody! So good to hear your voice. I'm fine mostly. I'm having some minor problems, nothing big. How's your new girlfriend? Zak told me about her."

Cody looked toward the shower. He imagined the water running over Victoria's body. "She's amazing, I gotta say. Don't know how I got so lucky. Hey, do you want to come up here for lunch? I know Zak wants to see you, too."

"The White Zombie is fully charged and raring to go. I can be there around 1:00. Does that work?"

"Sure. I'll tell Zak. See you then."

The rain had abated by the time the Zombie pulled into Zak's driveway. Zak charged his LEAF in his garage, but years earlier, he'd installed a plug specifically so his friend could make the round trip from down south. The White Zombie was set up for sprint racing, not long distance, but Mel could easily make the one-way trip to Seattle, charge his car, and then go back home.

"Mel! Come in, come in!" Zak greeted everyone heartily, but Mel warranted a big hug and a slap on the back. "Cody, Mel's here."

"Be right down," he shouted from upstairs.

Zak noticed a stoop to Mel's shoulders that hadn't been there before. His grey beard and ponytail were longer, too. "Here, sit in my chair. Coffee, tea?"

"Earl Grey if you have it. Thank you, my good man."

Mel made himself comfortable while waiting. He picked up an old copy of the Seattle Times folded to an op-ed on the assassinations. He'd just started reading it when Cody came in.

"Mel! Way too long, man!" Cody bent over and hugged Mel, who remained seated.

"You're a sight for sore eyes, young man. How are you doing? What's it been? Almost a year, right?"

Cody stood up. "I was down in the spring to see mom and dad, and we went out for lunch. You let me drive White Zombie, remember? Goddamn that was fun! Never felt that much power before. Hey, you raced the Tesla Ludicrous yet?"

Ludicrous was the absolute top-of-the-line Tesla, capable of hitting 60 mph in 2.8 seconds. It was faster than any other sedan in history and faster than any production car on Earth.

Mel looked up at Cody through his granny glasses. He'd never really changed the style since his hippy days. The wrinkles in the corner of his eyes deepened as a big grin spread across his face.

"Funny you should ask." He continued in the slow, laconic storytelling voice Cody remembered from his days learning chess and hearing tale after tale, all true, from his well traveled friend.

"As you can imagine, there is a dearth of Teslas in our fair metropolis of Eatonville. So, up until this morning, I hadn't seen one of the Ludicrous models. But, to my surprise, I happened upon a black one less than a mile from here. As it turned out, he knew of me. The stickers gave it away. Anyhoo, at a light, he actually got out and handed me his card. He told me he wanted to see how he could do against the Zombie." Looking over his glasses again at Cody, he said, "I guess we're going to find out."

"I want to be there! You gotta let me know, OK? I haven't even seen a Ludicrous yet. I'll watch for the black one."

Zak lumbered in carrying a tray with Mel's tea and coffees for himself and Cody.

"What's this about Ludicrous?" Zak interrupted. "Don't tell me you're going to buy one of those big-ass cars!"

"Nah, he just got invited to race one," Cody said. "We're all going to go watch."

"What else is going on, Mel? How's your health?" Zak had talked to Mel a month earlier when Mel was having some stomach pain.

Mel slowly brought the tea to his lips, blowing across the top to cool it, and took the smallest of sips, taking care not to burn himself. He set the cup down on the side table before making eye contact.

"Seems I've got a touch of the cancer. Nothing too big, only stage four. I think there are what, ten stages, right?"

Zak and Cody looked at each other, then back at Mel.

"No, man, that's fucked up." Cody immediately regretted the lame response. "Mel, I'm... I don't know what to say. How bad is it really?"

Zak knew how bad it was. Mel wouldn't be making light if it was nothing. Hell, if it was a simple cancer that had a high probability of survival, he probably wouldn't have even mentioned it.

"Well..." Zak looked at Mel. "I guess this means Cody and I get to fight over who gets the Zombie."

That worked as intended. Mel let out a good laugh. That Zak could joke about serious subjects was what had endeared him to Mel in the first place.

"C'mon, Mel, this is serious," Cody pleaded. He was devastated by the news and saw no humor in it.

Zak stood up, saying, "Be right back."

Mel raised his eyebrows and stared at Cody as if to say, "Yeah, what're you going to do?" Cody understood. He learned as a ten-year-old that Mel could impart a lot of valuable information with a simple arch of his eyebrows. All the important information had already been communicated.

Zak walked back in with the bong. "Time for your meds, old man."

They passed the bong around twice. Mel was going to be there for a while so they might as well enjoy the time.

"So, what kind?" Zak asked.

"Pancreatic, liver, and so on." Mel replied. "I have a few fun-filled months left. I'm not done being a pain in the ass to people who need it. I also want to see what this Gambit fellow does next. I'd probably check out earlier if it weren't for him."

"Wow," Cody thought. He felt good knowing his actions gave his friend something to live for. "Who do you hope he kills next?" he asked. "Do you think he killed Scalia, too?"

"No one killed Scalia. He died of pure meanness. Just came several years too late. He did a lot of damage to a lot of people. As for who's next, boy, that's a fun question! The Koch brothers have earned top billing probably. If you take it internationally, there are many players who need to go. But I'm sticking with the Kochs for now. I'd go to my grave a happy man if those guys were removed from the planet."

Cody, nodding, asked, "You up for a couple of games? It's been awhile since we played live and I've been reading up on some openings I wanna try."

"Sure, set 'em up, little buddy." Mel and Cody had played online for years on Red Hot Pawn, one of many excellent chess sites. It was a way to stay in touch and have some fun, but they always preferred playing live.

Zak excused himself to go write in his study. Mel and Cody settled into their chess.

"What's it like to know you're dying? Does it hurt a lot yet?" Cody asked quietly after a few moves into the first game.

"Not a lot of pain yet. I'm on some powerful painkillers that do the trick when it gets tough, but all in all, I'm pretty comfortable physically. Mentally, it goes back and forth. I've lived a long time and I've done some fun things. I'm not ready to give that up. On the other hand, with the direction the world is going, it's getting harder and harder to maintain a pleasant state of mind. There's so much pain..."

"I know what you mean. I'm having a lot of trouble dealing with it myself. The VA hasn't been much help with the PTSD. There are some people there who try, but the system is pretty fucked up. They can't handle the volume, not even close."

"That's what happens when you start a bunch of goddamned wars and don't pay for 'em."

"Yeah, you taught me that when I was a kid. I never forgot it."

They played in silence for a while.

Cody was squirming. He was having trouble concentrating on the game. One of his best friends was soon going to die. To sit quietly and let it happen seemed wrong, but what could he do? What would make it better?

Cody knew death. Boy did he know death. But other than a couple of buddies in the war who were killed, and his grandparents, the only person close to him who'd died was Jazzie. Mel was another thing altogether. He'd instilled in Cody much of what made him who he was. Cody's parents had raised him to be a good kid, but Mel, with some help from Zak, had made him a radical willing to try to change the world.

It seemed only fair. Cody would tell him.

"Mel, can you keep a secret?"

Mel stared at the board. "Well, if you're gay that's one hell of a fun closet you've been living in."

Cody tried to muster a laugh. No luck. This wasn't funny. Mel continued studying the board.

"The Kochs."

"What about 'em?" Mel looked up at Cody.

"They're next."

Cody said this with such seriousness. Mel's eyes narrowed and he stared at Cody. Neither said a word for a good twenty seconds.

Mel remembered the manifesto was signed "Gambit" and had used the term "reveal check." He tried to reconcile the inevitable conclusion with the young man sitting across the table. A man whom he'd helped raise. The boy who took to chess like a champ. "Gambit!" Mel thought. "He's fucking Gambit!"

Cody never took his eyes off Mel. "No one else knows. Just you," he said.

The game, which had been going in Mel's favor, was now forgotten. Mel tried to come to grips with the enormity of it all. He understood Cody was telling him this because of his terminal status. It was his way of telling Mel that he, too, was terminal.

"I...I want to be clear. Are you telling me this because I'm dying, or because you want my help?"

Cody wasn't sure why he told Mel. "I don't know. Maybe both. Yes, your dying triggered it, but help?" He paused. "This has been a very hard secret to keep."

Mel's eyes rolled at the understatement. "No shit! How long have you been planning this... these assassinations?"

Cody was glad Mel used "assassinations" and not "murders," because the connotations of murder were bereft of the political ideas catalyzing Cody's actions.

"After reading those books over the past few years, seeing "Merchants of Doubt," and reading every fucking day about these assholes getting away with killing people and harming the planet, it just pissed me off like crazy! Every day I got madder, and the feeling of impotence was overwhelming. Reading Klein's "This Changes Everything" only made it worse. Her 'solutions' were not scalable. I guess what cinched it was seeing people ignoring the problem. Even the so-called enviros are still using dirty energy and acting as if it's someone else's fault. Someone needed to do something. I didn't see any other solution."

Mel took a moment to think about this. He couldn't come up with a counter argument, especially since he agreed with virtually everything Cody said.

"What was...is your endgame?" Mel replied using the well worn chess term. Surely Cody had thought that through.

"When I first thought about killing these guys, there was no endgame other than me killing as many as possible before getting caught. I didn't think of the manifesto until after I killed Rush. Now my endgame is to encourage vets to take up the cause. There isn't much chance I can do many more of these before getting caught, and once that happens, the bad guys will go back to what they were doing. If they think their security detail might kill them, well, maybe that'll have an effect."

"And Victoria?"

Cody stared at his lap, shaking his head slowly. "You know, I met her the night before I left. She just waltzed into my life and made everything better—for me. But the shit going down in the world, the suffering, is only getting worse. I'd already made up my mind. She made me rethink everything, but in the end, I had to act. I really, really want to spend my life with her and forget all this, but I can't. It's too late. This is more important than my needs. People are dying. Lots of people."

Cody was getting very depressed. He began to second guess his confession, not that it mattered. Once a secret is out, it's out.

Mel's heart rate had increased hearing Cody's confession. He rarely got excited—either for good or bad. But in an instant, his world was turned upside down.

He had to respond to his friend and protégé who'd just confessed to a global assassination plot. It was more than a plot: he'd already killed a sitting senator and one of the most reviled shock jocks in the country. What the hell do you say to that?

"Cody," Mel spoke slowly and with deliberation, "you understand better than most what's happening in the world. This journey you're taking probably does not end well... for you. We don't know how it'll end for the Earth and its inhabitants, because it's too early to tell if we're going to change our collective ways. But we do know how it'll end without someone doing something." He shook his head. "It's not going to be good. The science, as you say, is clear." He continued in a more conspiratorial tone. "You say the Kochs are next? How? Where? After all of this, how do you expect to do it?"

Mel's look indicated he expected a real answer, not some half-baked move that would end badly for Cody. "Well, I'm not all that sure. Koch Industries is in Wichita, but I think the brothers live in Manhattan. Going there is out of the question. No way to get a rifle anywhere close to anyone important without getting caught. I think an attack on their headquarters is doable—mostly to scare them. Some targets are going to be hard to get without being on the inside. That's why I reached out to the vets. If nothing ever happens, they'll at least have it in the back of their heads that it could happen. And if even one vet gets in and kills someone, that'll scare the shit out of 'em, big time!"

"Kansas? Jeez, too bad you have to go to such boring places for your job." Mel could do black humor.

Cody actually smiled. But when he spoke, the sadness was still evident. "It's not too far from where I got Inhofe—just a few hundred miles north. I've been studying the campus. I might use a drone with C-4."

"Explosives on a drone? What do you know about that?"

"I had a friend in Iraq who was our unit's EOD specialist. Explosive Ordnance Disposal. He taught me how to handle C-4. It's not too hard. Acquiring it is the problem."

After a beat, Mel said, "I might know somebody."

Was Mel offering to become a conspirator? "You really want to get involved?"

"Do I have a choice? I'm on my way out of this world, and while I've done some things to be proud of, what you're doing has the potential, tenuous as it is, to change things for the better in a very big way. Or not. Regardless of whether some big asshole is stopped, the scare factor, as you said, is worth the effort."

"One thing we must do: Zak and Victoria need to be protected from any involvement should things go south."

Cody immediately agreed. "Yes! No one else knows, and there's nothing to connect them to what I've done. That said, shit will get ugly for them no matter what."

Zak heard the last remark as he walked back in the room. "Shit's gonna get ugly for who?"

Cody quickly responded, "Trump or Cruz, man. They're gonna get creamed in the general. It's going to be fun to watch!"

Zak grinned. "It's already fun, and gettin' funner every day!"

Chapter 23

Cody was intensely interested in how vets were reacting to his manifesto. He lurked online in veteran forums and saw that those who were willing to write were heavily against him. He'd assumed that would be the case but was not particularly happy to read it

He had signed his manifesto "Gambit," so many assumed the assassin was a chess player. Cody had had second thoughts about using the term, but millions of people played chess, so he hoped it wouldn't become a problem. He was much more likely to get caught because of security camera footage of the van or of him on the bike leaving the site of the Limbaugh killing.

In fact, the manifesto was a hot topic in veteran groups. It was generally assumed the perpetrator was a vet, but no solid evidence supported this. The FBI assumed the killer was a vet, and they were infiltrating veterans groups to learn whether vets were sympathetic to the manifesto.

Some were. They were generally keeping to themselves, not wanting to raise any flags, but the manifesto spoke to the anger many felt over being sent to fight a war for corporate interests and not for the reasons the Bush administration had claimed.

Most vets, however, were livid over the manifesto. They were the low-intelligence guys who generally swallowed anything the military leaders and right-wing media told them. They followed Limbaugh and Fox News and considered their words gospel. These vets were pissed someone had the audacity to say the war was not a patriotic war. They had killed people, and they had friends who'd been killed and maimed in that war. How dare someone impugn the word of George Bush, Dick Cheney, and all the rest with such lies!

Three weeks had passed since his return, and Cody began to plan his attack on Koch Industries in Wichita. Cody didn't look forward to that long drive, especially in a gas-guzzling van, but he believed his methods would work once again.

It took Mel another week to acquire the C-4. He and Cody researched the type of drone they'd need to carry the payload to the main building. Cody ordered the drone online through a dummy account and had it delivered to a PO box in Olympia. C-4 was easy to use if you were properly trained, but Cody had only been taught the bare minimum and had no real experience with it.

As this planning occurred, Cody and Victoria grew closer by the day. She still watched him sometimes when she thought he wasn't looking, but she was as happy as she'd ever been and seemed happier with every passing day. Spring was in full bloom, the weather was warming up and drying out, and on their runs they were building strength and speed for their first race together, the Snohomish Women's Half Marathon on Mother's day. Victoria had been a decent runner, but having a track athlete for a boyfriend helped her get much stronger, something she needed to run a half marathon.

Take It Off, Victoria's company, was one of the race sponsors, so she wanted to make a big splash by wearing her provocative new line of running gear. The company offered fit women the opportunity to wear running shorts and tops that accentuated their sexiness. Cody had mentioned to her that he'd run behind really fast women in road races before—trying to keep up just so he could watch them from behind. He said it had helped him run faster times. Victoria had guessed correctly that this was pretty common among male runners, so she had designed shorts and tops to take advantage of their desire.

Cody was dealing with his Jekyll and Hyde persona pretty well, but not perfectly. It helped immensely that Mel was now in on the secret, and his assistance in procuring the C-4 was invaluable. But Cody had trouble when it came to Victoria.

He began to feel a pervading doom as his plans took shape. He'd have to set a date, make up another lie about going to LA for a visual effects job, and then compound the lie every night with calls to Victoria, a woman with whom he was deeply in love. And worse, there was a nagging fear he'd be caught or killed.

Would you kill Hitler? Even if it meant you might be killed in the process? These questions were always underpinning his thoughts. The answer was always yes.

"Fucking assholes!" thought Cody. "They screw up everything. I wish they'd all drop dead over night so I wouldn't have to go."

As he'd predicted, the security apparatus across the country had stepped up dramatically. He read articles discussing the psychological tests given all veterans who were signing up by the thousands for the new security jobs his manifesto had generated.

A few vets were being turned away after being deemed too risky. One article even highlighted a vet who admitted in his interview he felt homicidal toward those who'd sent him to war. Those stories only helped get the word out to more vets who were similarly disposed to act. Knowing others thought along the same lines increased the chances one or more of them would do something. It'd only take one disgruntled vet assassinating someone to make all hell break loose. Cody hoped such an event would soon spur other vets to step up and make their own attempts.

He also searched media for stories of things getting better so maybe he wouldn't have to leave his new wonderful life and risk getting killed.

There was some good news. Solar and wind energy were still steadily dropping in price. Both were on par with dirty energy or close to it.

Also, the second generation of modern electric cars was months from the showroom. It was widely expected these were the cars that would bring the masses into the EV fold. Even better, autonomous vehicles were only a few years from perfection, and the idea that these cars would replace millions of privately owned vehicles was promising and exciting.

All of that was good news, indeed great news if you believed things would go smoothly. But the Kochs, of course, had other plans. They intended to disrupt and slow the transition to EVs as much as they could. The result being that their favored fuel—oil—would continue being extracted, shipped, refined, distributed, and eventually burned in a billion filthy cars, trucks, and SUVs.

Cody could not allow that to happen without making every effort to stop it.

As a surprise for Victoria on March 14th, Pi Day, Cody brought home a beautiful cherry pie from his favorite bakery, A la Mode Pies. He wanted to make her a nice dinner and finish it with the pie. Then he'd tell her that he'd have to leave for another gig. Zak was out of town for a couple days, so they had the house to themselves.

"Cody, that's the best dinner you've ever made for me, and the pie! Wow! We'll have to go back there for sure."

"Yeah, it's been a favorite of mine since Zak took me there once. Wait until you try their blackberry cobbler when blackberries are in season. Incredible!"

"Mmm, can't wait. We've got lots to explore together, you and me!" Her gorgeous eyes melted Cody every time.

"Well, I've got some good news/bad news, sweetie."

"Oh no, what's wrong? Are you injured?" Injuries to a runner were always bad news if common.

"No, nothing like that. I got another VFX job down at DD. I gotta to go to LA again. Probably only two weeks, maybe less this time. The pay is great, though, that's the good news part."

"That is a mixed bag. When do you leave?"

"In about a week. We have some time to play and get in some good hard runs. I won't be able to run much when I'm there, but I'll take the bike, so I can at least get some workouts riding to and from the studio. You should definitely keep up your training, though. I want you to shine at Snohomish. Have you decided what you'll wear? I love that turquoise singlet you showed me!"

Cody tried to deflect any questions about the trip. It was still painful to lie to Victoria.

"I love that top, too." She smiled at Cody. "But I'll be wearing a running bra underneath in the race, so it won't be quite as sexy as when you saw it. Probably that with a pair of my new tight shorts. You know, the ones you like to grab." As she said this, she walked around the table and stood next to Cody turning slightly, inviting him to grab her again.

Cody, still sitting, took the invite and grabbed her tight butt with both hands, pulling her close and kissing her long and hard. After breaking apart, they practically ran upstairs to his bedroom.

****

Cody spent the next few days gathering everything together for his trip. He decided against bringing the rifle. He didn't need it, and it might complicate things if he was stopped.

The day before his departure, Mel arrived at his door with the C-4. They'd planned this meeting for when Zak was across town with a client.

"You get plugged in?" Cody asked, noticing Mel's backpack.

"ABC: always be charging," Mel smiled. He'd been building his own EVs for decades and knew very well the need to find access to energy, especially with the short range vehicles he built.

"Great, come on in. Coffee, tea?"

"I'm good, thanks. I do need to pee, though."

After returning, Mel noticed Cody had brought down the Winchester and placed it against the wall by the door.

"That the weapon?"

"Yeah," Cody answered in a low voice. "I need you to hide it for me. It shouldn't be in the house in case..."

"Right. I'll deal with it. Do you think you'll ever want it back? I can hide it, or I can get rid of it. Either way, no one will ever see it unless you want it back."

"Don't destroy it; hide it. I might need it again." Cody tried to remain positive. But he knew any attempt from here on out was likely to be much harder to execute without capture, or worse.

"Got it. Worst-case scenario, I'll die soon anyway, so no one will find it after that." They exchanged a solemn look, acknowledging their similar fate.

"Now for the pack," Mel said as he lifted it onto the coffee table. "How much do you really know about this stuff? My guy says it's pretty safe, but you do need to know what you're doing."

"Let's see what you have here," Cody said, digging into the pack. "Looks like about a half-kilo of explosive. Is there a detonator? Yeah, there it is. This is good. I'm pretty sure I can make it work.

I really appreciate it, Mel. Just gonna blow some shit up, probably won't even hurt anyone. Maybe I'll get lucky and trigger something else."

"Oh, you've already done that, my friend. The whole country is going bat-shit crazy over the actions you've taken. The trigger you want now is for disgruntled vets to come on board."

"Got that right! I hope I get one or two, at least."

"When do you leave?" Mel asked.

"Tomorrow morning." Cody looked pensive. Was it Victoria, or was it fear of getting caught? Both.

The day had been warm for a Seattle spring. Everyone was saying it was climate change, and probably there was a bit of truth to that, but weather could always be up and down in the Pacific Northwest in spring.

Victoria took off work early to cook a nice dinner at her house. She was excited—not sad—because he was just going away for a couple weeks, not forever.

Cody rode his bike to her house, carrying a bottle of wine and some Euphoria chocolate truffles from his favorite chocolate store in Eugene. He'd had a dozen FedExed. As he locked his bike to the front railing, he stooped down and plucked a few daffodils from her garden, and when she opened the door, he thrust the flowers into her hands and kissed her full on the lips. It wasn't until she pulled away that he saw she was wearing the turquoise top—with no bra. Her nipples were quite evident, partly from the chill of the evening, and partly because of that kiss. They were going to be apart again for two weeks and both needed to get as much of the other as possible to last until his return.

They took the time to put the flowers in a vase, but not time to add water. The chocolate would wait till later. Cody and Victoria hurriedly undressed each other in their race up the stairs.

Over dinner, they talked about their future, the political race and assassinations, and the half-marathon they were going to run together in a few weeks. Neither brought up him leaving.

Later that evening, Cody pulled the heavy comforter up over their heads to ward off the cold. As their conversation drifted off, his beautiful girlfriend did so as well. Cody's mind, however, turned to killing more people. He hated what he'd become.

Victoria's warm body felt so good to his touch. He tried to concentrate on that alone, but the more he tried, the more the crazy thought of leaving in the morning intruded. He had felt so resolute after the party; why was he having second thoughts now? The question remained unresolved as he fitfully fell asleep.

There was a steady cold rain outside Victoria's bedroom window when they woke. The two lovebirds took their sweet time getting out of bed. Both had recovered enough from last night's sex to go at it again.

Eventually they tired and hankered for caffeine, so Cody jumped in the shower while Victoria got the coffee started before joining him. After drying off, he helped choose Victoria's outfit for the day, starting with her marvelous underwear drawer. He had to chuckle at the dozen or more sexy items, any one of which would be fine, but he had her try on five before settling on a green thong. It wasn't even his favorite, but he was having such a good time watching that he just happened to end on that one. He pulled out his phone and took a few shots so he'd have something to look at during the long drive to Kansas.

The rain kept coming down, and if anything, it was falling harder as they finished up breakfast.

"Let's throw your bike on the car, and I'll drive you home. No need to ride in this muck." Victoria offered.

"Works for me!" Cody replied with more cheeriness than he could inwardly muster. His relief in knowing he wouldn't have to get cold and wet made the difference.

"Damn, that wind's cold!" Cody exclaimed as he quickly loaded the bike on her rack. Victoria was dressed nicely in the outfit Cody picked out for her, but this being Seattle, all of it was covered with a big raincoat and hood. They both jumped into the car.

He was so in love with this woman! Everything about her was perfect. Why did he have to leave? Would he be able to return?

When they pulled up to Zak's house, Victoria stopped him from getting out.

"Since you're going to be gone so long, I want a kiss to remember you by!" she demanded with that sexy voice of hers.

He leaned in, and with his right hand gently pulling her face toward his, he gave her the nicest, softest kiss he could, and then pulled away. They gazed at one another as if trying to memorize every pore, every stray hair.

"I love you, Victoria!"

Her eyes widened and her face blossomed into a great, big smile.

"Oh Cody!" She took his face in both her hands, and they repeated the wonderful goodbye kiss.

"I'll call every night," Cody promised as he climbed out of her car. He wondered: was this the last time he'd see her? He could hardly bear the thought.

"Oh, baby, I'm so happy!" Victoria jumped out and ran over to him. She grabbed him in a bear hug and buried her head into the crook of his neck.

Chapter 24

Zak suspected nothing and gave Cody a ride to the U-Haul place so he wouldn't have to deal with the rain. He spent the morning packing for the trip and getting all his food and drink stowed. The drone and C-4 were stashed in a roller suitcase beneath his clothes.

Once more Cody drove a lumbering van out of Seattle. His route would take him down through eastern Oregon into southern Idaho. Cody checked weather reports and the conditions over the mountain passes to make sure all was clear. Still early spring, and the mountains could get heavy snow into June.

The first two days were uneventful. He called Victoria often. She kept herself busy at work, but always took his call when it came, day or night.

On the third day, he was driving across Colorado, marveling at the beauty of the Rocky Mountains. He'd been listening to NPR for news and music the whole way, not wanting to pollute his mind with the moronic drivel spouted on the AM dial.

Mary Louise Kelly, NPR's national security correspondent, was detailing the FBI's minimal progress in solving the Gambit case. While still big news, the assassinations were relegated to back-page updates as the presidential race regained its place on mainstream media's front pages.

Republicans were crying and running scared. They'd paved the way for the cartoon-buffoon Donald Trump to run away from the 18-person pack of candidates and essentially take over the Grand Old Party, leaving it in a not-very-partying mood.

The idea that their security guards might shoot them in the head added to their anguish.

The left had their own problems, but the fight between Bernie and Hillary supporters paled by comparison. Cody was sure the Democrats would win the presidency and probably the Senate. There was even talk that the House could fall, giving either Bernie or Hillary all the power they needed to stack the Supreme Court with liberal judges for a generation or more.

All this good news buoyed Cody's attitude considerably, and gave him and Victoria plenty to talk about before and after their phone sexcapades.

But the closer Cody got to Wichita, the more he wanted to turn around and go home. Go back to his lover, adopt a rescue dog, and live out his life as though nothing bad had ever happened.

He wanted to be just like the vast majority of Americans who, because of their gross selfishness and greed, wanted to ignore the horrendous problems they were causing and live out their lives in ignorant bliss, or as close to bliss as their meager assets could afford them.

After a very cold night in the mountains, he descended into Denver with its brown smog and heavy traffic, a harsh transition from the Rockies' near pristine environs. A high-pressure system was holding the pollution close to the ground as it often did in the Mile High City.

Cody could make it to Wichita if he drove late into the night, but he didn't feel the need to rush things, so he pulled over in Hays, Kansas, and stopped in the Vineyard Park Nature Area. He'd need a good night's rest before scouting the Koch Industries' site and this location was far enough from the freeway to allow a quiet, uninterrupted sleep.

****

Another half day drive and Cody arrived in Wichita. Koch industries was on the north edge of Kansas' largest city. Wichita has several general aviation airports and has been the center of private airplane manufacturing since the 1920s.

In 1940, Koch Industries, then known as Wood River Oil and Refining Company, was cofounded by Fred C. Koch. Two of Fred's sons, Charles and David, run the company today. It's the second-largest privately held company in the U.S., with virtually every subsidiary in its conglomerate involved in polluting the environment. It's no wonder environmentalists considered it the embodiment of evil.

Since Cody knew that both brothers lived in Manhattan, he didn't expect to find them there. But if he was able to blow up an office on the top floor of what looked like the main building on the sprawling campus, that might shake them up.

Cody needed to scout, so he drove out Hwy 96 about a mile east of I-35 to make a full circumnavigation of the campus. It was late morning, and traffic was light. The facility had four main entrances that Cody clearly would not be using.

He needed to study the area on his computer, so he pulled into Stroud's Restaurant and Bar, a slightly rundown eatery catering to Koch employees. He drove his van around back, where a large parking lot abutted a small pond. The tiny body of water was littered with debris and garbage. The locals must've been using it as a dump. Nevertheless, some birds were singing in the trees lining its banks, providing Cody a welcome touch of nature.

Walking into the restaurant, Cody immediately felt out of place. The stench of stale cigarettes permeated the room. Did they allow smoking?

It was a little early for the lunch crowd, but they'd be arriving shortly. He was seated at a window table and handed a menu. Nothing but meat! He was disgusted, but ordered a baked potato and iced tea. While waiting for the food, he scanned his email and news feed. The lunch crowd began ambling in. Some were actually smoking. Cody couldn't believe it! He was about to get up and leave when the waitress, an older woman who looked beaten down, delivered his potato.

Feeling sorry for the woman, Cody handed her a $20 bill and asked for the food to go, explaining he couldn't eat in a room where people were smoking. She was surprised, even smiled a little, and took the food away. She returned with a styrofoam box and what looked like a used plastic Slurpy cup.

"Sorry for the cup, mister, but we don't have anything else to put the tea in. Yeah, the smoke is pretty bad sometimes. I guess I've gotten used to it after all these years."

"It's OK. I just can't handle it. Please keep the change. I hope you have a good day."

He walked out into the sunshine, where the parking lot was filling up with people from Koch Industries driving solo in their big pick-up trucks and SUVs.

"They can't even carpool to lunch," Cody thought. He was growing angrier by the minute.

Near the van, two young men about his age were drinking beer by the pond. One of them hurled his bottle into the water and turned just in time to see Cody walk to his van. Cody stared at him, trying to think of what to say. The man stared right back at Cody as if to say, "I fucking dare you!"

As much as Cody wanted to tell the guy off, he knew it wouldn't go well. There were two of them and, besides, Cody had more important things to do. Getting arrested for fighting in this god awful place would not serve his mission. He turned away and climbed into the van.

He needed to calm down before he did something he'd regret. Looking at the map, he saw a large animal shelter less than half a mile south, just on the other side of Hwy 96.

Cody had never seen such a beautiful shelter! They combined the city and county shelters with the Humane Society into one huge facility. He parked in the shade of a scrawny tree. The tree didn't provide enough shade for the van, but it was cool enough that Cody could roll down the window and eat his potato.

Several cars came and went, with people carrying cat carriers or with dogs on leashes. Cody needed some animal time, so he finished off the potato, locked the van, and walked inside. The place was mildly busy with volunteers helping families choose animals, cleaning cages, or walking the dogs.

At the counter, Cody asked if he could see some dogs. One of the volunteers, an older gentleman, walked him down the hall toward the kennel.

"You looking for a big dog or a small dog? We got all kinds."

"To be honest, sir, I'm hoping to just spend some time with a dog or two. Walking them, playing with them, giving them some attention. I'm traveling across the country, and I miss the animals back in the shelter where I volunteer."

"I get it. I been around dogs my whole life and can't understand people who don't like them. I really can't understand people who abuse them."

"Me neither." Cody though of the dog-fighting scum he'd murdered. "I think abusers should be dealt with..."

"We just got these two lab mixes in the other day from a farm family. The father passed, and the kids didn't want 'em. Sad. I mean, they were in the family for several years." From their looks, the two black labs probably had a little shepherd in them. Both dogs were jumping for joy as the men walked up to their cage.

"We hope to find someone who can take 'em both. Hate to separate them. They've been together all their lives."

As soon as Cody entered the cage, the dogs were all over him. They were full of nervous energy from being cooped up hours on end. There was much tail wagging and face licking. Cody wished he had four hands so he could pet them both as much as possible.

"Is there a someplace I can walk them? You allow that?"

"Yeah, sure, but you have to fill out an application. Follow me." The man led Cody back to the front of the building.

After Cody filled it out, the man took him back to the two dogs and gave him one leash while he took another.

"Watch out when I open the kennel. They're kinda jumpy. You get the one on the left, and I'll take the other."

They fixed the leashes and walked the two dogs down the hall, where the man opened the door to the fenced dog run.

"You can take 'em off leash in here. Have fun!"

The dry, dusty ground was littered with balls and chewed-up toys. One dog grabbed a ball as soon as Cody let him off leash. Cody's mood quickly lifted as he repeatedly threw the ball for the dogs. They loved it, too, running hard and play-fighting with each other, but dutifully retrieving the ball for Cody. They'd been well trained to fetch.

Cody spent the better part of an hour with them. Other shelter volunteers, and a couple trying out a dog they were thinking of adopting, came in with their dogs to play. Cody's animals got along with everyone. He thought it likely they'd be adopted together once the right person came along. There were lots of farmers and ranchers in this part of the country with plenty of room to run dogs.

Cody reluctantly took them back to the front desk. The older gentleman said, "So how'd you like these two boys? Wanna take 'em home?" The man was a gentle soul, perfectly suited to his volunteer role. Cody knew people like him back in Seattle who would come by now and then to help out, some staying for months, some for a week or two, but all of them wonderful people. Animal people were of a kind, a good kind.

Feeling better about the world, he climbed into the van, pulled out his laptop, and brought up Google Earth. He had to figure out his plan.

After his drive around the perimeter, he knew he couldn't access anything on the property with the van. Gates and cameras controlled and recorded every vehicle. The maps, however, showed a Union Pacific railroad line crossing the property on a diagonal from the southwest to the northeast. Better yet, the tracks were adjacent to the animal shelter less than 100 meters from where he was sitting.

Zooming in, Cody saw a cluster of trees close to the tracks that looked like they'd provide decent cover for him and his bike. If he parked the van in the shelter's parking lot and left before dawn, he could ride along the track right of way until he got close to the trees and then walk the bike to the trees before daylight. From there, he should be able to control the drone as it travelled to the property's tallest building.

Cody didn't know what happened in the building, but it was the tallest, therefore it must be important, he reasoned. An explosion on the top floor would scare the shit out of them, and anyone important enough to be there was, by definition, a target. An explosion in the middle of the property would also draw all security there and away from the perimeter. No one would be looking for a bicycle. They'd be looking for someone on-site. That was sound reasoning, Cody thought. He'd just be some guy on an early morning training ride. There were bound to be some competitive bikers in a city the size of Wichita. He wouldn't look too out of place.

His plan set, Cody looked for a place to sleep the night. He contemplated staying in the shelter's lot, but it was likely he'd encounter a security guard. Surprisingly, he kept coming back to Strouds, the stinky restaurant with the polluted pond out back. It wasn't very far from the shelter, and if he waited until well after closing, there would be scant chance of anyone finding him in the back parking lot. If they did, he'd just tell them he was sleeping off a drunk before driving home. He'd move the van to the animal shelter before dawn, minimizing the chance of a security patrol catching him there. If he left before daylight and rode to his hideout in the trees, his chances of being seen would be close to zero.

Once the explosive was detonated, he'd ride the short distance along the tracks back to the shelter. It should take less than five minutes. Cody figured no security personnel would be on the perimeter roads in the time it took him to get back to the van, load his bike, and get the hell out of there.

Another perfect crime by Gambit.

Now Cody had the whole afternoon to chill and bide his time. He wanted to go back in the shelter and be with the dogs, but as much as that appealed to him, he needed to be careful. Familiarity with that nice older man might come back to bite him. Instead, he saw what looked like a long bike trail nearby that meandered through some neighborhoods and a school with a track. He wanted to burn off his nervous energy, so he decided a run was in order.

Cody drove to the Bio-Communications Research offices, a group of futuristic geodesic domes less than half a mile from the shelter. The company had a big parking lot, and the bike path was a short walk through the woods out back.

After changing into his running shorts and a couple of t-shirts to ward off chill, Cody set off on an easy jog through the small grove of trees. Once on the path, he picked up the pace to an easy run. He was in Kansas—which is pancake flat—so there was no way to get a hard workout without pushing the pace. Cody kept thinking of Victoria and their upcoming half marathon. He pushed thoughts of the next day out of his mind, wanting only to think of his sweetie, their runs together in Seattle, the race he'd pace her through, the fantastic sex they'd have that night, and all the other wonderful things in his future.

Cody believed he was still the good kid who loved Jazzie, the kid whose love for his dog and his family mirrored his love for all life. He compartmentalized the murders. He had to commit those atrocities, but he was not that man. He had been forced by circumstances to take action against those who, for love of money and power, were destroying the ecosystem. Because of them, thousands of species were going extinct every year, millions of people were dying horrible deaths. Their grip on power was absolute, as evidenced by the Koch brother's willingness to spend close to a billion dollars on the upcoming election.

Almost absolute.

Cody had found a chink in their armor—men who'd been trained to kill by the military-industrial complex, including some of the very people he'd named as targets. He was the first to exploit this breach, and his idea of encouraging suicidal vets to infiltrate security companies was the real solution—if it worked.

His mind drifted to the dark side as he ran. He thought of evil people and the destruction they caused. The more he thought about them, the faster he ran. He was nearing oxygen debt, so he backed off the pace.

How long had he been in that state? Where the hell was he? When Cody started the run, he made sure to pay attention to his surroundings so he could find his way back to the van, but his mind had drifted and now he found himself in a strange neighborhood with no idea where he was.

"Damn! Why didn't I bring my phone?" he thought. The safest way out was to reverse course. How many times had he taken a turn off the main trail? He found himself tiring and slowed down even more to conserve energy. Gradually, he began to recognize things. That tree over there, those houses off to the north, until he knew he was close to the geodesic structures.

The sun was setting, and the cold breeze blowing across the prairie gave him a chill. People were leaving the facility, walking to their cars. A few eyed him with curiosity. They didn't get a lot of strangers there, especially someone in a rented van who dressed in running clothes. Someone who actually ran.

Cody didn't make eye contact with anyone. He quickly took off his sweaty t-shirts and threw on a clean dry one. He started the van and drove off, hoping no one was suspicious enough to note his license number.

It felt good to have gotten a run in, and his fantasies involving running and having sex with Victoria returned to replace his dark thoughts of evil people.

Cody needed to find someplace quiet where he could park and call her. First, though, he needed to gas up the van so when he left the next day, he could drive far before having to stop.

He yearned to listen to NPR for reports on his latest action. He understood why some people murdered the famous, or became mass murders—it was for the notoriety. Having the whole country, or the whole world, pay attention to something you did was pretty heady. Of course, this wasn't why Cody was killing. He had a rational, and in his head, very reasonable reason for killing these people.

"If you could go back in time and kill Hitler..." It always came back to that.

After gassing up, Cody found a quiet street near where he'd run earlier and parked. Virtually no one was out, just an older woman walking her small doggy. She didn't even look at the van.

Cody pulled out his phone and hit Victoria's number with FaceTime.

"Hey, sweetie, how you doing?"

"Cody, so good to hear your voice and see your face! So sexy! Are you coming home tonight?" She was teasing him.

"I wish! I'm so hungry for you, I can't wait to get back to Seattle! I'm going to have to get a real job there so I don't have to leave any more."

"That'd be nice. I'll hire you to monitor the changing rooms in the store. It only pays minimum wage, but the benefits!" Victoria was in a playful mood. Cody liked that. Just hearing her voice made him feel better, but with FaceTime, he was able to see her, too.

"I can live on minimum wage as long as it comes with loving you."

"Oh, baby, you make me so happy! That was such a nice thing to say! I love you like I've never loved anyone before. Who died and made you god?"

The god reference was an inside joke, both of them being atheists to the core.

"When I'm around you, I feel god-like. It's as if I'm a little kid and the whole world is wide open. So many things we'll get to do together." Right then, Cody realized he wanted to marry Victoria. The thought came to him like a flash of lightning, but without the thunder. He almost blurted it out, but caught himself. This was not a question to ask over the phone. Especially not tonight. He decided he'd pop the question in person as soon as he got back to Seattle and could plan the perfect time and place. The decision to ask her to get married elated him. He was so happy, he wanted to dance right there in the van.

"Well, mister, we'll just have to get out some travel brochures and do some planning when you get back. Ever been to the south of France, to Provence?"

"No, never been out of the country except for Iraq, and I don't count that as a vacation."

"Let's not go there." Victoria responded.

"Right, sorry to have mentioned it. You've been to Europe?"

"When I was a teenager. My parents took me. They were trying to spark up their marriage. Sadly, it didn't work for them, but I lost my virginity to a nice young French boy, so I guess it wasn't a total loss."

"Really now? Do tell me more!" And with that, Victoria recounted her summer vacation in France between her junior and senior years. A skinny young French boy made eyes at her. He was only a couple years older and claimed to be training for the Tour de France. Whether that was true, or just a line he used to bed American teenagers on vacation, it worked. Cody relished every word, imagining himself in place of the young French boy.

This call ended as did all of their calls, with mutually timed orgasms.

"That was good!" Victoria exclaimed. "They're all good, but that one, wow!"

"Yeah, hard to beat a good orgasm, right?"

"Pleeeeze come home soon, baby. I want you here right now! I wanna fall asleep in your arms."

"Soon, and then we'll spend all of our time together." Cody almost slipped and said the "rest of our lives together," but that would've given away his big surprise. He wanted to give some thought to how he would propose. It had to be special.

"Sweet dreams, pretty boy!"

"Goodnight, gorgeous girl!"

Cody wanted to fall asleep right then and there, but feeling he'd be safer at the restaurant, he drove over to Stroud's.

Strouds' parking lot was empty. Not a soul in sight as Cody pulled around to the lot, stopping next to the pond. He turned off the engine and climbed out of the van. The wind had died down, so it was still and very quiet. Walking to the edge of the water, he could hear crickets chirping and even detected a frog.

In the dark, Cody couldn't see the garbage strewn around the pond, so hearing the sounds of nature gave him the pleasant sense he wasn't just half a mile from one of the most destructive companies on Earth. He thought about his phone call with Victoria, her beautiful face scrunched up in orgasmic bliss. He wanted to leave and drive back to her open arms and warm body.

But then he remembered that the evil in the world does not stop unless someone makes it stop. He was chosen for this task—not by some made-up deity, but by reason and logic. He understood the harm being done to people and the planet, and he'd come up with a solution, meager and unrealistic as it was.

He began to cry.

Chapter 25

His phone alarm startled Cody out of a pleasant dream. It was pitch black outside, a good hour before dawn. It took him a moment to orient to his surroundings. He desperately wanted to go back to sleep and finish the dream, but the spell was broken and he had work to do. Horrible work.

A big sigh escaped from deep within his soul as he began to pull on his riding clothes and prepare for the day. He downed an energy drink and ate a banana.

He then drove to the animal shelter and parked in a far corner. No one would arrive for at least two more hours. He didn't want contact with anyone when he returned from his target, so he positioned the van with its sliding door facing away from the building. If anyone was watching, they'd see him ride up, but not see him store the bike. Minimize the variables.

Dawn was breaking and Cody wanted to get to the hiding place before daylight, so he had to hustle. He pulled out his bike and leaned it against the van. He then grabbed the backpack with the drone he'd carefully packed inside. The C-4 was already affixed to the drone, and his controller was placed on top of that.

C-4 is a very stable explosive. It can be dropped, shot with a rifle, even thrown into a fire, and it will not explode. In order to make it explode, you needed to shock it with a smaller explosive, such as a blasting cap. The C-4 Mel had procured came with two fuse-type blasting caps. Mel's source had told him the fuses took 60 seconds to detonation. This didn't provide Cody a very reassuring margin of error.

Cody had practiced flying the drone a couple times during his drive out, learning how to navigate the wind and added mass, and timing its travel over the distance he'd calculated from his hiding place to the tallest building on the Koch property. His timing had to be near perfect: the 60-second fuse was going to be close. Once he'd lit the fuses, he'd need to get the drone airborne quickly and hope like hell it reached its target before exploding.

It was getting lighter by the minute, so Cody double checked everything and rode off. No fences or barriers prevented him from getting onto the railroad right of way. After crossing Hillside St., he rode along the gravel path parallel to the tracks. The trees where he intended to hide and launch his attack were about a mile northeast of the animal shelter. His mountain bike's tires had no problem with the gravel, but it did slow his pace.

As Cody rode alongside the Koch property, he was surprised there was no fence separating it from the railroad. This was helpful, since he wouldn't have to spend time negotiating his bike over barbed wire.

After four minutes, he recognized the trees off to the left. He looked in all directions and saw no one. It was getting close to sun up, so it was crucial he get into the trees as soon as possible.

He dismounted and pushed the bike into the tall grass. The main tree was a large oak. Its spreading canopy provided plenty of shade and smaller trees provided great cover for both Cody and his bike. Someone would have to be pretty close to spot him, and there was nothing indicating people ever came near this spot.

He leaned the bike against the tree and took off his pack. As he carefully removed the explosive-laden drone, he doubled checked its payload, making sure the half-kilogram rectangular plastic block was securely affixed to the drone's underside. He then pulled the two blasting caps from a plastic bag and, thinking back to how his Army buddy had inserted triggers into C-4, he carefully pushed them, one after the other, into each end of the clay-like substance. That was a scary moment. While two blasting caps were embedded in the C-4, only one was needed to trigger the larger explosion.

Cody's military training enabled him to block out all thoughts except those that contributed to his mission's success. This was possibly a life-or-death scenario for someone. The Kochs would clearly have beefed up their security, and a shoot-to-kill order was likely in place. There was also the chance he would kill or injure an employee. He didn't take this lightly.

The drone was ready. Cody retrieved a Bic lighter from his pants pocket and set it on the grass next to the controller.

"Here we go," he thought.

He tested the drone's capacity to lift the package with the added blasting caps. He'd practiced with the C-4 alone, so he knew it could handle that weight, but he wanted assurance the drone would lift off once the fuses were lit. There would be no going back; only success or failure in flying the device, hopefully close enough to do some damage and scare people. Google Earth had labeled the building, "Koch Sulfur Products."

Cody took a long look around, even walking back to the tracks to see if a train was coming. All clear.

He walked back to the tree, pulled out his iPhone, and set its timer for 60 seconds, placing it on the ground next to the drone and its controller. He kneeled on the grass, picked up the lighter, pushed start on the timer, and flicked his Bic.

The first fuse sparked to life with a hiss, briefly startling Cody. He was extremely nervous. He quickly lit the second fuse, grabbed the controller, and maneuvered the drone into the sky. It wobbled slightly while Cody tried to steer it toward the building, about 300 meters to the northwest. Sparks were trailing off the fuses, but there was no visible smoke.

Once the drone cleared the tree's canopy, Cody flew it to the height of the building's top floor. Then he jammed the controller to maximum forward speed and watched as the drone sped toward its target. It quickly flew out of earshot and after about twenty seconds, it was just a speck in the distance. Cody watched the timer on his phone count down from 60...45...30...15...

It was 7:48 am, and while some people had arrived to work, most were still coming through the gates or in transit. On the Sulfur building's top floor, several early-arriving executives and managers were assembling for a weekly production meeting. Their seventh-floor conference room had an expansive view to the south. Three men were discussing the latest Donald Trump craziness when one of them, who'd been facing the windows, noticed movement out of the corner of his eye. He turned to look just as the first fuse reached its destination and set off the blasting cap. A bright light filled his vision and, instantly, the large picture window imploded into the room, embedding bits of safety glass into everyone close to the windows.

Cody saw the explosion about one second before the sound hit.

"Shit, that's gonna shake 'em up!" he exclaimed. He couldn't tell how much damage he'd done, but it looked like he'd gotten close. The smoke seemed to be right at the top floor, maybe just this side of it.

Cody quickly grabbed his pack and scanned the ground, picking up everything he'd brought with him. It would be hard for anyone to determine where the drone had been launched from, but he knew they'd be thorough in their search.

He threw on his pack and walked his bike quickly back through the tall grass to the tracks, where he mounted the bike and started pedaling hard.

People heard the explosion well over a mile away. Everyone on the sprawling Koch Industries campus heard it, and first responders rushed to the scene. The conference room was chaotic. Several men had been hurt by the flying glass, but none sustained serious injuries.

Just as Cody had surmised, security personnel raced to the blast site. He, on the other hand, was pedaling like a mad man, retracing his ride back to the animal shelter.

Koch Industries had, in fact, strengthened its security. Within seconds of the explosion, a call was placed to local police, followed by calls to the state police and the FBI. All available security personnel went on high alert. They first assumed someone had gotten onto the property. This person was still at large and potentially capable of further damage.

The explosion occurred on the south side, at the back of the building. From the ground, first responders in front reported no visible damage, but several in back reported a huge hole where plate glass windows had been blown out. Sirens were blaring from fire trucks stationed on site and police on their way.

It had taken Cody a minute to get his bike together and another three minutes to ride back to Hillside. He was getting close to the shelter, listening to the growing chorus of sirens behind him. Another siren sounded from the direction of downtown Wichita to his left. Then he heard a train whistle coming from the southeast. The crossing guards began clanging and dropped, stopping all traffic on Hillside. Cody had to cross the tracks.

"Shit!" Cody spat. "Bad fucking timing!"

The train was too close to risk running across with his bike. Besides, the engineer had spotted him and was laying on the horn.

Cody reached Hillside, where a few cars had already stopped. After the locomotive passed through the intersection and its overbearingly loud whistle stopped blaring, Cody noticed the siren to his left. He'd just ridden up to the intersection, paying attention to the train on his right, when a police cruiser arrived behind the line of cars. The officer pulled to the left, positioning himself to race across the tracks as soon as the train passed. This way he could slip through as soon as the train cleared the intersection.

Cody was sweating bullets. He'd glanced at the police car and could see the officer rolling down his passenger window and staring straight at him. Cody looked away, but the officer had picked up his radio. He was telling dispatch to send back up. There was a "person of interest."

The officer's radio had been crackling with information about the explosion, but he only knew something had blown up. Initial reports suggested the explosion wasn't accidental and that it might be a terrorist attack.

The train finished rolling through the crossing, its sounds receding as it rolled down the tracks in the direction from which

Cody had just come. The crossing guards were about to rise, but the cruiser was not moving.

"Shit!" thought Cody. "Why isn't he going?"

The crossing guards lifted, the clanging bells stopped, and confusion ensued because the officer's cruiser was now blocking oncoming traffic.

Cody had to do something quick! The traffic on his side of the road, after initially hesitating, started to move. Cody began to ride with them to see what the officer would do. As soon as he began to pedal, the officer hit his siren: he wanted Cody to pull over.

"Fuck, fuck, fuck!" Cody thought as he bolted in between cars and then through the line of cars heading towards them. He couldn't go directly to the shelter parking lot because they'd find his van, so he flew down the right of way, hoping like hell the cruiser couldn't follow. The line of cars heading south was still stopped because of the siren and lights, so the cruiser couldn't move. The officer screamed at the lead car to go, motioning wildly with his left arm. The confused, scared driver hesitated before stomping on his accelerator. The next car started to go, too, but the officer just wanted the first car to go so he could turn left and follow Cody.

The commotion bought Cody a few more seconds, and he was now a good 100 meters down the tracks and looking for an opportunity to cut over to the back of the shelter's parking lot. He saw an opening and jammed across a narrow grass berm. Several shelter employees were just arriving.

The officer finally made it through the line of cars and was barreling down the right of way, throwing gravel every which way. Cody wondered if the car could make it over the berm. He was now pedaling hard through the parking lot to the front, where he'd parked the van. Looking over his shoulder, he saw the cruiser's front wheels as it bounced over the grass embankment, its engine growling, its siren blaring.

"Shit!" Cody said. The workers in the lot watched, mouths agape, as the chase unfolded in front of them.

Cody's heart and lungs were maxing out. If caught, he'd be shot or captured. Either way—his life would be over.

The cruiser was now closing in on Cody as he poured everything into riding around the building to his van.

"Fuck me! No!" Cody saw a second police car, lights flashing and siren blaring, race into the parking lot from the other side. Now Cody knew it was over. He was exhausted, in oxygen debt, and out of options. He made it to the van and dismounted, just ahead of the first police car. The second officer screeched to a stop on his other side. Both officers scrambled out of their cars, guns drawn.

"Get down on the ground now!" the first officer shouted. Both were screaming at him, and Cody, his mind reeling with what had befallen him, fell to his knees, put his head in his hands, and cried.

"Victoria! Baby, I'm so sorry." he said through his sobbing.

Chapter 26

Back in Seattle, Victoria had just opened the store and was in her office with the radio on when news of the explosion broke on NPR.

"This is Peter Overby reporting. There has been another apparent attack by the Gambit terrorist. Koch Industries, headquartered in Wichita, Kansas, was the site of an explosion early this morning. Damage to one building appears to be moderate. Several minor injuries were sustained, although there are no reports of deaths. We'll have more as information becomes available."

Victoria stopped to listen. "Damn, another one, and this time it's the Kochs. Right on!" She picked up her phone and called Zak.

"Zak, did you hear the news? NPR says this Gambit guy blew something up at Koch Industries."

"Whoa, the Kochs! Hot damn, that's good news. Any chance the brothers were hit?"

"It just happened, so they don't know much. Lots of damage and some people were hurt, but no deaths, evidently. Cody doesn't want to be called at work, but I can't wait to call him tonight and talk about it."

"I'm turning on NPR right now," Zak said. "When did it happen?"

"It sounds like just a few hours ago. I gotta get back to work, but I'll keep the radio on in the background. Talk to you later."

"Bye."

Victoria went on with her work, helping customers pick out sexy underthings, briefly forgetting the news until, as she was getting ready to close, Peter Overby broke in with an update.

"NPR has learned that Wichita police are reporting the capture of a suspect in this morning's attack on the Koch Industries site. We have more details from Dina Temple-Raston, who has been following the story."

"Thank you, Peter. Wichita Police say they captured the suspect approximately one mile from the explosion. He was on a bicycle, and there was a brief chase ending in the man's arrest. They identified the suspect as Cody Benson of Seattle, Washington. The suspect is..."

"What? No!" Victoria screamed, scaring the two women in her store. One asked if she was OK.

Her face frozen in disbelief, Victoria stared at them. "My boyfriend was arrested!"

The two women hadn't paid attention to the radio report. They looked at each other, and one said, "Should we leave? Are you going to be alright?"

"I have to go. Very sorry, but I've got to go." Victoria ushered them out of the store and locked the door just as her phone began to ring. It was Zak.

"Oh my god, Zak!" she said. She was shaking uncontrollably. "What the fuck! Can this be real?"

"I don't know. Maybe there's been a mistake. Do you want me to come over?"

"No, I'll come to you. Are you home?"

"Yeah… wait. Hold on, it's Mel. I'll patch him in." A moment later Zak said, "Mel, I've got Victoria on the line. Did you hear?"

"I'm driving up right now. The three of us have very little time. Meet me at the house in an hour. Do not talk to the media or the police until I get there."

Victoria arrived at the house ten minutes later. She was still shaking. On the way over, she listened as NPR reported more details. Her phone rang constantly as her friends learned about Cody. She ignored the calls.

Zak met her at the front door and ushered her inside. "I hope Mel gets here before the FBI. They can't be too far away. Let's go look in his room and…"

"Zak! What's happened? How can this be?" Victoria was falling apart and still trembling uncontrollably. The love of her life had been arrested for blowing up Koch brothers property. And it began to sink in—she and Zak would be implicated. They'd definitely suspect her of involvement. She thought about Cody's anger, his silences. Things began to piece together.

"This isn't going to be good for us," Zak said. "I didn't know anything, and I assume you didn't either?"

She could feel the lead curtain of shock descending. "He was supposed to be in LA working on that film. Oh shit, he was gone when the first two guys were shot! Oh fuck!" She realized the timing of Cody's first trip coincided with the Inhofe and Limbaugh murders.

"Could Cody really have killed those people?" she said.

The answer was becoming clear. Both their cell phones were ringing non-stop. They ignored the calls.

"C'mon, let's see what's in his room," Zak said. "Might be something we need to get rid of." They ran up the stairs.

They looked through everything but found nothing that could be considered a problem. Cody had been pretty thorough making sure there was no evidence in the house.

About 20 minutes later, there was a knock on the door. Zak peeked out of Cody's window and saw the White Zombie in his driveway. He ran downstairs and let Mel inside, looking up and down the street for any police cars or vehicles that might be the FBI. Victoria joined them in the living room.

Mel motioned for them to sit, then took a chair himself. "Everything I'm about to tell you is not to be repeated," he stated sternly. "I learned Cody was Gambit last week—the day before he left. After I told him I was terminal, he confessed. He was desperate to confide in someone. He was severely conflicted about leaving." He looked at Victoria. "Because of you."

She looked down and sobbed.

Mel continued, "He was adamant you both remain ignorant of his actions. I've taken care of everything I could. The weapon will not be found, although at this point, it's no longer relevant. I'll be implicated, but there's a chance they won't have enough evidence for an arrest. It all depends on how thorough they are. Regardless, I'm only going to be around for a few more months. It doesn't matter." Mel looked away.

Zak and Victoria were stunned over how Cody had kept such a secret. They were full of questions and began peppering Mel with them, one after the other.

Mel did his best to answer everything he knew until they were interrupted by a loud knock.

"Sounds like they're here," Zak said as he walked to the door. "Nobody tell them anything. We all need counsel. I'll help with that as soon as I can."

Zak opened the door to two FBI agents. Three police cars were parked out front and two more blocked the street on both sides of the house. Several officers stood outside. Unknown to Zak, two officers were also in his backyard.

"Howdy! What can I do for you gentlemen?" Zak played friendly, but he knew his rights and would make them go by the book—not that it mattered much.

"I'm Agent Briscoe of the FBI, and this is Agent Reynolds. May we come inside?"

"Do you have a warrant? What's this about?"

"We don't have a warrant. This is regarding Cody Benson. May we come in and talk to you?"

Zak opened the door wide, inviting them in. Victoria and Mel stood up.

"Agents Briscoe and Reynolds, this is Mel and Victoria. May I get you folks a drink?"

Shaking hands with Mel and Victoria, agent Briscoe replied, "No thanks, we just want to ask you some questions about Cody Benson."

And with that, while their lives were not over in the way Cody's was, or in the way Mel's would soon be, their lives were changed forever. The next few weeks would see them in the news a lot.

The investigation was intimidating. Everything they'd touched over the past year was thoroughly scrutinized. Victoria's business records, every phone call she'd made, and every person she'd–talked to were questioned. Even though she'd talked to Cody several times during both trips, they found no evidence he'd shared any of his actions with her. Suspicion remained, but nothing could compare to the unceasing ache she suffered over the loss of her first true love.

Zak's life was similarly upturned. His practice, all the cases he'd worked, all the people who had been at the party: everyone was interrogated to discern if they knew of Cody's involvement. No one knew anything.

Zak took it as a badge of honor that he'd been involved with Cody. Wasn't much they could do to erase the pride he felt for his part in everything.

****

Three weeks after Cody's arrest, Zak was back at work. The FBI would contact him several times a week about this or that for months to come, but eventually, things got back to normal. His practice grew over time from people who respected Cody's message.

Zak, along with Mel, had helped transform Cody. Many found the manifesto resonant, including Millennials, Gen-Xers, and even Baby Boomers. A cadre of "Cody's People" formed and grew into hundreds of thousands as his message about how to solve the world's problems took hold.

Sales of electric cars and solar systems grew as people took to heart their part in the problem. The eventual delivery of the second generation EV along with the vertical integration of

SolarCity with Tesla would lead the way to a sustainable future, although it was still unknown if it would be too little too late.

As Cody had predicted, security for organizations and people listed in the manifesto dramatically ramped up. Cody was not specific about who in certain corporations would constitute a target, so tens of thousands of presidents, VPs, CEOs, COOs, legal counsel, directors, and even mid-management officers hired security teams. Everyone was scared the first few weeks.

As demand for security guards increased, vets constituted a high percentage of applicants, as Cody had hoped. The better security companies employed psychologists to look for disgruntled people, but not all of the new outfits jumping into the booming guns-for-hire business were that picky—and a lot of guys with guns saw a way to make a quick buck opening a fly-by-night security operation.

After his arrest, Cody was held in the local Sedgwick County Jail for two days before federal marshals relocated him to Leavenworth Penitentiary. He remained there while awaiting trial. Given the numerous crimes he'd committed, two of which were capital offenses, the trial would be over a year away. Victoria flew to Kansas to visit monthly.

Zak would represent him for a second time, but instead of breaking a high school bully's leg, Cody had killed two prominent men who were bullies on a global scale. A Kickstarter fund grew to over two million dollars in the first month, enabling Zak to partner with a large criminal-defense firm sympathetic to Cody's message. They would need all the firepower they could muster just to keep him alive.

Mark, Debra, and Jennifer were devastated. The media camped outside their home for weeks after Cody's capture, preventing them from any semblance of a normal life. They became outcasts in Eatonville. Although some of their friends were supportive of Cody's message, few would say so out loud. The town was too conservative.

Cody parents weren't as radical as their beloved son, but they respected his message. Debra would fly into a rage at locals who challenged her about Cody. She reminded them that he'd been a good boy until bullies assaulted him without repercussions.

As feature stories delved into Cody's past, the public learned of his being bullied in high school, Jazzie's death, and the two soldiers Cody had shot in Iraq. Some in Eatonville would come to realize they had been complicit in turning Cody into a man capable of killing.

Mel's involvement was more complicated. There was no direct evidence he knew about Cody's actions, but when they searched his computer and phone records, they discovered a guy who was known to the FBI as a potential source of illegal explosives.

Mel's attitude was "So what?" His health was fading, and he didn't care what happened to him. He was honored to have been part of Cody's efforts and, before his life came to an end, he decided to write his own manifesto. Since he was part of the Cody Benson story, the manifesto would be published far and wide.

Chapter 27

IN DEFENSE OF CODY BENSON, by Mel Beckman

I abhor violence as much as the next person, but Cody Benson was right to do what he did. For too long society has been led by tyrants who care little for the welfare of people and the planet.

Cody identified the problem, and he proffered a solution of sorts.

Many have denounced his solution saying violence solves nothing, but most of these people are themselves guilty of violence against humans and nature. The use of dirty energy causes harm. This was Cody's main point, and it's why he specifically called out those who refuse to switch to non-harmful energy sources. The survival of billions is at stake because of wars over oil; pollution that sickens and kills; and the eventual warming of our atmosphere. If you use dirty energy, you are complicit in all of this violence.

In "On Liberty," John Stuart Mill argued that your right to do what you want ends at the point that your action infringes on someone else's rights. Using dirty energy severely infringes on other's rights. For most everyone, the use of dirty energy is the worst thing that they will do in their entire life.

In the past, there were few alternatives, but today there are many. That you have not switched to these alternatives is the problem. This is why you are complicit with the corporatists. Instead of fighting them, you continue funding their efforts by buying their products.

Too many of us are contributing to the problem, too few contribute to the solution.

There is no reset on planet Earth. When the damage you're causing reaches its ultimate end, your children, their children, and all who follow will curse your inaction.

Cody was the first to take this critical action against our common enemy, but he won't be the last. As the full effects of climate change begin to manifest, others will follow in his footsteps. Societal evolution will see to that.

Some of you don't currently have the means to switch to clean energy. But though your economic status or the lack of EV-charging infrastructure and other issues might present problems, you must still work on practical and political solutions to change your energy source. At the very least, you can reduce the amount of energy you use through efficiencies.

The world has many problems, but none approach the severity of climate change, and none are as easy to solve as switching your source of energy. You have control over who gets your money for energy, and at the moment you're funding the most vile, evil people on the planet, all while contributing to the deaths of millions. Is that the legacy you wish to leave?

Cody was willing to give up his life for this cause. What are you willing to give up?

Los Angeles Times

TUESDAY, AUGUST 23, 2016

Three more assassinations in NY, TX, CA

In what the FBI is calling a coordinated attack, three high-profile energy executives were shot to death by members of their respective security teams. One person is in custody, two others were shot to death by police.

About Paul Scott

I grew up in the south, memories of Memphis being my earliest. We moved around a bit going first to Mobile, then San Antonio, Arab (small town in northern Alabama), then back to San Antonio. I stayed there through high school and college before striking out for Eugene, Oregon. I found "home" there in 1975. I fell into volunteering for a recycling group and ended up working in that industry for many years. There was satisfaction in converting a societal liability, garbage, into its components, each with a use and value, creating jobs in the process. After a decade in that business, I was ready for a change. Through a fortuitous series of events, I stumbled into a tiny, four-person computer animation company in the mid 80s and eventually became its president. Visual effects eventually took me to Los Angeles where I reside today.

In 2002, health problems initiated another career change, this one lasting in some form for the rest of my life. As I grew aware of the severity of climate change, and especially of its potential for catastrophic damage over the coming decades, I felt I had to do something that would make a difference, at the very least mitigate the worst of its effects. It was clear that the use of carbon-based energy - coal, oil, and gas - was the cause of the problem. After installing a solar PV system and buying my first electric vehicle, I started selling solar systems to residents and businesses, telling them of my personal experience with technology. I also told them of the coming electric cars. Cars that would be available in a few short years.

In 2011, the cars did come and I began selling the Nissan LEAF. I sold about 500 of them directly, and probably caused several thousand more to be sold through my writing and speaking. I helped form the EV advocacy group, Plug In America, and had a small part in the Chris Paine documentary, "Who Killed the Electric Car?". I was on a mission to get as many people to switch from dirty energy to clean energy as I could. Powering your home with clean energy and driving an electric vehicle was as close to perfect as you could get.

These jobs were at once satisfying and frustrating. It felt good to be cleaning the grid and removing internal combustion cars from our roads, but I was frustrated every time I read a report about how quickly we needed to scale this technology. If we were to head off the worst of what was to come, it was essential we switch to clean alternatives at a much higher rate than we were doing. Selling electric cars and solar energy was effective, but the damage being done requires scaling this effort as quickly as possible to mitigate the worst of what is predicted.

Fast forward to today, I'm retired and three years into my last and most enjoyable career yet. I became a novelist. Holy cow, I wrote a book! And what a book it is. I have taken some chances. It feels like a dangerous book. I consider it the First Amendment equivalent of carrying a loaded AR-15 into a Walmart. I did this with a purpose, to bring attention to the problems concerning dirty energy, and to offer solutions.

Made in the USA
San Bernardino, CA
21 April 2017